FOR THE RECORD

NEDBANK

I would like to thank my bank
for their generous support of this project
GARY TEICHMANN

To my father, my mother and my wife

FOR THE RECORD

Gary Teichmann

WITH EDWARD GRIFFITHS

JONATHAN BALL PUBLISHERS · JOHANNESBURG

Photographic Acknowledgements

All photographs not itemised here are
the personal property of the Teichmann family.

Touchline Photo Agency: *Front and back covers,*
 pages 4, 5, 6, 7, 8, 9, 10 – top, 11 – bottom, 12, 13 – top, 14 – top
Huw Evans Picture Agency: *Pages 11 – top, 15 – bottom, 16*
Beeld: Jan Hamman: *Page 10 – bottom*
SARFU: *Page 13 – bottom*
Sean Laurenz: *Page 14 – bottom*

All rights reserved.
No parts of this publication may be reproduced or transmitted, in any form or by any means, without prior permission from the publisher and the copyright holder.

© Gary Teichmann, 2000

Published in 2000 by
JONATHAN BALL PUBLISHERS (PTY) LTD
P O Box 33977
Jeppestown
2043

Reprinted 2000

ISBN 1 86842 098 1

Design by Michael Barnett
Typesetting and reproduction by Book Productions, Pretoria
Cover reproduction by Collage Graphics, Johannesburg
Picture section by Ince (Pty) Ltd, Johannesburg
Index by Naomi Musiker
Printed and bound by CTP Book Printers (Pty) Ltd,
Caxton Street, Parow 7500, Cape Town.

Contents

	Foreword	vii
	Introduction	ix
1	Rhodesian Roots	1
2	Hilton	14
3	The Slow Road	27
4	Uprising in Natal	36
5	Losing the Lottery	76
6	François' Footsteps	88
7	André Markgraaff's Captain	112
8	Carel du Plessis' Captain	122
9	Team of the Nineties	142
10	Nick Mallett's Captain	163
11	The Record	187
12	Dream Denied	198
13	New Dawn in Newport	218
14	Home Thoughts	226
	Career Highlights	231
	Index	235

Foreword
Henry Honiball

'Forward!' said Gary Teichmann. For me, this became a familiar instruction. In so many matches for Natal and South Africa, he was the captain, I was flyhalf and forward was the direction he wanted me to get the team moving.

When I think of 'Teich', my first image is of a man at the centre of the action, keeping his cool under pressure, behaving properly, giving everything. When many toys are being hurled from many cots, he manages to do the right thing, say the right thing and maintain his dignity.

His name is engraved deep in the annals of Natal rugby, one of the icons of the Team of the Nineties, a captain who will always be held in great affection by the people of the province, particularly those who frequent King's Park.

Did he ever let Natal down? No. Did he ever conduct himself in a way that reflected poorly on the province? No. The image of a beaming Teich, raising the Currie Cup above his head, springs swiftly to the mind's eye.

At national level, he was the constant presence that held the Springbok team together through the traumas of 1996 and 1997. Coaches came and went, players came and went, but the captain not only maintained his high standard of play as one of the world's leading eighthmen but also retained the admira-

FOR THE RECORD

tion of his players. In tough times, this was a remarkable achievement.

And, more than anyone, Teich guided the team to happier times, winning the Tri-Nations title in 1998 and equalling the world record of 17 consecutive Test wins later that year. If ever anyone contradicted the dictum that nice guys come last, it was Gary Teichmann. He was nice, and he was triumphant.

The fact that he has captained South Africa more times than anyone else and led the Springboks to more Test wins than anyone else, settles incongruously with the reality that he never had the chance to play in a Rugby World Cup.

That has been the tournament's loss.

At one stage of my career, I seriously considered retiring from rugby. Then Gary Teichmann telephoned. He said I should play on, said we would have many great times together. That inspired me again. No-one else could have persuaded me to keep playing, but Teich has always been easy to follow.

By his dignity and honesty off the field, by his courage and skill in action, Gary Teichmann has been an extraordinary leader to hundreds of Natal players, and he has emerged as an indisputably great Springbok captain.

He has been an example to me.

It is a privilege for me to get this book moving forward. I have no doubt this particular move, Teich's autobiography, will finish beneath the posts.

Introduction

The day dawned bright and sunny in the capital of Wales. It was 6 November 1999, and, in my mind's eye, I had been there many times before.

Ever since accepting the Springbok captaincy, the thought had lingered at the back of my mind that, in a perfect world, the occasion of the fourth World Cup final would be the ideal time and place to end my international career.

And I was there in Cardiff, watching the match on television in the home we had rented since arriving from Durban to play for the Newport club side; the Springboks were in town too, most of them watching on TV at the Angel Hotel as Australia beat France in the stadium barely 400 metres away.

The image had materialised – except the jerseys worn by the triumphant players were gold with a green trim, when they should have been green with the gold trim, and the man with the cup was not me, but John Eales.

We were in Cardiff that day, but the fates had given neither me, nor the Springboks, the central roles in the showpiece occasion that we had eagerly envisaged. As everyone discovers at some stage of their lives, whatever they do and wherever they live, this is not a perfect world.

My Test career, launched 11 weeks after the 1995 Rugby World Cup, had followed an unbroken course through almost

FOR THE RECORD

four seasons and been concluded on the eve of the 1999 tournament. It is a fact that I was privileged to captain South Africa in more Test matches than any of my predecessors; it is also a fact that I was fortunate to lead the team to a record 17 consecutive Test victories; and it is also a fact that I never took part in a Rugby World Cup. My Test career could not have fitted more snugly between the 1995 and 1999 events.

It is strange, but true.

Nick Mallett, the Springbok coach who I respected so completely and with whom I had worked so successfully, took the decision to omit me from the 1999 World Cup squad. It was neither the right decision nor the wrong decision. It was simply his decision, and he made it. He was doing his job.

The history of sport – every sport in every country – is littered with tales of controversial selections, public outrage and injustice done. My situation was not unique. These storms regularly blow through the national consciousness, whipping up emotions before eventually settling down into sepia history.

South Africans will recall the weeks of outrage when heroes Clive Rice, Jimmy Cook and Peter Kirsten were omitted from the national cricket squad for the 1992 World Cup, outrage so hysterical that the selectors recalled Kirsten, who emerged as the team's highest scorer of the tournament; and, of course, nobody will easily forget the flood of public opinion polls and letters to newspapers that followed the still unexplained and rash decision to discard François Pienaar, the World Cup winning captain, at the peak of his career in 1996.

And Gary Teichmann was dropped on the eve of the 1999 Rugby World Cup. Such things happen. Life would be boring without controversy and, after the initial disappointment subsides, life soon trundles along again. It is no crisis, was no crisis, has never been a crisis and will never be a crisis.

So why write a book?

For two reasons, both of them being for the record.

In the first place, the achievement of the Springboks who

INTRODUCTION

established the record of 17 consecutive Test victories between August 1997 and December 1998, equalling the world record set by the All Blacks in the late 1960s, deserves to be set down. It has long been common practice to build monuments or statues that commemorate remarkable achievements. In this case, I am eager that the efforts of Nick Mallett and the players are faithfully recorded.

So, this book is written for the record: of 17 successive wins.

Secondly, the manner of my dismissal as Springbok captain occasionally rankled, with unkind suggestions that I had become more interested in playing golf than rugby and was physically damaged beyond repair. On the premise that nobody wins a fight in the newspapers, because every side becomes tarnished, I have strived to steer clear of public debate. Now, as time passes, I would like to set down precisely what took place, if only for the record.

There are other strands to the tale. At the age of 23, I was still sitting in the highest row of the open stand at Loftus Versfeld, Pretoria, a face in the crowd as Natal defeated Northerns to win the Currie Cup final. My rugby career fired soon afterwards, and my experience should serve as encouragement to everyone who develops more slowly than his or her peers. It matters not whether you take the slow or the fast road, so long as you reach the destination.

It is also right and proper that the emergence of Natal rugby should be set down, the story of a union that first sipped the cup of glory that warm afternoon in Pretoria and became hailed as the Team of the Nineties.

For all these reasons, this book is written. And it is written for people, too; above all for my wife, Nicky, who has so often been so strong in awkward times, and who has been ceaselessly supportive ever since the slightly blurred evening when we first met and she refused to let me buy her a drink.

It's for my parents, Jack and Mickey Teichmann, and my

brothers and sisters, all of whom have given much and asked so little.

It is written out of gratitude to the coaches who gave me the chance to feel the adrenalin from sport at the highest level, from Klein Strydom and Andy van der Watt at Hilton, to Brian Bateman at College Rovers, to the inimitable Ian McIntosh at Natal, through to the three men who placed their confidence in me as Springbok captain: André Markgraaff, Carel du Plessis and, most successfully and happily, Nick Mallett.

And, it is written in solidarity with the thousands of team-mates who, with me, have played this most precious and distinguished of games.

Lastly, I am particularly grateful to Edward Griffiths for his assistance in putting the book together, and to Henry Honiball for contributing the Foreword.

So the story of my rugby career does end in Cardiff, just as I hoped it would. A few of the details might have been different, but the story is absolutely complete, and whole, and fulfilled. The branch is full-grown, maybe in a fresh and unpredicted direction, but it is full-grown nonetheless.

Gary Teichmann
Cardiff

1

Rhodesian Roots

There is something about Zimbabwe that engages the senses and emotions of anyone who spends a considerable amount of time there. I spent the first 12 years of my life in this remarkably fertile, beautiful country, and I have felt every twist and turn of its intensely frustrating history ever since.

The colonial masters called it the 'bread basket of Africa'. Where farmers down south dared to plant three maize plants to the metre, the Rhodesians felt confident enough to sow ten to the metre. The Eastern highlands, the Vumba, Victoria Falls, Nyanga, Kariba; to so many, this was God's own country – not only for the whites but for the vast majority of its black citizens as well.

Of course, the inherited challenge for us fated to be living in southern Africa at the end of the 20th century and the start of the 21st could not have been more daunting: to transfer power, and with it prosperity, from the minority to the majority as peacefully as possible. This is a task that, history will sadly record, the people of Zimbabwe have so far struggled to achieve.

In two decades, the country has been transformed from bread basket to basket case, to the detriment of its entire population. President Robert Mugabe has established a virtual one-party state where, until the referendum on a new constitution earlier this year, election results had been utterly predictable. Mass unemployment, corruption at all levels, petrol queues, a massively devalued currency, spiralling inflation, an oversized army and a runaway AIDS epidemic: these are the open wounds in the flesh of modern Zimbabwe.

Far be it for me, a professional rugby player, to attach political blame for this desperate waste. Maybe the whites were reluctant to change; maybe they could have offered concessions before they were demanded, but I cannot help but believe Mugabe has been a huge disappointment. Compared to Presidents Mandela and Mbeki in South Africa, and their constructive, conciliatory approach, he has failed to grasp the challenge of his time. His personal wealth and luxury appear to be in proportion only to the misery among so many of his people.

In a different age, when, in fairness, Mugabe was giving the best years of his life to the liberation struggle, my parents were among those settlers who put their trust in the country they knew as Southern Rhodesia. Both born and reared in the rolling Natal Midlands, they married on 13 April 1957, and immediately headed northwards, in hope, arriving to start a new life in Umtali (now Mutare).

The Teichmanns had arrived in Africa from Germany, sturdy Protestants fleeing what they regarded as the declining moral and social standards of 19th century Europe. In their minds, Africa represented an opportunity to start again, to correct past mistakes and to build the kind of ideal society envisaged by their uncompromising ethics and religious codes.

And yet, during a century when Germany and England spent so much time at war, the family became curiously anglicised. By the late-1950s, the Teichmanns were settled in the Natal Midlands, thriving amid a community that happily stood to sing 'God Save the Queen'. Even if we did live in the province dubbed 'the last outpost of the British Empire,' we never regarded ourselves as British. Nor did we easily identify with the Afrikaners who, through the National Party, had ruled the country since the 1948 general election.

We were South Africans, first and last. On one occasion, Dr Danie Craven asked someone to tell him the result of a rugby match between Natal and the touring British Lions team. 'Who won?' he rasped.

'*Die Engelse*' (the English), came the reply.

'*Ons Engelse of hulle Engelse*?' (Our English or their English), Craven enquired again.

The Teichmanns were emphatically *ons Engelse*. During the First World War, my great grandfather fought for the Allies against the Germans in what was then South West Africa, now Namibia.

Jack Teichmann, my father, was born and raised in Ladysmith, one of two sons in a family that worked hard to secure a living. He suffered life-threatening pneumonia as a child, left school at the age of 16 and went straight into work. If the white man's life in Africa is often depicted as being luxury piled upon luxury then that is a gross distortion. For Jack, and his brother George, it was clear from their earliest years that every pleasure would be earned. Resourceful and clever, they made their own fun and fed off a tight, committed family.

In turn, my father resolutely set out to instil proper manners in his own children. When my parents entertained guests, we ate our meals in the kitchen. There was no debate. At every stage of our childhood, we knew where we were meant to be and we would feel our parents' displeasure if we erred. A powerful sense of right and wrong, delivered in reams of unconditional love, seems to be the finest gift any parent can give a child. My brothers, sisters and I received it and now, as a father myself, I strive to hand it on.

My father trained and worked as a stock auctioneer, becoming respected and popular among the farmers with whom he worked; and, even though he was often away from home, there could not have been a more supportive presence standing on the touchline when any of his children played sport. When business was quiet during the Rhodesian war, because rural travel was too dangerous, he even turned up to watch my rugby practices at school. I was always thrilled by his presence, always was then and always have been ever since.

Indeed, if I close my eyes and conjure an image of my father through my childhood, it would be of playing a rugby or cricket match and being alerted to his arrival at the ground by his trademark cough. He would clear his throat and, without even having to look, I would know he was present.

In later years, it would be harder to hear his cough when he took his seat to watch the Natal Sharks among a crowd of 45 000 at King's Park, but somehow I felt sure I could hear him. He has been absolutely reliable, and I am certain he would have considered all his efforts to be completely worthwhile even if I had risen no further than playing stalwart club rugby for Maritzburg Varsity.

That I played provincial and international rugby was a bonus; that he was able to amuse his weekly tennis partners by wearing the Springbok training kit I had given him was no more than that: amusement.

With the benefit of 20/20 hindsight, I feel I should have involved him more in my rugby career, meeting my team-mates and colleagues; but, for one reason or another, I have always wanted to keep my family in the background. This was never a consequence of being ashamed of anything – I just felt they should keep their distance from what effectively had become my work place. Now, nearing the end of my career, I wish I had shared more with my father.

That said, I never stopped hearing his distinctive voice and, for me, Jack Teichmann's opinion of any situation has always weighed more heavily than any other. It is not his nature to venture opinions on every subject under the sun but when he speaks, I listen. In 1996, my first reaction to being appointed Springbok captain in succession to François Pienaar was that I didn't want the job. While I was concentrating on securing my place in the side, I didn't welcome the task of replacing a national icon amid all kinds of outrage and controversy.

At this critical time in my career, my father did have an opinion. 'Take your opportunities when they come,' he said, 'however inconvenient they may seem, because there is always a chance they will never come again.' He was right and, paternally emboldened, I accepted the Springbok captaincy.

My mother has been the smiling, gracious focal point of our family. Well known in the Natal Midlands, she seems imbued with the spirit of community that runs deep in this part of the world. It's a spirit that welcomes people who 'drop by' and simply sets another place at the table, a spirit that brings up the children to be decent and bold, an outward spirit that cares for its own.

She was born Clare Lund, but has ever been known as Mickey, and her childhood was spent with three sisters and a brother on a farm, Montrose, not far from Howick.

Her father, Guy Lund, was at one with the land, a farmer who rose early every morning to tend his dairy cattle and worked until sunset. It might be difficult for a child of the cyber-age to understand such profound attachment to the land, but in the 1950s, farmers were widely respected as pillars of society who, together with the mining houses, provided the engine for South Africa's prosperity.

It would not always be so … one afternoon in 1963, Guy Lund was informed that the government had earmarked the farm Montrose as land to be developed into a township, to be called Mpophomeni. The officials regretted the inconvenience, of course, and they offered my grandfather a similar farm not far away as part of a compensation package. In his mind, however, there could be no compensation for the loss of his land. That was the point: it was *his* land.

After a protracted and painful process of appeal, the government decision was confirmed. Montrose would be developed. My grandfather was devastated by the finality of the news, and he quickly arrived at the decision that he would rather die on his land than leave it. Ah, but this land is beautiful, Alan Paton wrote, but its soil is stained with blood and tears, with inestimable pain and sadness. Guy Lund died, quite literally, for his land ... like so many before and so many since.

By the strangest of coincidences, three decades later my construction company, Teichmann Civils, would secure a contract to build roads and provide sewage and water services in, of all places, the township of Mpophomeni. My grandfather might have appreciated the irony. I should have asked the council to name a street after him.

My mother's family carried on with their lives as the tightly knit farming community rallied round. Her brother and my uncle, Jub Lund, who played Springbok polo, emerged as a pillar of support, and an important figure of authority in the family.

As the years passed, my mother excelled on the tennis court. In later years, she would hold coaching courses on our tennis court at home; at least she would try to coach while her mischievous children were causing unending distraction and irritation. My parents' enthusiasm for sport inevitably bred equal enthusiasm in their children.

I thank them both for that but, perhaps of greater importance as my name started to appear in more and more headlines, I am grateful to them for treating me in exactly the same way as they always had done. I might have been playing for Natal or even South Africa on the Saturday, but if the entire family gathered together for lunch on Sunday, we would talk about rugby no more than we would talk about whatever the others had been doing that week.

Throughout these past few years, I have constantly borne in mind the very shallow and transient nature of sporting fame. It's easy to be seduced by the few days of glory and fame, tempted to believe you really are somebody special. Two weeks of retirement is often enough to prove the nature of that illusion. The right approach is to enjoy the good times while they last, but always to recognise that they will not last forever and to acknowledge that we are only rugby players who kick an odd-shaped ball around. We're not special. Fortunately, my family have consistently assisted me in maintaining a stable perspective.

When my parents settled in Umtali, they soon set their minds to starting a family and my two older sisters, Robyn and Lindsay, soon arrived. Both of them would eventually marry and settle into a Natal farming life. Robyn, who trained as a nurse, became Mrs Charlie MacGillivray, and then Lindsay became Mrs Clive Alexander. There have been many occasions over the years when I have had cause to be grateful for their concerned sisterly guidance, even if – such is the nature of sibling rivalry – I have generally neglected to let them know.

My parents produced two girls in Umtali, but in 1963 they moved to live in Gwelo (now Gweru), a small town perched on the main road between Salisbury (Harare) and Bulawayo, and proceeded to produce three boys within seven years. There must have been something in the water. Ross was born in 1965; on 9 January 1967, at the Gwelo hospital, I arrived and, when David was born three years later, the complement of five Teichmann children was assembled – and my parents were confronted by two decades of noise and bustle.

The pros and cons of large families are well documented.

In my experience, you swiftly learn to make your own way and protect your own corner; and, amid all the inevitable quarrelling and fighting, there is a spirit and support base that rarely fails. There is safety in numbers; strangely there is also privacy because everyone in the family is often so busy with their own business they have no time to interfere in yours.

My mother insists that I was a noisy and active child, and she was there so she should know, although this is hard to reconcile with the reality of my much quieter nature in later life. I

FOR THE RECORD

remember reading in the biography of Naas Botha that he did not utter a single coherent word until his third birthday, and that his parents had started to worry whether there was something seriously wrong. There wasn't. The future Springbok captain did start to talk and, as admirers of his television work know, he has since made up for his early silence.

It appears as if the reverse has been true in my case. I may not say much these days, and the reason is obviously that I used up all my words as a child. In any event, that's my story and I'm sticking to it!

The nature of my childhood will be familiar to many of those who grew up in southern Africa during the 1970s. The South African Broadcasting Corporation only flickered across our TV sets in 1974, and our world was one that somehow had to get along without television, shopping malls and computer games. I can't imagine how we survived without such modern necessities!

I do remember that we spent most of our time outside, playing in the *veld* and in the rock outcrops behind our house. Zimbabwe is known all over the world for its distinctive rock formations: huge rocks that appear to have been piled one upon the other. These are miracles of nature, and it was among such an amazing landscape that I spent most of my leisure time.

Many of today's children will be familiar with the computer game brand Pokemon. Well, my first pet was also a small, lovable creature, but his name was no more marketable than 'Stinks'. He was a real, live bush baby and I won't deny that he did often smell terrible. That was his nature. He urinated on his hands to make them sticky so he could more easily climb up trees. Nature is a bit like that. It does smell. But I was fortunate to grow up in the midst of it.

Mine was, at times, a precarious childhood. We learned by trial and error as much as by instruction. We laughed, we played and, on occasions, we sailed close to the wind.

RHODESIAN ROOTS

We were not careless, maybe just carefree.

On one occasion, I was lucky not to lose my leg. A pillar of the agricultural community, my father had been elected as chairman of the Gwelo show society and we would happily play among the equipment while he went about his duties. I was sitting on a tractor, being driven around slowly, when I slipped and my leg was briefly trapped between the wheel and the chassis. The driver stopped and I was extricated. In point of fact, I had been inches from disaster.

On another occasion, my brother Ross was not so fortunate. We were all messing around at the Bulawayo athletic club, and Ross and I were running from the main lounge out to the patio. One of the large plate glass sliding doors was open and the other one was closed, but neither of us could see anything because the sunlight was so bright outside and the room was dark inside.

I ran through the open window, Ross crashed through the glass. That was my good fortune, his poor fortune. His leg was sliced open, and it required 120 stitches and three operations to restore it to working order. His aspirations of playing sport at the highest level were, however, hampered by the permanent restriction of movement in his foot. The sight of my brother's leg gashed open, the blood and his pain still stay with me. It might have been me who hit the glass.

Sport in all its forms preoccupied our family. While my mother had always relished her tennis, my father had played first team rugby during his school days at Maritzburg College. They loved sport; we loved sport. We were lucky enough to have a swimming pool and tennis court at home, and the games began. As the oldest, Ross would take on both David and me at cricket, swimming, soccer and tennis, and any combination or derivative we could develop. In Rhodesia at that time, rugby was not permitted for boys under the age of ten.

In our young minds, the prospect of playing among ourselves appeared vastly more exciting than watching a match from the stands. However, my father was a keen follower of Springbok rugby. He had a pilot's licence, and would often get some friends together and fly his company Cessna aircraft down south to watch Test rugby in South Africa. Sometimes our entire family would join the crowd of several thousand at the annual school rugby derby in Gwelo, between Chaplin and Guinea Fowl. On other days, my father would pack us into the back of our Toyota station wagon and drive us to watch the Rhodesian side play Currie Cup matches at the rickety, beloved Queen's Club in Bulawayo.

We were unashamedly proud to be Rhodesians. Ours may have been a small country but we managed to produce many excellent sportsmen, people like Ray Mordt, Ian Robertson and David Smith on the rugby field, golfers Nicky Price and Mark McNulty and many others. Their success sustained our spirit.

Ian McIntosh was a respected figure in Matabeleland rugby circles at the time and my father knew him well enough to greet, but not much more. 'Mac' was a person to be respected. In the years to come, when we shared so many great days with Natal and the Sharks, I would realise precisely why.

Rhodesia competed vigorously in the Currie Cup through the 1970s, rarely failing to give the strongest South African provincial teams a tough game, and it was the combative and bearded scrumhalf, 'Bucky' Buchanan, who captured my young imagination with his wholehearted performances.

I attended Cecil John Rhodes Primary school in Gwelo, one of many institutions named after the country's founding father. I suppose our lives were structured in such a way that it was very easy to forget we were living through a civil war in which more than 50 000 people would die.

There is no escaping the fact that Rhodesia was a country where whites were afforded much greater opportunities than blacks, but the country seemed to sustain a more relaxed racial atmosphere than was prevalent in South Africa. I was never brought up to believe black people were in any sense inferior, even if the only black people with whom I enjoyed regular contact were the maid and the gardener ... and they were virtually members of the family.

If my carefree life was not much affected by the war, my father was faced by much greater problems when sporadic terrorist attacks on farms made travel in rural areas downright dangerous. For a stock auctioneer who needed to be on the move to thrive, this amounted to a serious blow to business. In 1977, as the internal security situation deteriorated further, my father arrived at a difficult but inescapable decision: that we should move to Bulawayo.

I didn't mind much – my life still revolved around the tennis court and swimming pool at home, and the areas of bush nearby – and I made new friends soon after enrolling at Hillside primary school in the town. Amid the broad avenues, the sense of community and a gentle life, I meandered inauspiciously towards my teens with scarcely a care in the world.

Cricket began to excite me at my new school and my surprise selection for the Partridges XI, a national primary schools team that competed at a week-long festival in South Africa each year, thrilled me beyond words. Like most of the side, I was a batsman and a bowler. We could hardly contain ourselves as we gathered in Salisbury before setting off for Cape Town, and were presented with our official caps by no lesser man than the Prime Minister, Ian Smith. Our captain in the Partridges that year was a celebrated batsman from Banket by the name of Graeme Hick, but I didn't know him very well.

I did know South Africa from our annual holidays in Natal, but this was to be my first sporting adventure down south and, even though I didn't tell anyone at the time, I was relieved when my parents announced they would accompany the side to the Cape. My cousin, Clive Hill, had been named in the Natal primary schools cricket team, so this would be a family affair. In the event, we won a few matches and lost a few. In the fashion of Rhodesian teams competing down south, we accepted defeat with equanimity and took unbridled delight in our victories whenever they came along.

Meanwhile my older brother, Ross, had started to attend one of this small country's exceptional boys' boarding schools, Plumtree. In my young estimation, there was no more exhilarating place in the entire world. The school was located near the border, in an exposed position, and we used to carry a small firearm in the car whenever we took Ross back to school. There was a civil war taking place, but for me this was just real life cops and robbers.

Ross would come home with stories of how the boys were woken in the middle of the night and instructed to sleep in the showers because terrorists were said to be in the area. The school was fired upon several times, but no one was injured. The attacks appeared intended only to disrupt white lives.

As the war rumbled on, my father enlisted as a police reservist and he was often called away to man a roadblock. Ian Smith had suggested our small white state would last for 1 000 years but, as the months passed, more and more people began to see through the fantasy of such propaganda. Black majority rule was inevitable and to deny it was merely to whistle in the wind.

I was due to start at Plumtree in 1980, and could hardly wait. But I never got there. My father began to realise it would be almost impossible for a stock auctioneer to make a decent living in the new Zimbabwe and, just a year before independence, we decided to join the exodus to South Africa.

My initial reaction was disappointment. My Plumtree dreams evaporated in seconds, but we were heading for the horizon. I helped pack up our belongings and, at the age of 12, sadly left the country of my birth.

Looking back, I have real affection for Zimbabwe, although the fact that I have lost touch with the friends I made at primary school means I have not had reason to visit during the past 20 years.

RHODESIAN ROOTS

It was not until Easter 1999 that I finally did return. Adrian Garvey, my team-mate for Natal and South Africa, and I were invited to be representatives of the Chris Burger Fund, with the task of presenting a wheelchair to a young man who had been injured playing rugby. Adrian had put together a video during one of the Springbok tours, and raised some money for the cause.

The country that I found was not the one that I remembered. We visited Harare, Bulawayo and Gweru and saw my old school and the hospital where I was born. Everything looked quite run down, but there remains a special spirit among the people. Despite all the continuing problems, Zimbabwe is still a special place, and the people who live there are a special people. It's easy to be pessimistic about the future, but the prophets of doom may be surprised.

When I was growing up, the limit of my ambition was to play either rugby or cricket for Rhodesia. From 1979 onwards, my loyalty was transferred to South Africa, and the colours of my boyhood aspirations to green and gold.

2

Hilton

If there were an archetypal upbringing for a top sportsman, it would probably be one where an impoverished childhood nurtures a desperate hunger for success. In the happiest stories, the result is relentless dedication, then fame and fortune and enough money to buy houses and cars for the whole family.

Well, I was not typical. Foreign exchange regulations meant we were not permitted to bring much money out of Zimbabwe, so the Teichmanns were not exactly the Rockefellers when we arrived in Natal. I suppose we were the other fellas. Even so, we had enough to get by and my father rented a house near Howick, north of Pietermaritzburg, and soon afterwards leased a farm just across the river where we started to grow vegetables and maize.

From my 12-year-old perspective, the move was scarcely traumatic. In Natal, we lived among the same sort of people and enjoyed the same kind of life as we had in Zimbabwe, and now there was family around, the Lund, Evennett, Phipson and Hill cousins. Their presence partially compensated for the fact that my elder sisters, Robyn and Lindsay, had stayed up in Bulawayo, lodging with friends of my father while they completed their schooling at Chaplin. I was oblivious at the time but our departure from Zimbabwe, though necessary, must have represented a major challenge for my parents.

The only adjustment for me was to replace Plumtree as the focus of my high school ambitions with one of South Africa's finest schools. My brother Ross had enrolled at Hilton College, and I and my younger brother David, were destined to follow. First, I had to negotiate a year of excited anticipation at Howick primary school; there, my cricket coach was a man called Digby Rhodes. His young, active son, Jonty, was often to be seen hanging around our practices and matches, possibly picking up a few tips.

Hilton is an impressive place. Brilliant white buildings stand out against the beautiful rolling green hills and, in the valley below, the Umgeni River sweeps down towards the Indian Ocean. Some days, a swirling mist would settle around the school, creating a mystical, magical impression. In this perfect setting, Hilton has developed exceptional standards in all fields.

'How can you tell if someone went to Hilton?' the old joke goes.

'Don't worry, he'll tell you.'

In my experience, the perception of arrogance was not accurate. The boys were forever being made aware both of their good fortune in attending such a school and of their responsibility to make the most of the opportunity.

I suppose the status of the school could perhaps be measured by the rows of gleaming Mercedes and BMWs in the car park whenever parents were around. It was the school of choice for many wealthy businessmen in Johannesburg, the place where rich boys would be groomed into rich young men.

Amid the expensive German cars, we parked our yellow Datsun 120Y. It was the most popular model in Zimbabwe at the time. We were not in the market for imported saloons then, but I can't say I bothered very much.

One fact, however, was obvious even to my young and raw sensibilities: my parents were making huge sacrifices to send us to Hilton. The fees may not have been quite as terrifying as they are nowadays, but they were substantial.

Oddly, my father had attended Maritzburg College, one of the famous rival schools down the hill in the city of Pietermaritzburg, but my grandfather and most of my uncles had been Hilton men. It was a smaller school, numbering 400 boys compared to almost 1 000 at Maritzburg College, and my parents decided it would better suit the young Teichmann boys from the sticks of Zimbabwe. They were right. I relished every day at Hilton College.

The school cannot have been more than 40 minutes' drive from our home, but both Ross and I were boarders from the start. In a sense, we had the best of both worlds because we would see our parents almost every weekend when they came to watch us play sport but we still enjoyed that sense of independence and adventure known only to boys who 'go away' to school.

It must be said that I was never overexcited by the academic challenge at school. My ambition was to get by with the minimum possible effort, to be tucked away in the middle of the field, always passing on to the next stage but never breaking into a sweat either of concern or effort. On balance, this was achieved. For me, the focus of my attention was always sport, and the daily routine at Hilton always struck me as being particularly well designed.

We would rise at six, wash, file to breakfast and start school at eight. The intense anticipation and planning of the sport ahead would extend beyond the break at ten o'clock until we finished for the day at half past twelve. After lunch, the afternoon – each and every afternoon – was reserved for sport. Prep followed in the evening, and proved an ideal quiet time to reflect upon the match or practice.

My preferred sport when I arrived at Hilton was cricket, and I set my mind on following in the footsteps of people like Mike Procter and Rob Bentley, both of whom were revered old boys.

It seemed as if I was making progress when I was appointed captain of the school under-14 team. This was my first experience of leadership. I was exhilarated, and probably not very humble.

Our first match of the season was played against Alexander High School, from Pietermaritzburg, and we batted first, setting our visitors a mediocre target of 112 runs to win in 40 overs. The captain (that was me) believed our only chance of victory was to bowl Alexander out, and that meant giving full rein to the bowler who our captain (me) believed was the most effective (also me).

Unfortunately the Alexander batsmen did not share my lofty opinions of my own ability and they proceeded to smash me around the ground. Four, six, four. Never mind, I thought, I will not be beaten. I put in three slips to increase the pressure on the batsmen ... and I kept myself in the attack. Six, two, four, four. It wasn't getting any better. I dug harder, the hole got deeper. I duly completed my allocation of eight overs, conceding 78 runs. Soon, the Alexander boys were back in their bus, their victory secured within 15.4 overs.

I thought I had been brave and tenacious in sticking to my task. Sadly our coach did not agree. Mr Jarvis immediately relieved me of the captaincy. This turned out to have been the critical moment in my cricket career. I had started the day dreaming of being the next Procter. I finished the day wondering whether my life would ever recover from the disaster of being sacked.

Salvation, I decided, would be found on the rugby field, and I secured my place as a backline player in the school under-14 team. Too light and thin to play among the forwards, I enjoyed myself at outside centre but the responsibilities of our team extended beyond simply playing the game. We were also expected to serve as ball boys, sand boys and water boys whenever the Hilton first XV were playing a home match. These duties were to be taken seriously.

I wish someone had told me! On one occasion, the first team were in action and I was detailed as a water boy, expected to carry bottles of refreshment on to the field whenever summoned. I have never been a great spectator and, bored during the second half, I was hanging around behind the main stand, chewing the fat with my cousin, Clive Hill. I gave no thought to the water.

Suddenly someone appeared, shouting at me. The players needed water. I grabbed the bottles and ran through the stand, emerging from the players' tunnel. In my haste I completely forgot about the steep incline between the tunnel and the touchline; to my huge embarrassment, I tripped, theatrically stumbling forward. I spilled the water and earned an ironic round of applause from the 3 000 people sitting in the main grandstand. This was my debut in big time rugby. It was a little less than auspicious.

The captain of the first team that year was Paul Rayner, who later played provincial cricket for Natal. As I gathered myself and collected the bottles with what remained of the water, I became aware of Rayner glowering at me.

'Where were you?' he asked, failing utterly to disguise his anger. 'You should have been watching the game.'

'Er, sorry,' I stammered.

'Come on, pull yourself together,' he said.

'S-s-s-orry.'

I suppose I should confess that I was emotionally shattered by this terrible humiliation, that it took me months to recover my confidence. The reality is that it took me a few minutes. My nature was simply not to get too excited by this sort of event. It happened. It was finished. No problem, no point in worrying. I brushed it off with a smile, accepted the teasing of my friends and carried on.

Rugby was soaking into my blood. In 1981, at the age of 14, I was one of the most eager boys in Churchill House, to get up early in the morning and watch the Test matches between the

All Blacks and the Springboks in New Zealand. It was the demo tour, and around ten of us pulled on our dressing gowns, tip-toed along the wooden corridors, down from the dormitories to the main lecture room, where we sipped coffee and gathered around the television. They were exciting times, watching our national team confront the ultimate test.

Even now, I can clearly recall our sense of outrage when Allan Hewson kicked that last decisive penalty at Eden Park. That moment seems to have been engraved on the lives of so many South Africans. Just as every American knows where he or she was when President Kennedy was assassinated, many of us seem to remember precisely where we were when the Springboks believed they were cheated out of an historic series win in New Zealand. I was in the main lecture room at Hilton College – and it hurt there too.

The following year, a group of us climbed into a minibus and travelled to Durban to watch the Springboks play the touring Jaguars side at King's Park. It was the first time I had seen the Boks play, and the first time I visited the venue that would become the stage for so many of my happiest days. It would simply not be true to say I returned to school vowing to become a Springbok, but I did enjoy the vibe and I could appreciate the sense of honour.

There were other moments of inspiration that, looking back, gave me the desire to train harder and realise my potential in the game. Murray Mexted, the flamboyant All Black eighthman, was a frequent visitor to Durban during the early 1980s and, on one occasion, he gave a coaching clinic at Hilton. It cannot have lasted more than 30 minutes, but being close to a leading player left a mark on my young and impressionable mind. I wanted to be like him.

Many years later, I would find myself in Mexted's position. I have heard people question the value of such celebrity coaching clinics, asking what effect a half hour can really have. From personal experience, I know it can make an enormous difference, and I have always kept this in mind when looking out over a crowd of youngsters. You never know who's out there.

As the years passed, and the memory of the water bottles fiasco receded, I moved up the Hilton rugby ladder to the point where I was surprisingly drafted into the first XV in standard nine, my penultimate year at school. Then, as now, the Hilton team was being coached by Klein Strydom and the former Springbok wing Andy van der Watt. I cannot overstate my admiration for the integrity and knowledge of these two outstanding individuals; it was they who pushed through probably the most important decision of my entire career.

Soon after joining the first team squad, I was called aside by the coaches.

'Gary, there is good news and bad news,' they told me.

'OK.'

'The bad news is that we think you're too slow to be a backline player, the good news is we think you're strong enough to be a forward.'

I was surprised by this total change in direction of my career, but I was in no frame of mind to argue. At that stage, the honour of wearing the white jersey with the black trim was the limit of my ambition and I would have played hooker if it were necessary to realise that goal.

'Absolutely,' I replied, 'I've been thinking that for some time.'

I shudder when I reflect upon my switch to the loose forwards. There is no doubt at all that, had I remained in the backline, my rugby career would gradually have faded away to nothing. In all probability, I would not have played the game very far beyond school. At such moments, lives are made.

As a Springbok captain earning many thousands of rand and always in the headlines, there is a temptation to be overwhelmed by vanity, to strike up the band, to shift into Sinatra mode, shake the shoulders and break into a chorus of that great anthem to egotism: 'I did it my way.' I won't do that. Credit must go where the credit is due. The simple truth of my rugby career is that I did it Klein Strydom and Andy van der Watt's way.

My first team debut was a blur, not only because I didn't really understand what was going on around me on the fringes of the scrum but also because the opposition Ixopo players seemed to take special pleasure in tackling me into the ground. I was relentlessly drilled and, far worse, Hilton lost. We were simply not expected to lose such fixtures. As the Ixopo players grinned over their cool drinks and laughed their way through the post-match dance, I stood quietly to one side, wondering whether I had been exposed as playing out of my depth.

Even my familiar carefree approach was failing me, but the brief crisis passed. The coaches kept faith with me, and I settled into the first team, slowly adapting to the pace and patterns at the back of the scrum.

The strength of South African schools rugby has often been celebrated as the rock-solid foundation of the game in this country, and it is impressive to see how even today, in this professional age, crowds of up to 15 000 people still turn up, year after year, to watch the traditional school derbies across the land. Many of our schools maintain stadiums and facilities that can be compared to the facilities of senior club sides in other parts of the rugby world.

And yet we should guard against complacency because there is a trend that threatens to undermine the traditional power and glory of the schools rugby structure: it is an apparent inability to involve former provincial and Springbok players at these levels, a problem both of demand and supply.

On the one hand, there is often reluctance among schoolteachers to accept former players into their areas of responsibility. Such territorial jealousy is counterproductive, because players recently retired from the highest level, with all their knowledge and experience, should be welcomed into our schools with open arms.

On the other hand, in the minds of many former players, coaching has become not so much a vocation, by which you can put something back into the game, as a means of keeping your snout in the trough of professional rugby and maintaining a high level of income beyond your playing days. Aware of the need to market themselves, provincial unions are more inclined to appoint the big name ex-player as coach rather than the guy who has worked his way through the coaching ranks. Such experiments invariably end in tears. There simply are no short cuts. However, in this environment, it is not surprising that a former Springbok with an inclination to coach will gravitate towards a lucrative provincial post rather than go back to learn his trade at a school.

The result of these two trends is a gradual erosion of our traditional base of top-class coaches at schools level, and this is bound to have a serious impact as future generations of players move through the ranks.

We only have to look towards New Zealand to see the way forward. In all my visits to that country, and there have been many, I have always been struck by the sheer number of familiar faces still involved in the game at junior level. It is common to find former All Blacks coaching school sides, strengthening the lower levels of the game and, only once they have developed themselves as a coach, being considered for posts at provincial or Super 12 level.

My career was made possible by the foresight and quality of my coaches at school, and the authorities must not assume these foundations of the game will maintain themselves. The traditional player base requires as much care and attention as the national teams and the development programme. We have the structure and we have the passion among the parents and public. If we can get the coaching structures and trends right, the game will thrive.

The highlights of every Hilton rugby season were, of course, the home and away derby matches against Michaelhouse. Win these and you have had a fine season. Win every match but lose against the red-and-white hoops and your year will quietly be consigned to the archives, never to be mentioned again.

Fortune smiled on Hilton during my years. We beat Michaelhouse home and away in 1983, when the Hilton captain was Paul Harrison, a remarkable and talented person, who was tragically killed in a road accident while studying at the University of Stellenbosch. Peter Mackenzie assumed the captaincy in 1984, and we won the home match but were left high, dry and disappointed when a flu epidemic forced the postponement of the fixture at Michaelhouse.

Each Hilton-Michaelhouse occasion, in my experience, followed the same traditions and unfolded as an entirely memorable day.

As members of the first XV, we walked tall in the school grounds. We were the elite, and, showing the bald arrogance of youth, we behaved as such. Among the specific privileges afforded us was the exclusive right to wear the school's distinctive white scarf with black trim, the luxury of having our boots cleaned and our playing kit carried by younger boys. We felt special. On the evening before the match, we would be invited for coffee and cake at Andy van der Watt's house, an event masked in my memory by the taste of Mrs Van der Watt's milk tart.

Match day was nothing less than a festival. Parents and old boys flooded down the N3 from Johannesburg, bringing French champagne picnics and keen memories of schooldays gone by. Attendance at the match was compulsory for all students of both schools, prompting fierce chanting competition between the rival banks of blazered supporters on opposite sides of the field. This contest became so serious that schools set aside time to practise their war cries.

Amid the cacophony of noise, an intense game of rugby would be played and lasting friendships were forged across the rivalry. Andrew Poole, Richard Church and Sean Hulett all played for Michaelhouse, but nonetheless became close friends, while Adrian Short, Wally Grindrod, Justin King, Angus Bell and Bryce Varner were among my peers at Hilton, sharing in our victory celebrations.

We lived from Saturday to Saturday, enjoying the status and relishing the challenge of establishing an unbeaten season. In 1984, my final year, aside from keeping Michaelhouse in their place, our team was strong enough to contemplate a rare honour for Hilton: victory against the larger and traditionally stronger team from Maritzburg College. Before another huge, partisan crowd, we competed well and led College by two points with a few minutes remaining.

As we sensed a whiff of glory, the Maritzburg flyhalf cleared his lines with a long 22-metre drop kick. The ball took an awkward and inexplicable bounce on the sun-baked pitch, away from our fullback and into the hands of their right wing, who raced through to score the winning try beneath our posts. I have not felt so devastated and disappointed on a rugby field. Incidentally, the College flyhalf that afternoon was a talented young player named Joel Stransky.

Joel was already emerging as a star of his generation, and I was delighted to be included alongside him in the Natal squad to attend the 1984 Craven Week for provincial high school teams, a week of rugby played in Bloemfontein. Shaun Gage, a hooker from Durban High School, and a bold lock called Steve Atherton, from Pinetown, appeared as other fresh faces in our ranks.

The traditional role of Natal squads at such festivals was to be the life and soul of the party in the evenings, but to lie down and be crushed on the field by the bigger, fitter, stronger, Afrikaner-dominated teams from Northern Transvaal, Transvaal, Free State and the Western Province. We did lose our big game of the week, against Province, but we showed enough tenacity and talent in our other matches to hint at the imminent glory years of Natal rugby. Nobody knew it then, but we would not be the 'soft English' for much longer.

Throughout 1984, I had been winning golden opinions for my performances as an effective loose forward, trying to read the game and link between the forwards and backs, but I did not take much notice. I was enjoying my rugby, but had no special determination to play at a higher level. It was fun ... and I would see how things went, but nothing burned inside. At the conclusion of the Craven Week, Joel Stransky was selected for the South African Schools team, and I was not in the least disappointed to have been omitted. That honour had not even appeared on my radar screen; it appeared out of range.

Towards the end of my days at Hilton, I even started to contribute to the school in areas that reached beyond sport. When the Theatrical Society staged a production of Gilbert and Sullivan's *HMS Pinafore*, they needed someone strong to carry the ageing admiral on stage; they looked no further than the rugby squad, and they found me. There were no words to learn, but my first (and, as it has turned out, my last) stage performance passed off without a hitch.

Midway through my final year, I was named as a school prefect, but I did gain the impression that this was more a reflection of the fact there was nobody else to fill the position rather than any general conviction that I was leadership material. I was not a high profile person at school. Mingling happily in the crowd, enjoying a joke and a drink with my friends, playing rugby, easily brushing aside the problems of the world; this was the pattern of my existence.

Within days of leaving Hilton, setting out to use my privileged education and make a mark on the world, I found myself in a police cell.

A group of us had cast aside our uniforms and decided to spend a few days, and frantic nights, at Angus Bell's farm on the north coast. Soon after arrival, we set out on motorbikes to buy cigarettes. With no helmets and no licences, we were flagged down by the police, thrown into the back of a yellow police van and swiftly deposited in the cells at the Chaka's Rock police station.

Angus Bell's father could have come and secured our release within a few hours, but I think he rather enjoyed the spectacle of seeing these young bucks from Hilton getting an early taste of the big, bad world; and so we remained in the cells until late afternoon, finally leaving quietly and soberly. My parents were not unduly troubled by the incident. My laid-back nature was hereditary.

The 1984 season had unfolded as a successful year for Natal rugby, not that I took any particular interest. That year, Natal won the Currie Cup B section and the semi-final against the runners up in the A section. The result was that they played in the final for the first time in their history, but lost to Western Province at Newlands.

I remained largely oblivious to these developments. Towards the end of 1984, I would have struggled to name or recognise any Natal players. We lived out in the sticks, beyond Pietermaritzburg, and thus felt removed from the action down the road in Durban. And, at Hilton College, we were far more interested in playing touch out on the rugby fields than watching television.

Natal rugby? So what?

It would not always be so.

3

The Slow Road

It is not unusual for a young man to leave school with absolutely no idea of what he wants to do with his life, and yet have hardly any concern for how he will survive in the big, bad world. When I left Hilton in 1984, I had no vision of what I wanted to be or do but this uncertainty was not exactly troubling me. That was not my nature; my inclination was to drift with the tide, to go with the flow.

The fact that I had achieved only a standard pass in Afrikaans meant I could not follow my brother, Ross, straight to university; a strategy emerged whereby I would first undergo my two years of national service, improve my Afrikaans and only afterwards go on to university.

National service had long been a fact of life for young white South African males and the prospect of fighting on the borders in some kind of unmentionable activity against Cubans, terrorists and sundry communists filled many school-leavers, and their parents, with dread. My view was simply that the two years in the Defence Force were unavoidable, so I should make the best of my fate.

My initial posting was to Kimberley and, not wanting to travel alone into the military unknown, I arranged my itinerary so that I could be dropped off in Durban and join my cousin, Geoff Evennett, on the train from there to the Diamond City. As luck would have it, he had received the same posting as me. If anyone asked, of course, I blithely remarked that Geoff needed company. In reality, of course, it was me who sought the comfort of a friendly face.

In the event, I was not particularly fazed by 12 weeks of basic training. We lived in appropriately basic bungalows, there were no comforts at all and the corporals stomped up and down for most of the day, but they were mostly bark and not much bite. Fortunately there were enough English-speaking guys at the camp, mostly from Natal, to ensure the Afrikaans vitriol from the Permanent Force soldiers was equally and thinly spread between us. I had played rugby for Hilton against Voortrekker Hoërskool in Pietermaritzburg, but this was by far my most prolonged exposure to Afrikaans culture. The divide between English-speaking and Afrikaans-speaking was obvious and glaring, but it has never caused me any significant problems.

The PF soldiers seemed physically tough and they were undoubtedly intense about the issue and responsibility of fighting for their country. They were driven in all respects and I suppose they could have been irritated by our more relaxed approach. Most of us were far from obsessed by the communist threat, insurgents or even 'terrorists'. Such matters did not play on my mind from morning to night. In fact, throughout my basic training, I did not even know the words of *Die Stem*, the national anthem ... but I survived.

For no apparent reason, I was then dispatched on an officer's course in the Intelligence section and on to a posting in what was then South West Africa, later to become Namibia. No explanation was asked, or given. The accepted pattern of distributing national servicemen around the SADF was that the talented rugby players would be sent to Pretoria, where they could play for Northern Transvaal, the beach bums would be sent straight back to Natal Command in Durban and, if they didn't know what to do with you, you headed for SWA.

THE SLOW ROAD

On reflection, I suppose I should have been disappointed to miss out on the rugby ticket to Pretoria but there were some huge Afrikaans loose forwards in my year and no-one seemed to notice the small eighthman from Natal. I simply was not big enough to get any attention, and I had almost accepted that that would be the eventual epitaph on my rugby career. We would see.

Our group and I finally arrived in the town of Rundu, in the north of South West Africa near the Angolan border. This would be home for 18 months. It may have sounded like a dramatic location, but the truth is I was never involved in any kind of threatening military activity. During my 18 months in Rundu, I only ever heard the sound of angry gunfire once – and that was over the radio from PF guys fighting much further up north. As far as I was concerned, this was not war; this was sitting in an office, day after day after day.

I was attached to Section 20, the group charged with protecting the inland border between SWA and Angola. This was a task massively eased by the overwhelming presence of friendly UNITA soldiers in the area. The Section 10 guys, based nearer the west coast, suffered a much harder time.

We did experience one moment of excitement, however. Soon after our arrival, for one or other reason that was not made clear to us, we were flown up to inspect the border and forcibly warned not to swim in the crocodile-infested Okavango River. But the sun beat down … it was unbearably hot that afternoon and a group of us decided to swim across, if only to be able to tell our friends back home that we had actually set foot on Angolan soil. The water was refreshing, and I was exhilarated to reach the opposite bank.

In this moment of triumph, I was stopped in my tracks. There was a rustle in the bush behind me. I turned and saw a camouflaged black soldier holding an AK47 and staring directly at me. An instant dive and frantic crawl later, I was back on the other bank, chastened and with my heart pumping. They had been friendly UNITA soldiers, but this brush with reality brought home the fact that we were a bunch of naïve kids thrust into a serious, in many cases tragic, situation.

Even in Rundu, rugby spiced up our lives. Section 20 duly formed its own team and, under the enthusiastic patronage of Colonel Ferreira, we were taken on serious organised tours of South West Africa, playing other military sides. Jean Engelbrecht, son of the former South African wing Jannie, scored most of our tries as we won a makeshift SWA SADF league and started to earn a proud reputation in this part of the world. Even in the dust, we found status. At one point, here in the middle of our national service, we embarked on a month-long rugby tour of the Western Cape. Time was flying by, and I was having fun.

By the end of 1986, the prospect of returning home appeared daunting and uncertain when compared to what had become relentless relaxation in Rundu, but my period of national service was ending. What next?

The uncertainty dragged on for some weeks and, after an occasionally vexed period of frustration and concern (I was frustrated, my parents were concerned), it was agreed that I would start working with my brother, Ross. He had left university after one year and, an entrepreneur at heart, started his own company producing diamond mesh fencing from coils of wire. Diamann Ltd was gaining momentum and securing a respectable list of orders, and I duly joined the payroll early in 1987. The plan was that, for an initial period, I would learn about production and Ross would make the sales. Thereafter, I would take over in Maritzburg, freeing him to start a new branch in Durban.

We worked hard to establish the business, focusing on the task at hand as we shared digs outside Pietermaritzburg, shared a *bakkie* and shared an office. Some brothers would have clashed in such circumstances. We didn't. It was exciting in a way, exhausting in other ways. And we stuck to the master plan, with Ross branching out to Durban in 1988. Our hopes were high but it slowly and sadly became clear that Diamann was fighting a losing battle. By August 1989, our main backers had lost faith and our tiny profit margins evaporated. We had always been vulnerable, but the closing of the business was no fun for anyone.

I felt desperately disappointed for Ross because he had invested so much emotional capital into the business, but there was no reason for me to worry on his behalf. He moved to Empangeni, and subsequently to Johannesburg, where he has since developed a successful steel merchant business.

As time went by, I started to sense people were feeling sorry for me. The fact was that I had passed my 21st birthday, and, in many ways, I hadn't really had much fun, and hadn't really made significant progress in any direction either. Straight from school, straight into the army, straight into work with my brother: there had been no respite from the daily grind and it was not as though I had been reaping any great rewards. My confidence was sagging.

My parents, however, remained calm. Where some mothers and fathers might have started to apply pressure and effectively transfer their worries to me, I think their strategy was to support me in whatever I wanted to do, outwardly relaxed in the knowledge that I would settle down soon enough. I appreciated their sympathetic approach during these uncertain times and, privately, resolved not to be a disappointment to them. Following Diamann's demise, I assessed my position and decided it was time to earn a professional qualification. Farming had always interested me, and I enthusiastically enrolled in the two-year farm management course at Cedara, an agricultural college out on the road between Pietermaritzburg and Midmar. I should add that reports of the social life at Cedara had also filtered through, and these were invariably favourable.

If someone had said to me on New Year's Day 1990 that I

would become a farm manager gently living out my life in the Natal Midlands, I would have been extremely content with that. I was playing rugby for the Maritzburg University open side and for the Natal under-21 team, and playing well within the confines of what was then an explicitly amateur game, but it appeared unlikely that I would even play for Natal and there was never any suggestion at all that I would ever reach international level. Nobody stood on the touchline and told me: 'One day, my boy, you will be a Springbok.'

The Natal under-21 team was regularly thumped by larger and stronger opposition, even if we did produce sporadic and therefore unexpected glimpses of the resolve that would usher in the glorious 90s at King's Park. At one stage, we actually took the lead in a match against Transvaal. The sense of shock was profound. Four or five times a season, the under-21s would travel with the senior provincial team and play the first curtain-raiser, kicking off at around 11:30 in the morning with a hundred or so people sitting in the stands. Such early exposure to the citadels of the game was undoubtedly positive for young players, and has always been a strong feature of South African rugby. Throughout this period, the Natal under-20 side was coached by Chukka Kember, an amicable Argentinean, but rarely earned either back page headlines or fulsome praise.

In the meantime, I was discovering the meaning of fun at Cedara. While my studies focused on soil science, there was no lack of opportunity to revel in the kind of carefree, light-hearted existence held so precious by students. Four of us were sharing a house not far from Hilton, although we tended to spend more time at the Nottingham Road pub than under our own roof.

I enjoyed a few beers, enjoyed a laugh and might have fooled around with a fire hose or two in my day, but we never became involved in any kind of fighting or violent behaviour. We were laid back, living for the next laugh.

Part of our second-year course was a project in which the

students were divided into groups and challenged to bring up a young steer. We would have to plan his diet, feed him and care for him, all with the goal of leading him in the Cedara Show and, if selected, taking him to the Royal Show in Maritzburg. At the outset, we were shown a precautionary video in which an earlier student had failed so miserably to nurture his steer that he suffered the ignominy of leading a pig around the parade ring. That student was Dick Muir.

None of our group particularly enjoyed getting up at five in the morning and driving for 20 minutes to feed our steer, but the animal didn't let us down and, with a little luck and help from our friends, we were all successful in securing our Cedara diplomas in farm management. The irony – and I was not to know this at the time – was that I would never use the qualification.

Through 1990, I continued to enjoy playing rugby for Maritzburg University and was picked on a handful of occasions for the Natal Duikers, effectively the provincial second team, but the measure of my achievement rarely amounted to more than a paragraph in the local *Natal Witness* newspaper.

Any faint hope I might have nurtured of playing provincial rugby appeared to be blocked emphatically by the outstanding form of Andrew Aitken, who was playing eighthman for Natal. He was not only younger than me, but he was also mobile, strong and talented. Aitken was being hailed as one of the stars of the side in a centenary year that gathered momentum and took Natal to a place in the Currie Cup final against Northern Transvaal, the favourites, at Loftus Versfeld.

My role, in what unfolded as a momentous day for Natal rugby, was not to be a member of the team, or even the reserves, but to be one of the many fervent supporters who travelled north more in hope than expectation.

Clive van der Spuy, a friend from Cedara, had contacted some friends in Johannesburg and arranged for us to stay with them on the Friday night. There was a bottle of whisky on the bar and, under pressure from our host, we agreed to drink the bottle dry in the unlikely event of a Natal triumph.

Match day dawned. We dressed in khakis and proudly carried branches of banana trees that we had painstakingly brought up the N3. The atmosphere in and around the streets of Pretoria that warm, sunny Saturday was outstanding. Everyone was relaxed; the home fans were confidently expecting to win and we were content to contemplate nothing more than a great day out. Few considered Craig Jamieson's Natal team stood a realistic chance of upsetting Naas Botha's Northern Transvaal side. The Blue Bulls had won the Currie Cup in 1987, 1988, shared the trophy in 1989 and had even planned their victory party for later that evening. Natal had never won the Currie Cup, not ever.

Our tickets took us to the very highest row of the towering open stand at Loftus but, even from those bird's-eye view seats, I was able to appreciate the strategy adopted by Natal coach, Ian McIntosh. He had created a large, physical pack of forwards, known affectionately in Durban as the 'macro pack', and the plan was to match Northerns up front, to meet muscle with muscle. The 'soft English' were fighting back, and, for us, it was magnificent to behold.

The minutes began to pass, and we remained in contention, making the tackles, holding the line. The victory that had seemed so unlikely became more and more possible with each second that ebbed away. Our group was cheering each and every ruck, each pass that went to hand. Speckled around the light blue stands, Natal supporters rubbed their eyes, and dared to believe.

Midway through the second half, our record-breaking wing Tony Watson skipped around a tackle just in front of us and wheeled around to score at the northern end of the ground. It was a moment of triumph now frozen in the history of Natal rugby. We had seized the lead, and we never lost it.

Maybe Northerns had been unsettled by the loss of centre

Pieter Nel, who was injured running onto the field, but all this was detail. Natal, for so long the bridesmaids, had prevailed.

Having screamed and yelled myself hoarse all afternoon, I can remember being content simply to watch the team parade around Loftus Versfeld. I had not been the most enthusiastic of supporters, indeed had hardly watched any games at King's Park. I had been happy to play for the under-21s and the Duikers now and then, but Natal rugby was scarcely engraved on my heart.

Maybe, along with many others, I had been infected by a sombre expectation throughout the fraternity that we would never actually win anything. Coaches would come and go, talented players would do the same, and we might produce one or two top-class performances, but we would never win.

The sight of Craig Jamieson's team holding high the Currie Cup at Loftus exploded these deep-seated convictions and inhibitions. For Natal rugby, this was the breaking of the dam; it was the start of an era in which everything became possible and silverware was confidently anticipated. For me, it was a moment of acute discovery. At once, I knew I wanted to be part of all this.

Not long after the Currie Cup triumph, I bought a newspaper and read that Andrew Aitken had decided to further his studies in Cape Town. The report said he would not be available for Natal during the 1991 season, and went on to offer the names of some candidates who might reasonably fill the vacancy at the back of the scrum.

'Gary Teichmann'.

There stood my name.

In black and white.

My heart skipped a beat.

My opportunity had arrived.

4

Uprising in Natal

More than anyone else, Naas Botha ensured Natal's Currie Cup triumph in 1990 would not be a freakish one-off, an historical anomaly, but would rather herald the arrival of a new power in South African provincial rugby.

'It took them 100 years to win their first Currie Cup,' said Botha, following the final at Loftus Versfeld, 'and it will probably take them another 100 years to win it again.' This remark served as perfect motivation for a Natal squad that was leaving behind the insecurity and inferiority of the past and fast getting into the habit of winning, and expecting to win, every match.

It was my excellent fortune to arrive on the fringes of the Natal team at this most exciting and invigorating period of the union's history. There was a new driving ambition and professionalism within the Natal Rugby Union that filtered through all levels of the game; in Ian McIntosh, the province had an inspirational, emotional and much respected coach who, through two spells in charge, would be able to measure his success in silverware.

During the 1980s, Natal had languished in the B section of the Currie Cup, season upon season being characterised by what seemed to be an annual promotion/relegation match against Northern Free State. This home and away tie between the winners of the B section and the bottom team in the A section invariably unfolded as a narrow win at King's Park followed by a heavy defeat at Welkom. These were desperate days, as eager, fresh-faced Natal teams were repeatedly physically dominated and bullied back to the B section.

A depressing defeat in Welkom was once infamously followed by a brawl during the post-match function when a Northern Free State official hurled a large television set at a group of Natal players making their way up the steps to the room where the cocktail party was being held. On the field, off the field, the consensus prevailed that the 'English' were just too soft for top class rugby.

Loftus Versfeld 1990 shattered that perception, and it fell to us, as Natal players of the 1990s, to ensure the mind shift would be permanent. It is a matter of immense pride for many people that we achieved our goal.

On reflection, my introduction to the Natal squad owed a great deal – if not everything – to Andrew Aitken's decision to pursue his educational and business career in Cape Town. Had he stayed in Durban at the end of the 1990 season, it is almost certain that I would have languished in the Maritzburg University club team, earning positive reviews in the *Natal Witness,* the local newspaper, but still not cutting much ice with the decision-makers in Durban.

Again I am eager to stress the truth, as I know it. It would be heartening to pretend that my rugby career has been a triumphal march to glory, paved by the unstinting admiration and respect of coaches and team-mates; heartening, but wrong. It is probably true that every career, in every field, owes something to being in the right place at the right time. I hesitate to use the word 'luck', and would refer instead to a 'happy confluence of circumstances'.

I benefited at school when coaches Klein Strydom and Andy van der Watt decided I should play loose forward rather than centre, and I was fortunate again when Aitken's decision at the end of 1990 created an opportunity in the Natal team. I had personally played no role in either event, and the truth is I might never have played top-class rugby had these cards fallen differently.

To a large extent, we are all the products of circumstance, and I have tried to bear this in mind when any inclination to vanity threatens. When things go well, we should be grateful and seize the opportunity; that's all.

My invitation to pre-season Natal provincial trials in March 1991 seemed to be my long-awaited invitation to the ball, and I was content with my efforts in the Rest of Natal XV playing against the shadow provincial side. I clearly recall a bubbling, infectious mood of confidence and excitement that evening. For the first time ever, we were the champions! Joel Stransky was on top of his game, running the show, laughing, marshalling the backline, taking decisions and, it seemed to me, getting everything right.

I rated my chances of being included in the team for the opening match of the season, against Free State in the Test Unions day at Bloemfontein, as being no more than 50/50. The consensus was that I was still too small – at only 97 kg, I would evidently need more bulk to earn a place in the 'macro-pack' – and the coach duly named a loose forward trio of Andrew Blakeway, John Plumtree and the captain, Wahl Bartmann. I travelled as a reserve.

Don't worry, I told myself, your chance will come. In fact, April came, May came and June came ... but not my chance. Ian McIntosh seemed initially eager to give older players an opportunity and then appeared reluctant to throw me into the heat of a major Currie Cup match. Whatever the reason for my continuing omission, I was becoming frustrated. My name had started to appear more often in the newspapers, and my club form remained at a respectable level, but the provincial chance remained elusive.

Be patient, I told myself. But McIntosh seemed to be trying every loose forward in the entire province, leaving me on the side! The fact that Natal battled in the Currie Cup might have offered some perverse consolation, but I simply wanted to get on the field. My trademark diffidence was melting away. I was 24 years old, and desperately wanted to play provincial rugby.

Towards the end of June, I played for Natal University in a convincing 26-4 victory over Wits University in Johannesburg. The match was televised and I had produced several of the distinctive surging runs and dramatic tackles that ensure you get noticed, and appreciated, by TV audiences – the hard gains in the bottom of the ruck might be more appreciated by your team-mates, but they tend not to leave an impression on the people watching at home.

I had been attending the first team practices at King's Park on Monday evenings, trying not to appear too irritated by my lack of progress, and nothing appeared much different on the Monday following the Wits match. One of the coaches said something complimentary about my performance but I had started to think there was more chance of a white Christmas in Durban than there was of Ian McIntosh including me in his Natal team.

Seven o'clock the next morning, my telephone was ringing. Who on earth would want me this early on a Tuesday? It was my mother.

'Congratulations,' she said. 'You're in the Natal team.'

She had bought the *Natal Witness,* and casually checked the side announced to play the Currie Cup match against Northern Transvaal in Pretoria on Saturday. There I was, at last. Eighthman: Gary Teichmann. Errol Stewart, the Natal cricketer, would also be making his debut, at centre.

These were the days of amateur rugby, of course, when players needed to buy the Tuesday morning newspaper to see whether they had been selected or dropped for the following Saturday match. There was a running joke among the players that, in Pretoria, you could even find out the Northerns side by buying the Monday morning newspaper, printed before the selectors had met. Quintus van Rooyen, the late rugby writer of *Die Beeld* newspaper, would telephone each of the five selectors on the Sunday evening, assess their views and calculate what would happen when they gathered. Nine times out of ten, he was right.

For me in Maritzburg, the *Witness* was the harbinger of good news and I quickly telephoned Lood Muller, the Natal prop, and arranged a lift with him to the provincial first team training session at King's Park that night. It was not until I arrived at the ground that evening that Ian McIntosh shook me by the hand and wished me a successful provincial career.

Just over eight years later, we would close our formal associations with Natal rugby on the same emotional occasion, at the same venue.

Spirits among the Natal side were not exactly buoyant. The defence of the Currie Cup title had been stillborn, with the team losing four of the first six Currie Cup matches. Maybe Naas Botha's prediction would prove right, after all. And, three weeks before, the team had been trounced 62-6 by Northerns in the Lion Cup final at Loftus Versfeld. As we prepared to travel north again, there was a discernible dread that we were in line for another bull whipping.

Ian McIntosh made an instant impression on me. His affection and simple enjoyment of the game was evident in everything he said and did; his charts and tables represented the hours of planning he committed to getting the job right, and he bestrode the training field in the manner of a slightly eccentric, but much loved schoolmaster. Everyone called him 'Mac'; players occasionally teased him, but he retained the capacity to put anyone swiftly in their place.

Craig Jamieson was the other dominant personality in the set-up. Feisty and sharp as a scrumhalf, he was a sympathetic captain who took care of his players on and off the field. With Wahl Bartmann, he went out of his way to make sure the new eighthman settled comfortably into the routine.

The preparations for my debut were smooth, but my fellow debutant Errol Stewart was not so fortunate later. It was his fate to room with Dick Muir, the experienced, up-beat centre who was sometimes not averse to drinking a can of beer on the eve of a match. Under duress, Errol agreed to join him and the order was duly posted with room service at the Pretoria Holiday Inn.

By chance, the coach was standing in the hotel foyer when he noticed a waiter striding from the bar to the lifts, carrying a tray with one Castle and one Lion. In a frightening moment of inspiration, McIntosh followed the waiter into the lift, discovered which room had asked for the two beers and, within minutes, the coach was knocking on the door of room 210.

Errol answered the door.

The coach stood impassive.

'I believe one of these must be for you, sir.'

As Errol later recalled, he might have got away with the incident if he had ordered a Castle, like Dick. He could have assured McIntosh they were both for his midfield partner, probably already recognised as a lost soul. But, with the two brands on the tray, Errol could only bow his head and blush.

After so many years in the curtain-raisers, I was thrilled to be playing in the main match and excited to perform before a crowd in excess of 40 000 at Loftus Versfeld. I clearly recall Naas Botha warming up before the game, kicking a ball in the long corridors outside the changing rooms. This would be the last season for the ultimate match winner, the player who, more than any other, had dominated South African rugby for more than 15 seasons. The sheer weight of his experience made me feel very new and raw at this level.

Every provincial debut is a blur, 80 minutes passing like 80 seconds, and mine was no different. Northerns scored in the first moments of the game as Uli Schmidt, the home side's ferocious hooker, seized possession straight from the kick-off, then stepped past, and maybe through, my tackle. He set up a maul, and the Northerns forwards were soon thundering over our line.

Welcome to the Currie Cup. I had missed my first tackle, Naas Botha had kicked the conversion and we were trailing 7-0 after two minutes. Natal teams of the past would have succumbed, but this side of the 1990s steadied, made the tough tackles and emerged with a 22-12 victory that demonstrated loud and clear that winning the 1990 Currie Cup title had not been a fluke.

My contribution had been mediocre, even if the coach was kind enough to compliment me for getting involved: he said it would have been easy for me to go out and hide but, at least, I had not been afraid to seek the work. Following two shattering challenges from Pote Fourie, the rugged Northerns eighthman, every aching bone in my body offered proof of my physical efforts.

I sat quietly in the visitors' changing room afterwards, taking my time to change, content to watch Jamieson, Watson, Reece-Edwards and the other Natal legends enjoying a result that compensated significantly for disappointing Currie Cup results earlier in the season. Only eight months earlier, I had been watching them win at Loftus from the highest row of the open stand. Now, I was sitting among them in the changing room.

Formal confirmation of my elevation to the Natal team would arrive in the form of the official cap and blazer when I had played five provincial matches, but the informal marks of progress were applied during an initiation ceremony. Some provinces instructed their debutants to stand on chairs at team meetings, sing songs, tell jokes at which everyone had in advance been told not to laugh and drink large amounts of beer before being slapped on the backside.

The Natal tradition was less complicated. On the morning following their first away match, the new players would be lined up on the tarmac immediately before the team stepped aboard the flight back to Durban, and beaten across the buttocks with a thick cane stick. Three senior players would administer this beating and, on a cool Sunday morning at Johannesburg airport, Rudi Visagie, Tony Watson and Steve Atherton duly stepped forward to administer the thrashing to Errol Stewart and myself. These traditions may sound barbaric, but they did build team spirit and encourage a sense of belonging. I might have been stinging as I took my seat on the plane, but I felt proud as well.

Our 1991 season ebbed away to nothing. A week after winning at Loftus, we lost 36-22 at home to Free State, our third successive defeat at King's Park. If we were to become a consistently competitive provincial team, we needed to turn our home ground into a fortress, and there was work to do.

I was, however, happy to secure my provincial colours after the 51-15 Currie Cup romp against Eastern Province at King's Park, my fifth match, and then set off to spend the northern hemisphere 1991/92 season in Ireland. Cliffie Egberink, teammate at Maritzburg University and my closest friend, and I had arranged a five-month trip to play for the Clontarf club, outside Dublin. Such trips epitomised rugby union: fun-filled and companionable.

These precious qualities have often been taken for granted in the game, and there is justifiable concern they may not survive the rigorous demands and hard-nosed strategies of professionalism, but they were alive and well when I was of an age and ability to take full advantage.

It happened like this: one evening, we were sitting at the University club, listening to Keith Walker, a silver-haired guy who played for the club long ago but still liked to watch the first team play and stay for a drink. He said he had long-standing friends in Ireland, people who he had played against many years ago, and they had enquired if there were any young varsity players who would be interested in playing a season with their club in the Irish league.

The Irish club would pay the airfare, provide lodgings and a little pocket money in return for wholehearted commitment on the field. This was the stuff of rugby, a life-enriching experience laid on by the brotherhood of the game. Such processes are entirely foreign to harsher codes, like soccer.

I enjoyed Ireland: the sheer friendliness of everybody I met, the easy resolve to enjoy every moment of every day, the absence of airs and graces. And I was relieved to play well for Clontarf, contributing to a run in an event called the Smithwick's Old Belvedere Floodlit Cup. To my great surprise – and everyone else's as well – I managed to score a spectacular and decisive try in the 14-6 semi-final win against Old Wesley, bursting clear, chipping ahead, gathering the ball and plunging over the line. I had run 45 metres! In seasons to come, any try that I scored from more than 2 metres would qualify as long-range.

As luck would have it, my stay in Ireland coincided with the staging of the 1991 Rugby World Cup, and I took the opportunity to watch Zimbabwe, land of my birth, take on Ireland at Lansdowne Road. Any international in Dublin seems to be as much a social occasion as a sporting event. The crowds pour out of the pubs to the ground, and pour back into the pubs after the final whistle. The spirit and atmosphere throughout the city is happy, and positive, maybe only equalled by the big-match mood in either Edinburgh or Cardiff.

The Springboks, of course, were not taking part, although there appeared to be no shortage of South Africans in and around the tournament eager to offer an opinion on how their heroes might have fared had they been allowed to compete. One well-known figure, who should have known better, suggested the excluded Boks would have defeated England at ten o'clock in the morning, then re-emerged to beat Australia at noon, and still had enough energy to whip the All Blacks at three. Such ill-informed arrogance would be ruthlessly exposed upon the Springboks' readmission to Test rugby in 1992.

My own assessment is that we would have struggled against any of the top three teams in the world. Ignorance was bliss throughout the years of isolation. Five or six of our leading players were regularly hailed as the world's best in their position but this was a meaningless and easy boast, since we were sure in the knowledge that the proposition would never be tested.

There was certainly no lack of quality in the 1991 semi-final between Australia and New Zealand at Lansdowne Road, a game won by the inspirational genius of David Campese. His astounding flick pass, over his shoulder to Tim Horan, has been engraved in the annals of the game, and hinted at standards that South Africa would have to match. I enjoyed that match from the stands in Dublin … you could say it was good practice for watching both the remaining Rugby World Cup tournaments of the decade.

Arriving home in March 1992, my primary goal was to cement my place in the Natal team and, as proof of my commitment, I left my digs in Pietermaritzburg and joined a group of friends renting a house in Durban. After so many years of uncertainty and drifting, I had become remarkably focused on the challenge of making the black and white No. 8 jersey my own – focused, at least, in relation to the amateur standards of the day. I ran as hard as anyone at training, but I did stay clear of the gym where I found the exercise so boring and monotonous. If I didn't want to go, I didn't go – life would not always be so easy. I still enjoyed myself every Saturday night having a few beers with my friends. Drinking and rugby, soon to be separated by professionalism, were still getting along.

I agreed to join the College Rovers club in Durban, where Brian Bateman was a driving force. It was not money that drew me to Rovers, but the promise of a job interview at the Natal Building Society. All went well, and I duly started work in the corporate division at the NBS. Every aspect of my life was falling into place, my parents had stopped worrying and I owed almost all the breaks to rugby. A few headlines, my picture in the paper every now and then, flying around the country with one of the top provincial rugby teams, fêted and praised wherever we went; life was good.

As the Natal squad sweated through pre-season training, we all assumed life was good for Shaun Gage as well. We had played at Craven Week together and he had developed into a fine hooker, playing 22 times for Transvaal before moving to Natal, where he had already won 24 caps.

It is hard to explain the sense of absolute devastation when we were told, before training on the Thursday before our opening Currie Cup match of the season, against Western Province at King's Park, that Shaun had died in tragic circumstances on his farm. My memories of him will always be of a bright, cheerful and talented team-mate.

Such tragedy, so close to home, put the apparently crucial importance of making a winning start to the season in perspective. There is always a danger of taking sport too seriously, but Ian McIntosh intelligently managed the situation so we would play our hearts out for Shaun, rather than be depressed by the loss of a friend who had been among us, and suddenly taken away.

King's Park was packed, and I was further fired up by the knowledge that Andrew Aitken was playing for Western Province. I wanted to show everyone that I was the equal of the player I had finally replaced in our side. Mercifully, the fates were kind. I was able to take the ball on the burst and assist Errol Stewart in scoring an early try, and we cruised to a 31-19 victory. Midway through the first half, I was flattened by a stiff-arm tackle, but not even a bloodshot eye could conceal the perception that Wahl Bartmann, Andrew Blakeway and I had thrived in the loose phases against Andrew and Tiaan Strauss.

The playing personnel in the Natal team has evolved through the 1990s, with guys constantly leaving or retiring and others arriving, but I have always appreciated a strength of spirit within the squad that has meant the players have consistently taken a collective pride in whatever we achieved. There have been no prima donnas or individualism at any stage, and this has ensured the whole has always been greater than the sum of our parts.

Our backline combined solid defence with a flair for scoring tries. There were years of experience and reliability, and no shortage of talent, at the back, with players such as André Joubert, Tony Watson and the flamboyant Cabous van der Westhuizen. Scoring tries was never a problem

Dick Muir was the midfield pillar of the team. Creative and positive, he never failed to deliver on the field, and he also managed to keep the mood light off it. With his sense of humour and mischief, more than anyone else, Dick ensured we were a team with a ready smile. His midfield partners, Pieter Muller and Jeremy Thomson, offered a contrast: the richly talented Thomson brought a touch of class to everything he did and, at times, Muller presented one of the hard, uncompromising faces that forever banished the perception that we would not rise to a physical challenge.

Joel Stransky had established himself as one of the most skilful and most consistent flyhalves in the land, and he was supported by the hugely effective Henry Honiball, who had seemed prepared to retire from rugby and return to his farm in 1991 but was persuaded to remain with the squad. Robert du Preez had been recruited to the cause from Pretoria, and I was particularly grateful to the tall, strong scrumhalf for accepting me in the side with such enthusiasm. He had been there and done that, and his absolute recognition of my potential gave me confidence when I needed it most. As a new eighthman, I was fortunate to have a scrumhalf prepared to take the knocks.

Six of this backline would become Springboks, and Tony Watson would certainly have gained national selection had he been born several years earlier and if his career had not been abruptly curtailed by the grotesque injuries suffered in a collision with Uli Schmidt. There was talent and resilience, and the sheen of quality throughout.

But, of course, the backs needed the ball, and Ian McIntosh had forged a pack of forwards able to hold its own against any team in South Africa. Gerhard Harding and Lood Muller were as tough and strong as props should be; the front row was completed by the arrival in Durban of John Allan, the fiery hooker who had played for Scotland in the 1991 Rugby World Cup.

Every pack needs a combustible character to fire the spirits, and John provided this dimension to our side. To watch him high-step out on to the field or to whirl his arms maniacally during the warm-up prompted thoughts that he might be one or two sandwiches short of a full picnic, or that his lift might not always go to the top floor. In reality, of course, he was a class act and a constant physical presence in every match. I used to think the level of confidence within the side rose in direct proportion to the blood in his neck. When he was firing, everybody fired and, more than anyone else, John Allan ensured the tag 'soft' was removed from the neck of the Natal team, once and for all.

Rudi Visagie was another player who brought streetwise qualities to the heart of our pack. He had played for South Africa against England in 1984, and was generally thought to be entering semi-retirement when he moved from his familiar berth in the Free State scrum to Durban. His performances, both in the lineout and on the drive, quickly dispelled that suggestion; what's more, his long years of experience rubbed off positively on a talented, emerging lock forward such as Steve Atherton. This was the team McIntosh built, and everywhere the balance between experience and youth was expertly struck.

The senior partner in our company of loose forwards was another stalwart of Currie Cup rugby from the past seven or eight seasons. Capped by the national selectors in 1986, Wahl Bartmann had emerged in Transvaal colours as one of the strongest and most effective loose forwards in the game. He played rugby as he lived his life. I don't remember him ever throwing a dummy or making any kind of sidestep. There was not an ounce of deception in his body. He simply put his head down and bravely ploughed through the opposition.

Wahl had assumed the Natal captaincy when Craig Jamieson retired, and his calm, essentially quiet style of leadership established a model that I would be happy to follow in due course. There are some captains with a natural ability to motivate and spur the team on with fine, inspirational words. In my career, François Pienaar stands alone in this respect. Other captains lead by example, by being unselfish and conscientious, by setting standards for others to follow. Problems arise when the latter type attempts to mimic the former breed. As captains, Wahl and I understood what we could do, and how we would do it. It might not always have earned the loudest applause, but that was good enough for us.

With Wahl at No. 6 and me at No. 8, the loose trio was completed by one of the hardest rugby players I have encountered. Andrew Blakeway, my room-mate, was a typical South African grafter. He was the sort who burrowed away at the base of the maul while the glamour boys – the wings who glided over the try line or the eighthmen who ranged free and wide – were combing their hair, waiting for the ball to emerge. Andrew was an absolutely honest player, who throughout his rugby career gave very much more than he received.

This was the core of the Natal team. The basic requirements of success were all there: players with talent, a coach with knowledge, and a union with the financial guts to secure top class players when it was required. The fourth item on our credit sheet was the King's Park crowd.

The Natal public had responded magnificently to the upturn in fortunes of the provincial side to a point where we were drawing crowds in excess of 20 000 to cross-section matches and rarely less than a full house 45 000 to every Currie Cup match at King's Park. Again the Natal Rugby Union should be credited with the development of their product as top-class family entertainment.

By providing the beer tents and facilities to transform the car parks around the stadium into happy, seething braai areas, the NRU succeeded in conveying a sense that Currie Cup day at King's Park was the best party in Durban. While fathers and sons took their seats in the stadium, mothers and daughters arrived to set up the braai in the car park. The result was a vibe unmatched by anything else in South African sport. The matches would end before five in the evening but people would still be partying at three the next morning.

At times, admittedly, the crowd's enthusiasm did boil over and fruit was thrown at opposition players. On one occasion, most famously, Naas Botha had to shield himself from the barrage of missiles by standing in front of a linesman while we were attempting a kick at the posts. That was unacceptable, but nobody was ever hurt and such partisanship in the stands represented welcome progress from the generally apathetic, blazered courtesy of years gone by.

What has this to do with rugby, you may ask. Everything, I would reply. Natal rugby was a happening place in the 1990s, and this smell of success would permeate from the car park celebrations through to the players. We once wanted to win, then we needed to win; in 1992, we expected to win.

The result was a tremendous season in which Natal finished on top of the completed Currie Cup log for the first time ever. Fired by the weekly momentum of the A section format, which was strength versus strength, we settled into a rhythm of hard training, top class performance and high-spirited celebrations. It was exhilarating to be involved, week upon week, winning and laughing.

We beat Free State at home, defeated Western Province at Newlands and then overcame Northern Transvaal at King's Park. Victory in Bloemfontein and a home draw against

UPRISING IN NATAL

Transvaal duly booked our place in the 1992 Currie Cup final, to be played against a confident Transvaal side at Ellis Park.

This big year for Natal rugby had also been big for South Africa, as tours by the All Blacks and the world champion Wallabies brought the Springboks back to official Test rugby after an absence of eight years. I watched the Test defeats against New Zealand and Australia, at Newlands and Ellis Park respectively, on television and was left with the same emotions as the rest of the population. We were clearly not as strong as we had thought we were. To an extent, we had been put in our place. We would have to build from scratch.

The inexplicable arrogance of the Springbok mentality had permeated through to Natal as well. It is hard to know quite what the All Blacks thought when they arrived in Durban for their tour match against us to read crazy newspaper headlines screaming: 'Welcome to your worst nightmare!' South African rugby was nowhere, but we were shouting the odds.

I was excited by the prospect of playing New Zealand, even if I did feel in awe of players like Sean Fitzpatrick and Zinzan Brooke. These were legends of the game, and I was pleased to be on the same field as them. John Allan, our hooker, had played against the All Blacks before and, throughout our build-up, he stressed the importance of rising to the physical challenge.

'These guys will elbow you in the lineout, tug at your jersey in the loose and accidentally push your face into the ground when they stand up from the tackle,' he told us, 'but they will always be completely in control. They will be subtle enough not to concede penalties, and their sole aim will be to harass us out of stride and reap the rewards as we lose our focus. We have to meet their fire with fire, give as good as we get, and always stay cool.'

This was the first time I had heard such advice before playing New Zealand, and it would be repeated incessantly for most of the seven seasons that followed. By the late 1990s, of course, it would be me doing the talking.

FOR THE RECORD

In the event, the 1992 All Blacks knew too much for us and, proving there is no substitute for experience, emerged as 43-25 winners. Defeat against the celebrity tourists was a disappointment, but the make-or-break match of our season would be the Currie Cup final versus Transvaal at Ellis Park.

Typically, Ian McIntosh sought a fresh approach to our preparations and, in the week before the final, he brought in a sports psychologist to sharpen our mental attitude. This guy sat us down and asked us each to draw a picture that depicted courage. Most of us proceeded to draw lions, but Andrew Blakeway was moving on a different track, and he produced a stunning image of a man facing a firing squad and showing one finger in the direction of the guns.

I confess to having always been a sceptic about psychologists in sport, but I can appreciate these processes work well for some players and I recognise they play an important role in the modern sporting environment. Maybe I am a product of the amateur age, when people didn't seem to take things so seriously, but I have never had a problem in motivating myself to play, and I have generally dealt with the pressure by being oblivious to its existence. Maybe I am simply too stupid and primitive to understand the complexities.

The coach also exhibited astonishing paranoia that opponents were forever sending spies to record what happened at our training sessions. As players, we would tease him mercilessly, saying we had seen a camera lens in a bush alongside the training field or pointing out some stranger to him. Before the Ellis Park final, McIntosh insisted that we train in private, at a school, but even in this protected environment he could never be completely relaxed.

In later years, as Springbok coach in Australia, he went so far as to send a posse of players sprinting off to hunt somebody he thought had been filming the training session from raised ground adjacent to the field. The players usually greeted such adventure with hilarity, but Mac was serious.

UPRISING IN NATAL

Ellis Park was packed to capacity for a match enthusiastically billed by the Johannesburg pressmen as the fairytale conclusion to a distinguished career. Jannie Breedt, a massively gifted eighthman, assumed the Transvaal captaincy in 1986 and guided an expensively assembled team to Currie Cup finals in that and the following year, but lost both. In 1991, he had once again stood only 80 minutes from seizing the golden trophy, but lost the final at Loftus. Now, on the brink of retirement, he would play in one last Currie Cup final. The only right and fair result would surely be victory for this lion of the game.

The destiny of the Natal team, ironically led by Bartmann, for so long a close friend and team-mate of Breedt, was to conclude a successful season by winning a second Currie Cup title in three seasons. The words of Naas Botha were still ringing in our ears. He had said it would take us another 100 years to win another Currie Cup. We had the opportunity at Ellis Park to show that he had been no more than 98 years out in his assessment.

We started in a blur, spinning the wall wide with pace and accuracy, and I took an inside pass from Pieter Muller before scrambling over in the fifth minute. What followed was the sort of tight, intense struggle typical of most finals and, as the closing seconds ticked away, we clung to a 14-13 lead. Late in the game, the referee spotted errant Natal hands striving to seize the ball in a ruck and, to our horror, he awarded a goalable penalty to Transvaal.

Such is rugby. Everything came down to a single kick. Our season, all the training sessions and matches, all the plans and commitment, came down to this one moment. If Theo van Rensburg kicked the penalty, we would lose the final and be recalled as a team that fell at the last fence. On a different scale, Jannie Breedt stood with his hands on his knees, knowing that this kick would determine whether he retired in triumph or as an unlucky loser, again.

Van Rensburg kicked, and missed. Within minutes, Wahl

Bartmann was raising the Currie Cup above his head at Ellis Park, a significant moment for him after the acrimony of his departure from Transvaal, and Breedt was standing to one side, once again applauding the victors in his moment of defeat.

Throughout our celebrations, I was aware of Breedt's situation. Perhaps it was because we played in the same position, perhaps it was because we were both eighthmen who strived above all to play the ball and form a link between the forwards and backs. Whatever the reason, I empathised.

I was born in 1967. If Jannie Breedt had been born in that year, there is no doubt that he would have captained South Africa in many Tests, and probably enjoyed the financial benefit, opportunities and honours that lay ahead of me. It was the accident of his birth that he was reaching the age of retirement not only as the years of our isolation were ending but also as the amateur code was being swept away by the professional era. It was my great good fortune to be arriving on the scene as the good times started to roll.

Thus the Natal season ended in triumph. Aside from an early season loss to Northerns and a draw with Transvaal, we had won all our Currie Cup matches and emerged as deserving champions, albeit by a solitary point in the final. I had enjoyed a successful first full provincial season and was heartened to read in the *Sunday Times* the following morning that their chief rugby writer, Dan Retief, rated me as a 'fine young player who this season has developed into a legitimate Springbok candidate'.

The idea that I would ever wear the green and gold had not even struck me, but I was pleased other people considered it a possibility. Some berated the selectors for omitting me from the Springbok squad to tour France and England at the end of the year, although I probably knew the reality that, after only one full Currie Cup campaign, I was not ready for such elevation.

The celebratory beer had started to flow in our changing

room at Ellis Park and it was still flowing when, on our return to Durban the next day, the players gathered at the Cattleman's Restaurant on the beachfront. In spite of my drunken stupor, this would prove to be a significant occasion in my life.

Two weeks before the final, I had met a girl called Nicky de Giorgio. She was staying in digs with a Natal player, Neil Penrose and his girlfriend, and we had started to talk in the bar. After a while, I offered to buy her a drink, which she declined. Although injured by this rejection, I was encouraged to see she was standing on the touchline when I played for College Rovers the next day.

Nicky insists she was always planning to attend the match, but I believe she just had to see me again. The following night, I arrived at her door with a bunch of flowers and insisted on taking her to dinner. She maintains that, at this stage, she thought I was some kind of struggling basketball player.

At any rate, we had dinner and she subsequently agreed to attend the Natal team's victory party at the Cattleman's. To her credit, she held her own as the celebrations swiftly degenerated. Tina Turner's anthem *Simply the Best* shook the foundations and I have a misty recollection of being thrown in the air and then caught by a row of team-mates. Nicky has since confirmed this did indeed happen and, despite such early impressions which cannot have been entirely positive, we were married several years later.

A trough must follow every peak, and it was perhaps inevitable that my personal success of 1992 would be followed by more difficult times in 1993. After the honeymoon of my rugby career, the bills started to arrive. The Springboks had drawn a Test series in France and been beaten by England at Twickenham, prompting the knee-jerk dismissal of John Williams as the national coach. When, after some confusion, Ian McIntosh was named to succeed him, everybody understood the consequences for Natal rugby would be severe. In a sense, the loss of our coach took us back to square one.

Undaunted, the Natal Rugby Union sought out and secured probably the most exciting young coach in the country. Harry Viljoen, a self-made millionaire, had guided Transvaal to the Currie Cup final in 1992, but then fallen out with the Transvaal president, Louis Luyt, and needed a new challenge.

He was bright, and he was dynamic. He introduced cash bonuses for the player who made the biggest tackle in a match, and he was constantly trying to keep things interesting and challenging, but there was nothing he could do to alter the fact that the players, used to McIntosh, needed to adapt. We had wanted to take up where we had left off in 1992, but that was not possible.

The new season with the new coach also brought in a new competition: the Super 10 between the leading provincial sides in South Africa, Australia and New Zealand. After decades of playing the same teams at the same venues in the Currie Cup, the arrival of the Super 10 had an invigorating effect on the body of South African rugby. There were new worlds to conquer.

Natal's campaign in the fledgling event began with a sound victory over Western Samoa and gathered pace with an impressive win against Otago at the renowned House of Pain, their home ground in Carisbrook. James Small had returned to the province, bringing his unique blend of commitment and talent to the wing, and he touched down the first try as we consolidated a 3-0 half-time lead and joyfully romped away to a 35-13 victory.

It amused us to read afterwards that the New Zealanders had not been taking the tournament seriously. I am not sure the day will ever dawn when any New Zealand team plays a South African side and doesn't take it seriously. At any rate, if the excuse soothed their disappointment, that was fine.

Four days later, we played Auckland at Eden Park and were overcome by what virtually amounted to a team of All Blacks.

UPRISING IN NATAL

The format and draw had been hard on us, and that away defeat placed us second in Group B, condemning us to stand by and watch as Auckland lost the final to Transvaal in Johannesburg. In many ways, the inaugural Super 10 had been unsatisfactory, but the concept was right and would swiftly make it a genuinely massive event.

Returning to contest the Currie Cup, I was finding life more difficult. Where I had found space and opportunity in 1992, opponents seemed to be closing me down in 1993. It is well known among senior players that your second provincial season is usually the most difficult, although no amount of warning appears able to convey the message to young sensations in their first year. Pride is invariably followed by a Year Two fall. It is the players with the resolve and courage to get back on their feet who advance to the highest levels of the game.

When newspapers speculated that I would be included in a preliminary squad of 25 players to attend a Springbok training camp ahead of the home series against France, the prospect arose that I might somehow avoid the second year blues. Ian McIntosh was in charge of the Boks, and I started to fancy my chances again.

In the event, Tiaan Strauss took his place at the back of the scrum and, when the Springbok squad to tour Australia was announced, it was the Northerns eighthman, Adriaan Richter, who was fitted out for a new blazer. Staying at home and playing in an under-strength Currie Cup competition, I had started to believe my career was slowing to a halt. With hindsight, I was cocky, and I was wrong as well. I wasn't slowing to a halt. I had slipped into reverse.

Harry Viljoen was speaking.

'Gary, I haven't been happy with the loose forward combination, and I am going to try another option. I'm sorry, you're going to have to sit out.'

Dropped!

In April, I had been on the brink of Springbok selection. In

June, while the Boks were celebrating a sensational Test victory in Sydney, I wasn't even able to hold a place in a Natal team missing seven regular players. Bartmann, Blakeway and John Plumtree: this was the new loose forward combination.

I hated the experience, suffered what I regarded as humiliation. You turn up to training as usual, but now you are not included in any discussions, people seem to move away from you and the first team trots across the field to practice the moves on its own. All your status and self-confidence are stripped away, and you feel like yesterday's hero, washed up and unwanted. That Monday evening at King's Park was among the hardest of my career.

Chris van Loggerenberg, one of South Africa's top physical trainers, had been brought by Harry Viljoen to condition the side, and he was sensitive enough to see my discomfort. 'Come on,' he said, 'let's run.' The gruelling one-on-one session that followed at once exhausted and refreshed me. I was not going to lie down and fade away. Five matches later, I was back in the side.

Despite my personal upheavals, Natal continued to prosper and we were able to secure a place in our third Currie Cup final in four seasons, to be played at the end of an exhausting domestic season against Transvaal in Durban. It was a match we expected to win and, where we had been relaxed and focused as the underdogs in 1992, suddenly pressure and nerves crept in ...

Harry Viljoen was feeling the pressure more than anyone. He had never won the Currie Cup as a player, and had lost the previous final as coach of the Transvaal team. It is not possible to approach a final as just another game, although that would be perfect, but I do feel Harry changed too many aspects of our preparation with the result that the pressure cramped us. During the week before the 1993 final, we were subjected to the power talks of not one but three sports psychologists, including an American. It was too much.

UPRISING IN NATAL

The new Transvaal coach, Kitch Christie, adopted an opposite approach, only bringing his side to Durban on the day of the match so they would not be overwrought by the intense build-up to the final. As a result, we struggled to get our engines turning over and, much to the disappointment of the King's Park crowd, François Pienaar and his side were able to take the Currie Cup back to Johannesburg for the first time in 21 years. Transvaal had enjoyed a fantastic year, winning the M-Net Nite series, the Super 10, the Currie Cup and the Lion Cup in a clean sweep of trophies unequalled before or since.

We were quiet in Durban. All our efforts had been in vain. But the rugby season was still not spent, and a Springbok squad was being chosen to set off on a two-Test tour of Argentina. My form in the closing stages of the Currie Cup had been such that my name was once again being touted. I had no idea if this was mere newspaper talk, or an accurate reflection of reality.

The Springbok squad was to be announced on a Saturday evening after we had played at King's Park but there was still no news by six o'clock when I joined my parents who were braaiing with friends in the car park.

There followed one of those experiences so memorable and special that the crystal clear memory of what happened will always remain with me.

I was sitting in the passenger seat, my father was sitting in the driver's seat and my mother and Nicky were milling around outside. There were others nearby but they tactfully kept their distance, anxious not to intrude whether the news was good or, as I half-expected, disappointing again. The radio sports news droned on. Still no announcement of the Springbok squad.

Finally, at around quarter past six, the announcer spoke ... 'and we have just received confirmation of the South African squad to tour Argentina.' He read out the names by position, starting at fullback through to scrumhalf, then running through the props to, last but not least, the eighthmen.

'Eighthmen ... Tiaan Strauss and Gary Teichmann.'

My father beamed, slapped me on the shoulder and shook me strongly by the hand. All your life, you want to make your parents proud and I think I derived less pleasure from the simple fact of my selection than I did from seeing my own mother and father so absolutely thrilled by the news. In an instant, I felt I had, after all, not let them down; I felt as if I had made something of my life. Over the next 48 hours, more than 80 people called to congratulate my parents.

No fewer than ten Natal players had been included in the squad of 26: André Joubert, James Small, Pieter Muller, Joel Stransky, Henry Honiball, Steve Atherton, Guy Kebble, John Allan and, in an attempt to provide some height at the back of the lineout, our young lock Mark Andrews, selected as a flanker. The most glaring omission was that of Wahl Bartmann, our captain. In every moment of celebration, there lies a moment of intense disappointment – although he was to be included in the squad at a late stage following a withdrawal.

My arrival for the first time at a Springbok gathering was made far less daunting by the fact that I knew the coach so well. The perception existed around the country that 'Mac' had filled the squad with Natal players, but I don't believe this was the case: firstly, he was only one of six selectors and, it later emerged, was frequently outvoted on matters of selection; secondly, Natal's success in provincial rugby merited a significant number of Boks.

Nonetheless, against all logic, the myth remained that Natal players were the chosen race during the McIntosh era, just as John Williams had called up the Blue Bulls, Kitch Christie would select Transvaal players and Nick Mallett would favour Western Province players. In each case, there might have been an element of the coach turning to players he had relied upon in the past, and knew he could rely on again, but I am absolutely sure each coach followed one simple and overriding goal: to select a winning side.

Provincialism was rife within the Springbok squad, to the extent that the Natal players ate breakfast with other Natal players, sat on the bus beside other Natal players, chose to visit town with other Natal players and, if possible, room with other Natal players. Players from other provinces tended to stick together as well, all following the precept of each to their own. Of course, we said hello, discussed rugby with them, but not much more.

It was simply easier to get along with team-mates than to meet the challenge of making friends with people who were enemies in the Currie Cup. One legacy of isolation, and the consequently ferocious domestic competition, was division within the Bok squad up until, probably, the 1995 Rugby World Cup.

It did not take long for me to calculate that, with no shortage of loose forwards in the touring squad, I would only play in the two midweek matches, and my brief discussions with McIntosh and François Pienaar, the captain, did not alter my assumption that I was travelling as a dirt-tracker.

This was fine. I needed time to find my feet in the national squad, and Argentina was the ideal place for such a process. It is a beautiful, hospitable country where rugby people are enthusiastic but massively outnumbered in a nation of devoted soccer fans. The round ball game is so dominant that there is no pressure at all on touring rugby squads. We could walk the streets, visit clubs and relax to a degree that was not possible in Britain or New Zealand. Springbok teams have traditionally loved Argentina, and I soon saw why.

With only two opportunities to prove I could thrive at this level, there was little room for error. One indifferent display and I might be forever set aside as 'a talented provincial player, but no more'. I doubt whether anybody in sport can be written off as mercilessly as a Springbok after one poor match.

It was, therefore, disappointing to play in the side that lost the opening game of the tour, against a Buenos Aires XV. I can declare without any fear of contradiction that the 28-27 defeat was caused by a refereeing performance of such appalling proportions that, when the three match officials stepped forward to receive their commemorative medals at the post-match function, most of the South African players audibly chanted the song *Three Blind Mice*. We were not bad losers. We were simply enraged at being cheated.

Jannie Engelbrecht, the affable Springbok manager, was more tactful, telling the media that the standard of Argentine rugby had certainly improved, but the same could not be said of the refereeing. We had conceded 34 penalties that afternoon, 14 of which were awarded consecutively without reply.

Our changing room was silent for at least 40 minutes after the match. It is said that the greatest silence on the planet is to be experienced on a still and clear night in the middle of the desert, a silence apparently so complete that it is deafening. I would put forward another candidate for the most silent of silences, and that is the stillness in a defeated Springbok dressing room.

No-one talks. No-one offers a wry smile, or curses their luck. No-one pulls anyone's leg or starts making plans for alcoholic excesses that night. There is a stunned silence, of big men staring blankly at the ever-increasing pile of dirty kit. There is a sense of desolation, as if each individual is contemplating the disappointment of his friends and family back home. The Springboks wear the pride of their nation on their sleeves; they feel defeat not only as a personal disappointment but also as a cause of national shame.

The tour of Argentina advanced from daylight robbery in Buenos Aires to open warfare at Tucuman three days later. While the shadow Test team set about the task of winning the match, I was sitting with the non-playing reserves in the middle of the main stand, and becoming increasingly frustrated by

UPRISING IN NATAL

the bloodcurdling aggression of the chanting crowd and, in particular, the insistence of a 14-year-old boy who kept standing up and blocking my view.

'Tu-cu-man! Tu-cu-man! Tu-cu-man!' The chanting was frantic, manic, and almost delirious. Sport was evidently engaging all the emotions.

I asked the boy to sit down. He ignored me. I put my hands on his shoulders and gently pushed him into his seat, upon which people sitting around us in the stand began to scream and shout. The police arrived and suggested we leave our seats among local supporters, and slowly make our way to sit with the reserves on benches beside the field, inside the security fence.

Tempers were fraying and, before long, the match had erupted into a wild and prolonged fist fight involving almost every player on the field and a few others who leaped from the bench to join the fray. And the crowd did not behave much better. By the end, the black tracksuits worn by our reserves were covered with the spit of spectators standing behind them.

The Battle of Tucuman, as the media unimaginatively christened the day, represented an appalling advertisement for rugby, but it was magnificent for the spirit and resolve of the 1993 Springboks. François Pienaar pulled the squad together afterwards, saying how, under threat, we must stand as one. Returning to the city of Buenos Aires for the internationals, we united.

And the result was two convincing Test victories over the Pumas. A year dominated by series defeats at home to France and away to Australia ended on a winning note, and even the dirt-trackers managed to restore some pride with an end-of-tour 40-26 victory over Rosario. I managed to score one of the five tries, and was happy to have contributed to a solid performance.

As 1993 turned to 1994, I returned to the Natal camp to find the province searching for a new coach to replace Harry

FOR THE RECORD

Viljoen, who would go on to enjoy deserved success with Western Province. The quest ended with the appointment of Noel Olivier, who had established a fine reputation as coach of the Crusaders team in Natal club competitions. I liked Noel, and respected his knowledge of the game. He was, however, being asked to bridge an almighty gap between the clubs' Moor Cup and the Super 10, between Glenwood and Auckland.

We retained a stable squad of players, however, and performed creditably in the Super 10, most memorably beating Auckland 14-12 at home and winning through to host the second Super 10 final against Queensland in Durban. Noel Olivier had intelligently maintained a strong, physical pack of forwards and backs who always threatened to score tries. With these qualities, we stood 80 minutes away from the title of 'southern hemisphere champions'.

It was the second major final at King's Park in the space of five months and, for the second time, we froze on the big occasion and allowed a premier prize to slip through our fingers. The reality is that, in any career, you don't get so many opportunities to win big finals at home and, whenever such an opportunity comes along, it must be vigorously and relentlessly seized.

The mathematics were that, with three minutes of a tight and bruising match left, we remained within a penalty goal of victory, but the undeniable reality was that a more focused and controlled Queensland team had slowly squeezed the life out of our ambition. Michael Lynagh intelligently controlled long periods of the game, and he calmly kicked the goals that mattered.

Natal 10 ... Queensland 21. The neon scoreboard flickered in the Durban gloom as our disappointed supporters slipped away, some home, most to drown their sorrows in the car park. Together with a few team-mates, I wandered among the braais and postmortems afterwards. There was less laughter than usual, but human spirits were being revived as bottled spirits emptied. The Super 10 was a maturing event, but the Currie Cup remained the greatest prize and the primary objective of the year was to bring the trophy back to Durban. Sadly, in a wholly disrupted domestic season, that task would prove beyond us too.

The Springbok challenge lay ahead, as two Tests were to be played at home to England, followed by the ultimate opportunity, a three-Test tour to New Zealand. I was playing well, I was hopeful of making a contribution to the national cause and I was determined to use Natal's match against the touring England team as a platform to state my case for an international call.

Natal 21 ... England 6. Every province was mauling the pale people from the north, but our victory was emphatic, even if the score boiled down purely to Henry Honiball kicking seven penalties out of eight attempts and Rob Andrew, England's flyhalf, goaling just two of his nine opportunities.

Ian McIntosh had watched the match, surely noting how I had not missed a tackle all afternoon and repeatedly punched holes in the England defence; I was duly selected to play at Loftus Versfeld on the day of the first Test between South Africa and England – but not for the Springboks, rather for a President's XV against Northern Transvaal in the main curtain-raiser.

The newly inaugurated President, Nelson Mandela, was taking his seat in the Blue Room at Loftus just as our game was drawing to a close. Inevitably, the honed provincial side had gradually overwhelmed the pick-up Invitation XV, and I was feeling particularly disgruntled as I walked off the field, passing what looked to me like a notably pumped-up England team in the corridor.

4 June 1994 had been set aside as festival day. As the country basked in the relief and joy of a successful transition from minority rule to democracy, in the triumph of what amounted

to a negotiated revolution, Mandela's appearance at a Springbok Test represented a soaring moment of national unity.

The pre-match introductions, hand shaking and anthems must have taken almost 20 minutes, not that anyone minded. There was little tension in the stands because a ritual slaughter of England, by at least 40 points, was so unanimously expected. The tourists had lost five of their six matches so far.

I showered and dressed in one of the changing rooms buried deep inside the grandstand at Loftus, only emerging to locate and take my seat in the stand with 25 minutes of the Test match played. I glanced at the scoreboard, and had to glance again. England was leading 20-0, and the stunned Springboks were heading for one of their toughest days since readmission.

Any hope of being called into the squad for the second Test at Newlands a week later was dashed when the selectors persisted with Tiaan Strauss. I could understand their loyalty to a talented and lion-hearted player, and was starting to wonder whether the tag of 'a fine provincial player just lacking international class' was not being imperceptibly but firmly placed around my neck. Ian McIntosh was only one of six selectors, and I seemed to be going down 5-1.

When the Springbok squad to tour New Zealand was announced, and I was omitted again, my response was to drop in at the Nottingham Road pub, not simply drowning, but flooding, my sorrows. People were saying I was too light to be effective in the heavy conditions, but two of my strongest performances for Natal had been in our Super 10 victories against Otago and Waikato, both eked out of the same New Zealand soil. When injuries caused no fewer than six replacements to be flown west during the course of the tour, and I was still left at home, I began to wonder whether I had insulted any of the selectors or committed any similarly heinous sin.

I watched events unfold from the outside, saw the team narrowly fail to win the first Test, saw them well beaten in the second and watched with sadness as Louis Luyt, newly elected president of the South African Rugby Football Union, flew to New Zealand and publicly executed Ian McIntosh. A creditable draw in the third Test would not save the coach from summary dismissal.

Few people leaped to Mac's defence in his hour of need, and I think some senior players at the time must live with the knowledge that they undermined the coach to save themselves. Personally, I wish I could have been more outspoken in his support, but I was not in a position of any influence at all, not being in the Springbok squad, not even being captain of the Natal side. History, however, has judged the coach more kindly than his contemporaries.

It is now common knowledge that he was frequently outvoted by his fellow selectors, and was therefore unable to coach the team he wanted. No lesser authority than his successor, the late Kitch Christie, frequently acknowledged the role Ian McIntosh played in transforming the Springboks from dinosaurs of a lost age in 1992 to a team with a world championship core 18 months later.

'There is no doubt in my mind that, had he been allowed to continue in his work, Ian McIntosh would have guided the Springboks to glory in the 1995 Rugby World Cup,' declared Christie, with great humility, in his biography.

Christie was clever enough to recognise McIntosh's difficulties and, before accepting the appointment as the third national coach since readmission, he was able to insist on an overhaul of the selection process. The panel was reduced from six to three, two of whom would be Christie and his assistant coach, Gysie Pienaar. In effect, quite correctly, the coach would pick the side.

But would they pick me?

The initial signs were positive, and I was pleased to be invited to a series of intensive Springbok squad training camps at the Wanderers, in Johannesburg, on successive Mondays. The new coach, appointed just eight months before the World Cup, had neatly described his challenge as 'an ambulance job', and it was clear that his primary medicines were discipline and fitness.

Christie had coached Transvaal to unprecedented success in 1993 and 1994, and he was clearly held in great affection by the core of players from that provincial team, but we, as outsiders, were new to his methods.

At one stage, Cabous van der Westhuizen called him 'Kitch', and the new coach turned on him and snapped back, saying: 'You either call me "Coach" or "Mr Christie", all right?' I was standing beside Cabous at the time, and we were both amazed by the outburst. Such stilted, old-fashioned authority was unknown in Natal where coaches were respected but 'Mac' had always been 'Mac'. I was not particularly impressed. Authority is more than a name.

At another point during this initial regime, André Joubert and James Small were sent home from a training camp for indiscipline. Again, the Transvaal crew regarded this as a welcome imposition of discipline on the far too relaxed players from Natal, but they were deluding themselves. The training was exhausting. To my mind, André and James simply enjoyed the break.

As time passed, Kitch Christie started to earn our respect for all the right reasons, because he spoke straight and acted straight, because he assessed an issue, decided on what action he would take and took it. Even though I might not have been his favourite player, even though I was not always in his team, my respect for the man never wavered below the absolute.

Tiaan Strauss retained his place at the back of the Springbok scrum in two home Test victories over Argentina, but I was extremely pleased to be included in the squad named to tour Wales, Scotland and Ireland at the end of the year. My overwhelming goal was to win a full Test cap and simply being in the tour group, playing in midweek matches, represented a major step in that direction.

Whatever happened, I resolved to be a positive member of the tour party and to seize my opportunity whenever and however it arrived. I performed well in the opening win over Cardiff and was encouraged to be named in what appeared to be a shadow Test side that overwhelmed Llanelli. My hopes of winning a place in the Test team, however, were effectively dashed when Rudolf Straeuli played magnificently in a tremendous victory over Swansea.

Rudolf's form carried him into the Test team, which beat first Scotland at Murrayfield and then Wales in Cardiff, leaving Tiaan Strauss to play as captain of the midweek side. When Tiaan insisted on playing eighthman, I was consigned to playing the remainder of the tour out of position, at flank.

There was no point complaining. Such things happen on tour, where your fortunes are so intertwined with those of your team-mates, and I understood what was happening. Kitch Christie was supposedly impressed by my attitude as the fates swung against me. I resolved to be positive.

The first announcement of a Test team brings about a low moment on every tour, instantly transforming one happy squad of 30 players into a delighted Test team and a depressed bunch of dirt-trackers. It was no different on the 1994 tour to Britain, and the response of the midweek team was to lose by a last gasp drop goal against Scotland A at rain-soaked Melrose. For the first time in my Bok career, I sensed some members of the team were not giving 100%.

We did pull ourselves together and, while the Test team achieved all their goals, the midweek side recovered and, led by Tiaan Strauss, put together three further emphatic victories on tour, the last win following an exciting, open display against the Combined Provinces of Ireland. Showered by a standing ovation from the crowd at Ravenhill, Belfast, our tour ended in glory.

I had thoroughly enjoyed myself, particularly when the not exactly shy and retiring Cabous van der Westhuizen arrived midway through the tour as a substitute for the injured Chris Badenhorst. Cabous was not the type to let a staid function get in the way of a memorable party, and his performance at a banquet hosted for the players in Edinburgh was particularly astounding.

When six kilted bagpipers entered the hall, our longhaired winger was standing behind them and, for no apparent reason, started trying to block the pipes of their instruments with his outstretched fingers. The spectacle of the broad Scotsmen wildly kicking out backwards, trying to drive away the Springbok who was blocking their pipes, was wonderful and hilarious.

All in all, the tour did not lack laughter: Uli Schmidt held a firework display in his Swansea hotel room, and Special Branch detectives flattened Rudolf Straeuli when he cut off the power supply to the post-match dinner in Edinburgh and briefly plunged Princess Anne into darkness. Such was life on an amateur rugby tour: unashamedly childish, but invariably harmless, fun.

Professionalism would take us into a terrifying, rigorous new era where highly paid players would be expected to behave like adults.

When the squad returned home only ten days before Christmas, every thought started to turn towards the 1995 Rugby World Cup to be held in South Africa, on our home grounds: the opportunity of a lifetime. I rated my chances of inclusion in the squad as being no more than 50/50. Yes, I was in contention but nothing less than a spectacular series of performances in the Super 10, and a lot of luck, was likely to dislodge Straeuli or Strauss.

The defining triumph of Kitch Christie's period as Springbok coach was the depth of the bond and trust between the coach and his core players. At the start, this 'chosen few' solely comprised Transvalers such as François Pienaar, James Dalton, Balie Swart, Kobus Wiese, Rudolf Straeuli, Johan Roux, Hennie le Roux, Japie Mulder, Gavin Johnson and others. But by World Cup time, this core had grown to include the entire national squad. This was a coach who would do anything for players he absolutely believed in, and his success was due to the fact that, in return, his players would do anything for him.

It is, of course, a matter of regret that I was never one of 'Christie's men'. I would naturally have liked to be included, but I understood why he selected other players. For me, this was never a matter for anger or recrimination.

Ian McIntosh had returned to his natural berth as the Natal coach, wiser for his trials and tribulations with the Springboks, and we performed effectively in the Super 10 competition of 1995. We were solid at home and we produced one momentous performance to beat Queensland in Brisbane. For the second year in a row, we reached the last four but, when we were drawn to return to Ballymore for the semi-final, we failed to repeat our heroics in the group phase.

Queensland advanced to retain the title, defeating Transvaal at Ellis Park, in another final where planning snuffed out any passion.

I had begun to assume the World Cup selection equation would boil down to one place resting between Tiaan Strauss, Ian MacDonald and me. In the back of my mind, I always assumed Tiaan would get the nod. After his efforts in the previous three seasons, he didn't deserve to miss out.

Yet, as the tournament drew closer, I remained with the Springbok squad and the story began to circulate that Tiaan would be unlucky. Maybe I did have a chance, after all. Christie had planned two potentially catastrophic fixtures to get his Springbok team match fit, against the full-strength provincial sides of Western Province and Natal on successive Saturdays. Where he might have arranged two invitation teams, the coach was bold enough to seek out real opposition, even if this raised the very real possibility of a demoralising defeat.

I was selected as eighthman in the Springbok team to play

Province at Newlands. Tiaan was playing for the home side. Was this the final eliminator for the last seat on the bus to the World Cup? We weren't sure. Neither of us lacked for commitment during a frantic, physical match, only won for the national side by Joel Stransky's last gasp drop goal. We would see more of those.

By general consent, I had performed well but my heart sank when, early the next morning, I received a request to be at Morné du Plessis' room at quarter past nine. Everyone knew the final World Cup squad was to be announced live on the SABC evening news that evening, and everyone knew four players would have to be sent home from the team hotel during the day. It was highly unlikely that I was being called to be told I would stay in the squad.

I knocked on the door.

'Come in.' It was the voice of Morné du Plessis, the widely respected former Springbok captain who had succeeded Jannie Engelbrecht as manager. I entered to find the manager and the coach sitting together.

'Gary, you know the situation and you are aware that not everyone can get into the World Cup squad,' Morné started, 'and I'm afraid you haven't made it. I'm sorry, but we simply cannot take everyone along.'

Strangely, I experienced no immense sense of disappointment. I had seen this decision coming for some time, and my emotional response was much less acute than it would be four years later when a similar disappointment arrived like a bolt from the blue.

Ironically, Tiaan Strauss was omitted as well, with the fourth place in the loose forwards going to Robbie Brink, the young Western Province star who had produced a string of fine performances in the Super 10.

Some people detected the smell of politics in the decision. Once Christie had decided to omit Strauss, did he feel an obligation to placate the enraged Cape Town public by including another Province player? Mindful that the crucial opening game against Australia would be played at Newlands, did he feel the need to make a gesture and secure the home crowd's support?

I don't think so. Robbie had been playing well. He probably appeared to be more of a prospect for the future than me, already past my 27th birthday. At any rate, it was a marginal decision and, for me, it fell the wrong way.

When Kitch had finished speaking, I stood up, thanked them both for letting me know their decision, walked back to my room, packed and, after wishing some of the guys in the team room luck for the tournament, headed to the airport in search of the next available flight home to Durban.

I slept most of the way home, the sleep of the sad.

I watched the SABC news that night, watched as my teammates from the previous day beamed as their names were read out and they took their place on a special stand, positioned in front of the slogan 'One Team, One Country'. They were at the start of perhaps the greatest adventure of their lives. I was sitting at home, on the sidelines, one of the unfortunate ones. Ian MacDonald was feeling the same way in Johannesburg, and Tiaan suffered in Cape Town. Little did we know at the time that the hair's breadth selection decision had cost us not simply a place in the tournament, but also many millions of rands.

The following Saturday, I played for Natal against the Springboks and, for the second week in a row, the national side squeezed home, winning 27-25. It was a strange feeling to play against the green and gold.

Of course, the events of the six weeks that followed will be remembered as perhaps the most remarkable in South Africa's sporting history. As François Pienaar and his side advanced through the tournament, a combination of their success and some astute management and administration provoked an astonishing reaction in every town and city, in every nook and cranny of the country.

For the first and perhaps only time, the entire population of South Africa rallied in support of the Springbok rugby team. When Nelson Mandela pulled the No. 6 jersey over his head, he pulled his country together. It was remarkable, it was morale boosting, it was gladdening, it was unforgettable just to be a South African, alive and kicking on 24 June 1995, the day of the final.

It did not matter that the Springboks were probably not the strongest team in the tournament; it didn't matter that they probably didn't play the best rugby. It did matter that the spirit within the squad was unmatched, and it did matter that, in June 1995, South Africa was a country whose time had come.

I managed to see several matches during the tournament, travelling to Newlands for the opening game as part of a group with my excellent employers, the Natal Building Society, and watching a couple of England's group matches at Ellis Park. In general, the event was competently staged but its unique point of difference was the sheer enthusiasm of the South African people. When most of the people don't care, the event takes place in a strange vacuum – as we would all discover in 1999 when the tournament was pitched across Europe.

The Natal Rugby Union provided us with tickets for the semi-final match between the Springboks and France on 17 June but several of us succumbed to the temptation, cashed in these prime seats with touts and, in a spectacular error of judgement, bought cheaper tickets for the open stand. As the incredible deluge of driving rain fell all afternoon, delaying kick-off by more than an hour, our group was soaked to the skin – not that we worried as the brave Springboks prevailed.

I watched the Rugby World Cup final at Brian Bateman's house in Durban, where everyone was wearing Springbok jerseys and entering into the spirit of the day. Even then I feared the All Blacks would be too strong, but that remarkable sense

UPRISING IN NATAL

of destiny remained with the South Africans, and the nation celebrated again.

A week after the 1995 World Cup final, I was appointed to succeed Wahl Bartmann as the captain of Natal.

Life would go on ...

5

Losing the Lottery

After a weekend away with Nicky in the Drakensberg Mountains, I arrived back in Durban to discover six messages on my cell phone. They could hardly have been more alarming.

'You have six messages waiting … next message.'
'Hi Gary, it's Guy Kebble. Please call me back. Bye.'
I pressed '7' for delete.
'You have five messages waiting … next message.'
'Hi Gary, Guy Kebble. Call me.'
I pressed '7' for delete.
'You have four messages waiting … next message.'
'Hi Gary, where the hell are you?'
I pressed '7' for delete.
'You have three messages waiting … next message.'
'Gary, you're going to miss out – this is urgent.'
I pressed '7' for delete.
'You have two messages waiting … next message.'
'Gary, we're meeting today – get hold of me.'
I pressed '7' for delete.
'You have one message waiting … next message.'
'Gary, my house at 12 – try and be there. Where are you?'
I pressed '7' for delete, and glanced at my watch. It was almost 11. I would make the meeting. Whatever the former

LOSING THE LOTTERY

Natal prop wanted to discuss would be revealed at noon. I had an idea we would be talking about money, the favourite topic of conversation among rugby players around the country.

Nominally, we were supposed to be playing an amateur game, within the laws laid down by the International Rugby Board. In reality, South African rugby had been semi-professional ever since the Cavaliers, an unofficial New Zealand squad, were expensively persuaded to tour in 1986. Through years of isolation, our game had adopted its own maverick strategies to survive.

An informal transfer market developed where players frequently switched provinces, chasing the bait of jobs, houses, fast cars and monthly salaries. Throughout the late 1980s, it became unusual for the Springbok team to play any match without first threatening to strike. This was the Wild West. A settlement in the region of R5 000 per player per match would usually be reached.

Into the 1990s, the four top provinces began paying match fees of around R800 per game, and officials would diligently pack clean bank notes into discreet envelopes far away from the eyes of the IRB. Together with other bits and pieces, an average provincial player could expect to take home in the region of R110 000 per year from rugby. This was not enough to give up other forms of employment, but the regular brown envelopes were starting to reduce the numbers of young players pursuing further education. An infinite number of degree courses were started, few were finished; and so the fabric of the game began to change. The days when leading provincial teams would be crammed with doctors, lawyers and accountants were gone.

Mischief makers would occasionally irritate the administrators, and amuse everyone else, by listing their employment in match day programme profiles as 'professional rugby player'. Initially, such miscreants were severely warned but, after a few months, no-one bothered. After all, it was true.

Readmission to the international rugby community in 1992 did compel South African rugby to hide away some of the brown envelopes, and tidy up its outward appearance, but the professional horse had long since bolted. As the days passed, players became impatient for the day when the old pretence would be ripped away, and professionalism could be embraced.

Week after week, we filled vast stadiums, attracting huge sponsorships and television rights. The envelopes were starting to lose their appeal as we longed for parity with soccer players and cricketers: we wanted contracts and money delivered into bank accounts. We wanted honesty.

South Africa's rugby administrators signally failed to respond to our need, hiding behind the amateur veil when it suited them, using and abusing players, operating within no moral or legal code. The gladiators in Rome had more rights than provincial rugby players in South Africa, as the provincial union presidents borrowed principles of fair employment practice from Nero.

The image that endures is of a young rugby player sitting opposite one of these intimidating union presidents. It's an intimate lunch for two, with wine, and the administrator is making the player an offer to join his province. He urges the player to make his decision there and then: 'Come on, don't mess around.' The player is stranded, confused. He signs over coffee. Deal done.

As a result, relations between administrators and players deteriorated to a point where the overwhelming majority of players would have had no problem in deserting the official structures to join a rebel organisation that paid well. The old administrators had played the cards of 'loyalty' and 'pride in the jersey' to a point where they were no longer worth anything. How could anyone be loyal to people who so callously exploited your position of weakness?

By the mid-1990s, the player body was fed up and ready to run.

LOSING THE LOTTERY

Rugby union's path towards status as an open, honest professional code was littered with newspaper cuttings, suggesting an entrepreneur would secure a backer and establish a rebel professional circus, pursuing the same strategy that Kerry Packer, the Australian tycoon, applied to cricket in 1978.

The players always read these reports with excitement, but so many grand plans and expectations had evaporated into nothing that we had grown cynical. Personally, I didn't pay much notice: if it happened, great; if it didn't happen, no problem. Understandably, it was the older players who scanned the news most keenly. The later the professional bus arrived in our game, the less chance they would have of being young enough and fit enough to climb aboard.

Early in 1995, at last, it seemed significant events were imminent. For several weeks, South African newspapers reported on a rights war within the world of Australian rugby league that prompted Rupert Murdoch, the powerful Australian-born media mogul, to develop plans for a Super League, a professional global rugby competition. NewsCorp spokesmen were quoted, saying the top 80 rugby union players in South Africa would be recruited.

'This is for real,' people muttered behind their hands. 'And we're talking big money. They're just waiting until after the World Cup.'

It was two weeks since the tournament had ended, and I was now driving to Guy Kebble's house. Was this the long-awaited revolution? I was intrigued, although not ready to bet my last rand on anything materialising. As I turned into his house, I recognised some of the parked cars. Through the day the entire Natal squad gathered. This had not happened before. Something was afoot.

Guy proceeded to outline the key principles of the World Rugby Championship, a global professional rugby structure that incorporated both a provincial and an international event. He outlined how our lives would not change dramatically, save for the fact that we would now be playing under the auspices of TWRC, rather than the official bodies, IRB, SARFU and the NRU – and, of course, we would be properly paid like professional sportsmen.

He indicated that the initial phase of the project had been to sign up the leading international squads, and I was impressed to hear the Springboks, All Blacks, Wallabies and England players had all signed contracts. The second phase, he continued, was to enlist the leading provincial players in each country, and that was why we were now being recruited into the organisation.

The pattern of such meetings is that the players are more concerned with the numbers than the words. As 27-page contracts were handed out to each of the players, everyone flicked impatiently to the page with the money.

I did the same.

There it was.

'Annual salary: $100 000'.

At the time, my total annual earnings from rugby amounted to something like R140 000. A threefold increase, at the prevailing US dollar-rand exchange rate, was not to be dismissed. On the contrary, it was to be eagerly accepted.

Of course, I am well aware that every contract should be handed to legal advisers, checked and rechecked and only signed after due consideration. But the adrenalin and excitement was pumping around the Kebble home and, by day's end, the entire Natal squad had signed on the dotted line.

I had not even read the contract but heh, Guy said everything was fine. There was security in numbers. The World Cup Springboks had signed the same contracts, Western Province, Northerns and Transvaal, even Free State players: TWRC was gaining momentum.

It was almost two when I left the house, and I was surprised to find myself genuinely excited by the prospect of playing in a proper, professional and modern organisation. It was everything we wanted.

Not long afterwards, we were summoned to another meeting and found Harry Viljoen, our former coach, and a lawyer from Johannesburg giving further details of the TWRC project. It became clear that Ross Turnbull, a former Australian rugby administrator, was fronting the organisation. They intimated that Kerry Packer was providing the financial muscle.

Within my understanding, events were starting to make sense. On the eve of the World Cup final, the three southern hemisphere unions – Australia, New Zealand and South Africa – announced they had sold their combined TV rights, at provincial and international level, to Murdoch's NewsCorp for a total of $550 million over ten years. That represented a major coup, but the administrators had then erred by not moving quickly to satisfy the players.

Once again, they seemed more concerned to pay the least possible rather than enter into fair and reasonable agreements, and this arrogance created the opportunity for TWRC to gain momentum. It made sense. Murdoch had secured TV rights from the established unions. Now Packer, his great rival, was planning a classic counterattack by bidding to secure the players. The TV rights would be worth nothing if the leading players deserted the structure.

Two Australians were jousting for global domination of the sport, and we appeared neatly positioned to reap the maximum financial benefit.

So we waited, and waited.

It was just an average Friday afternoon at King's Park, and the players were starting to arrive for training, in dribs and drabs. John Allan didn't just arrive. He blew in to the changing room like a hurricane.

'The bastards!' he exclaimed, at the top of his voice. 'The Springboks have signed with SARFU! The bastards have looked after themselves, and they have stabbed the rest of us in the back.' John was not simply angry; the hooker was incandescent with rage and he would not be calmed.

I was aware that the Springbok World Cup squad had that morning gathered at a hotel near Johannesburg, because André Joubert, Mark Andrews and James Small, the Natal Boks, had been excused from training for the day. It appeared as if the national squad had reached a momentous decision.

'They have shafted us,' John Allan repeated over and again. We trained poorly, and the players dispersed in confusion and concern.

The situation became a genuine crisis within our team when Mark, James and André rejoined the Natal squad the following week. I could see several of the guys would not even bring themselves to look at them, let alone talk to them.

'We need to discuss what to do now,' John Allan said, 'and I don't think the Springboks should stay in the room. They have done their own thing, and we must sort this matter out on our own.' I could see the three players, our friends and teammates, were taken aback by the aggressive approach, but I don't know what other reaction they could have expected. They left the room.

An animated discussion followed, other meetings were held, Guy Kebble became involved again, but nothing could change the fact that TWRC was not going to happen without the world champion Springboks. In turn, the Wallabies and All Blacks started to sign contracts with their unions and, before long, our TWRC contracts were not worth the paper they were written on.

It would later emerge that NewsCorp had prevailed upon Louis Luyt, president of SARFU, to match the TWRC offer and secure the Springboks as soon as possible. Murdoch wanted to crush the Packer project once and for all. Luyt moved quickly, telling the Springboks that he would match the massive offers they had received from TWRC. Suddenly, the national squad was being presented with a chance to secure the best of both worlds. They would remain within their familiar structures and surroundings, but their earnings would soar. In every possible way, the Springboks had won the lottery.

As provincial players, we had lost the lottery. With the Springboks safely signed, SARFU and the unions now held all the aces. We had nowhere to go, no bargaining power. Packer retreated: TWRC was dead in the water.

I was as angry as anyone. The Springboks had been selfish and SARFU had sunk TWRC but stored up inestimable problems for the season ahead. How could anyone defend a situation where Mark, André and James were playing for Natal during August and September and earning anything between six and ten times as much as their team-mates, sweating in the same side?

Springboks would like to say: 'Jealousy makes you nasty,' but how should we have reacted to this appalling inequality? Should we have congratulated them on the skill of their negotiations and asked for a loan?

Eventually SARFU distributed more of the Murdoch millions to the unions for distribution among the provincial players and, by the end of 1995, my earnings had doubled to more than R200 000 per year. That was much better! I was now earning almost one third of what a Springbok earned.

And the discrepancy was not simply founded in the numbers. Provincial players were invariably given one-year contracts, but we soon discovered the Springboks, some of whom were hovering on the brink of retirement, had been given the security of three-year deals. There was more. Our deals were loaded towards match fees rather than monthly retainers. The Springboks, on the other hand, would receive exactly the same money whether they were in the national side or not; whether they were in their provincial side or not.

Strangely, I don't recall ever sitting down with Mark, James or André and talking through my sense of disappointment at their behaviour. The subject was simply never raised: maybe they were too secretive and I was too angry. There is no doubt, however, that for some time the issue poisoned relations between the three super-wealthy Boks and the rest of the Natal squad.

Happily, time heals. Maybe we'll talk about it one day.

If the impact of the Springbok contracts was damaging at provincial level, it was nothing less than catastrophic within the national squad. There is no doubt in my mind that the side's poor performances during 1996 and 1997 were largely caused by the underlying, cancerous inequality of employment. We spent far too much time talking, worrying and arguing about money.

Anyone who has played rugby at any level will understand the absolute impossibility of developing team spirit when half the team are being paid twice as much as the rest, or when half the team are playing happy in the knowledge that they have total security while the other half have no security. I still fail to understand how SARFU could effectively reward a squad for winning the World Cup by giving them contracts stretching three years into the future. The problems might largely have been avoided if the World Cup players had received a one-off payment for winning the tournament, and then been offered the same contract as their team-mates in the national side through 1996, 1997 and 1998.

That was not done, and we all suffered the consequences.

At one stage of the troubled 1996 season, Morné du Plessis arranged a meeting at Ellis Park between Louis Luyt, president of SARFU, and several of the World Cup Springboks. They were having problems in the implementation of their contracts, but I can't say I was either interested or sympathetic. As an excellent Springbok manager who wanted to restore calm, Morné asked me to attend the meeting as the representative of players without contracts.

This was new territory for me and I was taken aback when Luyt began the meeting by speaking aggressively and without pause for five minutes. The idea did strike me that, even if the World Cup players were raking in millions, they were earning their money – working for an employer as hard as this.

Luyt suddenly focused his eyes on me.

'What are you doing here?' he bellowed.

Morné intervened: 'Dr Luyt, I asked Gary to come because …'

'He's not a contracted player,' Luyt thundered. 'Please leave now.'

I left the room and spent the next hour and a half standing in the car park at Ellis Park. We had all travelled together, and Morné had the car keys. I was not going to interrupt the meeting to ask for them. Crazy times.

The World Cup players eventually emerged and I was told to go back and negotiate with Luyt on behalf of the players without contracts. It was me against him, and the full and frank negotiations unfolded as follows:

'Right,' he said, 'We will offer the players without contracts a match fee of R30 000 per match. That is our final offer. You can take it or leave it. If you don't want it, let us know and we will find some other players.'

'OK,' I said.

That was it. I returned to the hotel and informed my teammates what had happened. It was widely accepted that my 15-second negotiating marathon with the ferocious rugby boss had been a triumph. I was thankful the ordeal was over and, after an afternoon spent in the boardroom, looked forward to the comparative relaxation of playing against the All Blacks.

As time has passed, I have often asked myself how I would have reacted to the SARFU offer if I had been a member of the World Cup squad. I must be honest in saying it would have been tough to stand up and say this is wrong because we are selling short the provincial players. When offered huge sums of money, under pressure, the human mind says thank you very much.

The other dimension to the dilemma is that, for all Guy Kebble's resolute assurances, TWRC was not a 100% proposition. Kerry Packer had not spoken publicly of his intentions, and the fact was that no-one had been paid a cent even six weeks after signing the contracts. If TWRC had been able to pay reasonable sums on signature, then the venture might yet have thrived.

Given the uncertainty surrounding TWRC, would the Springboks ever have forgiven themselves if they had declined the SARFU offer in solidarity with the rest of us, and then ended up with nothing because TWRC turned out to be a lot of hot air? When opportunities arise, you seize them.

There again, even though TWRC had collapsed, the players might still have secured acceptable terms simply by sticking together.

Some years later, I would gain another perspective on this traumatic time from Ernie Els, one of the outstanding golfers in the world. We were sitting next to each other at a banquet, and discussing how some sportsmen seemed to be securing much greater financial returns than others.

I asked him if he did not feel frustrated when Tiger Woods, riding the wave of his incredible popularity, announced yet another multi-million dollar sponsorship or personal endorsement. Ernie's response surprised me.

'Not really,' he said. 'When Tiger does one of those deals, he is helping the rest of us by expanding the market and setting new benchmarks for people who want to endorse or sponsor top golfers. He helps himself in the short term, but I think we will benefit from his success in the medium term.'

The same may have been true of the 1995 Springboks. They got lucky, they won the lottery, but they also set a new mark for paying top rugby players in South Africa. SARFU officials repeated endlessly throughout 1997 and 1998 that the 1995 deal had been a one-off and would never be repeated, but they have been proved completely wrong. When the World Cup contracts expired in 1998, regular Springboks were earning at least as much as the famous lottery winners of 1995, if not more. Player salaries continued to grow.

By then, of course, the turmoil of 1995 was long forgotten. If only it could have been avoided ... the most unpleasant off-the-field experience of my career.

6

François' Footsteps

The measure of any captain is the esteem in which he is held by his team-mates. It doesn't really matter how eloquently he delivers the post-match speech or how well he comes across on television. These factors help, but the core challenge is to motivate and direct the players, individually and as a group. Esteem is the only currency that counts, and it comprises 30% affection and 70% respect.

Judged against these criteria, I believe François Pienaar was a great captain. His presence, his capacity to motivate his team, his sheer desire to be successful, all contributed to an aura that I had sensed during the Springbok tours, to Argentina in 1993 and to Britain the following year, but that I only truly felt during the preparations for my long-awaited Test debut.

I was pleased to have played in François' team, but there have been times over the past three years when I have considered it a particular burden to have succeeded him as Springbok captain, and to have suffered by comparison with his reputation. Many people have sought to compare our styles of leadership, but I have never strived to emulate him as a captain – we are different people, with different talents and different faults.

I am grateful, however, that we have never allowed the sad history of rivalry between successive Springbok captains to sour our relationship. I have never had a bad word to say about him, and he has never had a bad word to say about me. On the contrary, at various stages, he has not hesitated to phone and offer encouragement and good wishes. I have always appreciated his support.

'Welcome, Gary!'

François Pienaar was beaming, stretching out his hand, in the foyer of the Sunnyside Park Hotel in Johannesburg. The Springboks were gathering for the first time since their moment of triumph, to play Wales at Ellis Park on 2 September, precisely 11 weeks after the Rugby World Cup final.

Out of the blue, I had been selected as eighthman. Mark Andrews was moved back to the second row, after playing the semi-final and final at the back of the scrum, and Kitch Christie apparently sought a classic eighthman. I had been thriving for Natal, and he had picked the form player.

The coach pulled me to one side. 'Just play as you have been playing for Natal,' he said. 'Your attitude was excellent when you had to play out of position in Britain last year and I have been waiting for the moment to give you a chance. I believe you can succeed at this level. Enjoy yourself.'

Ellis Park seemed to be filled with a shared resolve that the 1995 Rugby World Cup would never stop. Once again, the stadium became an ocean of new South African flags and, once again, the foundations rocked to the familiar tune of 'Hier kommie Bok-ke! Hier kommie Bok-ke! ...' The mood was wonderful, remarkable, almost as though 60 000 people were indulging themselves in the recollection of a special time, and desperate to retain the memory. Maybe this was my taste of World Cup fever, my consolation for missing out.

I relished my Test debut. When you wear the green and gold jersey, you feel the pride and passion of the colours, but when you play in a Test, there is an added sensation, the sheer weight of responsibility. A Test is not something that can be lost and talked away. It matters, and you feel the pressure building up in your muscles. It is perhaps the great Springboks who transform the pressure into a positive force, and the also-rans who are overwhelmed.

Jacques Olivier, on the wing, and I were the only new players to the side, the only ones without SARFU contracts in our back pockets. News that we would each be paid a R30 000 match fee soothed any misgivings.

We defeated Wales comfortably, producing sporadic moments of superb rugby even if the overall display lacked fluency. I was satisfied with my own performance, relieved to have fitted in without difficulty and wholly delighted to have made no glaring errors. More positively, I had scored a try midway through the first half, turning up in the right place at the right time to crash over from several metres out. The sense of joy in grounding the ball was immense.

Before and during the game, I had not wanted to let down Nicky or the members of my family in the stands, and we were able to enjoy our celebratory meal at the Randburg Waterfront afterwards. At the dawn of my international career, I recognised that winners have fun. Losers don't.

The following morning, Jacques and I left the team hotel while the rest of the team stayed behind at the hotel for meetings with various financial advisers. It felt strange. The lottery winners/losers divide was emerging.

When Natal began to mine a rich seam of Currie Cup form, powering to a home final against Western Province, I started to contemplate the prospect of a place on the Springbok tour to Italy and England at the end of the year. When I raised the Currie Cup at King's Park after we had overwhelmed Province in wet and muddy conditions, I began to believe I was on a roll.

I wasn't. Hours after winning the Currie Cup, the Springbok touring squad was announced and I was not among the 21 named to play the two Test matches, with no midweek fixtures at all. I never received any official explanation for the decision although various theories were relayed to me.

One held that I was some kind of dry-weather player, unable to thrive in wet conditions – my strong performances in New Zealand, throughout my career, exploded this proposition. The other revolved around Kitch Christie's supposed concern about England's height and reach at the back of the lineout, prompting him to move François Pienaar to No. 8, and draft in Fritz van Heerden, the tall Western Province loose forward, at No. 7.

Whatever the reason, I was disappointed to have broken into the Test team against Wales, played well and then been discarded without any explanation. The decision may have been no reflection on me, simply a result of other circumstances, but someone should have said so. In any event, coming on the night of our Currie Cup victory, the omission from that tour was a greater blow than my omission from the 1995 World Cup squad.

There was, however, significant compensation.

Released from the obligation of an end-of-year tour, I had been able to make a greater contribution to the arrangements for my wedding, something that is, of course, every man's dream. I had met Nicky in late 1992, and we started to see each other regularly some time thereafter.

Our relationship steadily developed and, standing on a beach somewhere down the South Coast, I carefully placed a small box on the sand and asked her to marry me. She responded by immediately bursting into tears. This momentarily panicked me. Had I upset her so much by asking the question? But all was well: her tears were tears of happiness. She nodded. I deftly directed her towards the box, and the ring was soon slipped over her finger.

We were married at the Hilton College chapel on 10 February 1996. My friend, Cliffie Egberink, had agreed to be my best man, and it turned out to be a wet and wonderful day. The beautiful Mrs Teichmann stole the show.

Nicky had had no particular interest in rugby but she soon accepted the often frustrating life of a rugby wife. There are many nights away from home, and the tightly knit squad lifestyle can leave little room to breathe. We have made a conscious effort to get away for weekends together as often as possible, if only to forget about rugby, and the associated drama and crisis.

She is a strong person by nature, and she has been a tremendous support to me in a million ways. At times, she would take things more personally than me, and maybe be more disappointed in the way a few people behaved, and I'm sure this has been good for me. Sometimes, I am too relaxed.

It is not unusual for a sportsman to be heavily indebted to his wife by the time he reaches retirement, for it is she who has made almost all the sacrifices in terms of settling the home, and maybe even bringing up children, while he has been living in luxury and generally playing in the limelight.

Sadly, I sense it might be unusual for a sportsman to acknowledge and repay the debt, but I have kept all the slips. Hopefully, I am aware of exactly what is owed and will start making repayments from the day I retire.

Rejected by the Springboks, accepted by my wife, I identified the primary challenge of 1996 as being to secure my place in the national side. I had been on the periphery for almost three years. It was time to advance or slide away, and not for the first time during my career, the happy and successful foundation of Natal rugby proved an ideal springboard for my international ambition.

Natal's progress towards the final of the new, enlarged, hyped-up Super 12 sustained my challenge and I was named in the Springbok team for the first Test of the year, to be played on 2 July against Fiji in Pretoria. François Pienaar had reverted to No. 6, Ruben Kruger was at No. 7 and I was installed at No. 8. By then, however, the Springbok coach had changed again.

It was widely known in rugby circles that Kitch Christie was fighting a long-term battle against cancer and, at times, had been hospitalised when severe regimes of treatment were necessary. His matter-of-fact approach to his illness, and the courage that never deserted him, inspired admiration from all sides.

When his health suffered another lapse in 1996, he announced he would step down as Springbok coach. I was disappointed by the news, for him above all but also because I had wanted to develop the sort of relationship with him that he had established with the players at the core of his Bok team. Given the chance, I knew I could prove myself to him. Straight, open and always prepared to follow his instinct, Kitch Christie was an outstanding coach and an even finer man. He died in April 1998, and was much mourned by the country to which he brought the Webb Ellis trophy and on which he left an indelible mark.

The young, ambitious coach from Griqualand West, André Markgraaff, had for several months been earmarked as his successor. Tall and broad, he had made his name by guiding his minor province to a series of notable victories against the leading provincial teams, some in the Lion Cup, some in pre-season friendlies. He had also secured a position of influence on the SARFU Executive Committee, emerging as a powerbroker for the small unions.

SARFU had been eager to facilitate a smooth transition from one coach to the next, and the agreed strategy was that Markgraaff would work as Christie's assistant during the 1996 Tri-Nations campaign, and only take over as coach for the tour to Argentina, France and Wales at the end of the year. But when Christie fell ill, Markgraaff was thrown in at the deep end. He had yet to coach a Currie Cup side, now he was coaching the world champions.

I had never met him or even spoken to him, and my first impressions upon watching him during the week of preparations before the Test match against Fiji were not particularly positive. He seemed to have graduated from the old school of South African coaches, where you were taught that if it was good enough for Oubaas Markotter and Danie Craven, it was good enough for you. Such men had been great men in their day, but this was our day now.

My heart would sink when André ordered the forwards to set 100 scrums in the week before a Test. The ancient wisdom held that such training would give you extra fitness in the last quarter of the match and ensure you scrummed well. Modern knowledge had since proven it simply made you tired.

He appeared dogmatic and inflexible, but this may have been his natural reaction to taking on such a major responsibility. As he settled down and grew in confidence, André started to listen to his players, taking on board what they were thinking and taking it on himself to advance their cause. The contrast between his attitude at the start of the year, and at the end, was striking.

Fiji were swept aside at Loftus, and the squad turned its mind to the huge challenge presented by a new competition in our calendar: the Tri-Nations series, an annual round robin competition of home and away matches between the All Blacks, the Springboks and the Wallabies. Created to provide six weeks of world class televised rugby for NewsCorp, the event swiftly became established as the premier annual rugby event on the planet.

François was determined to maintain the momentum from 1995 into 1996 but, though he would never have admitted it at the time, this was not possible. A new coach means a new start, new structures and new levels of trust. You have to build from the ground floor. There are no short cuts.

When the players arrived for training, they found not the familiar figure of Kitch Christie and the familiar drills. They found Markgraaff and a new way. While we were adjusting, we could probably have kept winning against any side except the two that headed our fixture list. The Wallabies and All Blacks, smarting from the 1995 World Cup, would allow us no room for error.

And we lost in Sydney, 21-16. There were doubtless factors of which I was not aware but, from the perspective of this eighthman, playing only his third Test, we were simply unprepared for the challenge. It was foolhardy to think that we could adapt to a new coach in the space of one friendly against Fiji and a couple of weeks training, and then compete against Australia.

   As we flew to New Zealand, it was conceivable that the wheels might have fallen off. Defeat places intense pressure on the relationship between what was an established team, and a new coach, but François accepted the responsibility and kept his Springbok show on the road.

   He arranged for the squad to watch a film together on the Thursday night before the Test, and had selected *The Rock,* starring Sean Connery. As we sat and watched the story of a group of men rallying behind their leader, I started to see some method in the captain's strategy. At one highly charged moment, the commander, played by Connery, was barking questions at his troops.

   'Are we going to survive out there?'
   'Yes, sir,' the soldiers shouted back, in unison.
   'Are we going to be defeated?'
   'No, sir!'
   'Are we going to help each other?'
   'Yes, sir!'

   In the changing room before the Test against the All Blacks, our captain started asking similar questions and the guys responded exactly as the soldiers had done in the film. There was an incredible electricity and resolution in that Christchurch changing room. I don't think I have ever seen a team become so motivated and pumped up. That was the gift of François Pienaar.

   We scored the only try of a tight, physical match, through André Joubert, and we ought to have won. Instead, Andrew Mehrtens kicked five penalties and, to our bitter disappointment, we were defeated 15-11.

It would subsequently become clear that the relationship between captain and coach had already started to fracture by the time we arrived home in South Africa, but I never saw any indication either from François or André that this was the case. The incompatibility between the two men has become legend, but my view is that they might have worked together very effectively. The problem was that they were put together at short notice, and the defeats against Australia and New Zealand kindled the greatest pressure and recrimination. It might have turned out very differently if, for example, we had started the Tri-Nations series with two matches at home, and posted two victories.

Team confidence was partly restored by a 25-19 victory over Australia in Bloemfontein, which was more emphatic than the scoreline suggests. Joel Stransky scored a try, converted it and kicked six further penalties, but I was disappointed with my own performance, probably my least effective in a Test so far. I couldn't get into the game, couldn't get the ball in hand and run at defenders.

As we left the field, victorious at the Free State stadium, we all assumed our season would be pulled back on course. A Tri-Nations Test against the All Blacks at Newlands followed by a full three-Test series against our fiercest rivals lay ahead, and there seemed everything to play for.

We were wrong. A series of controversies off the field, incompetently and disastrously mismanaged by SARFU, served to destabilise the team, distracting attention from the task at hand; and we became stuck in a cycle of losing. August 1996 would unfold as an exhausting and desperate month.

It is hard to overstate the importance of sound administration and team management to a successful team. These elements, handled correctly, enable the players to concentrate solely on playing the game. Handled incorrectly, they spread confusion and mistrust, and undermine performance on the field.

FRANÇOIS' FOOTSTEPS

In 1996, our troubles began on the morning after the Test in Bloemfontein when Morné du Plessis, our team manager, expressed the side's disappointment that so many old South African flags had been waved by spectators at the Free State stadium. It was a perfectly reasonable statement, distancing us all from symbols that were widely interpreted as support for apartheid.

However, when right-wing groups started to complain, SARFU issued a statement indicating Morné had been speaking in his personal capacity and thus implying the union did not agree. François was drawn into the dispute when he was asked if people had the right to wave the old flag, all of which meant that far too much of everyone's time and energy was invested in the flag issue when it ought to have been focused on the task of defeating the All Blacks.

Morné, François and the players: we had all been let down by an absolute lack of leadership, conviction and support when it was sorely required, and team spirit began to suffer. We were not a happy side. Quite apart from broad divisions created by the World Cup contracts, quite apart from trying to adjust to a new coach, we were constantly being distracted.

And yet, and yet, this redoubtable group of players regrouped again and unleashed a whirlwind on the All Blacks at Newlands. New Zealand had already secured the inaugural Tri-Nations title, having won three out of three, but the concluding match offered us an opportunity to restore lost pride and to set down a marker before the three-Test series that lay ahead.

Japie Mulder and Os du Randt scored excellent tries as we raced away to an 18-6 lead. After an hour, we were in charge.

Then François Pienaar plunged low to make a tackle, and was struck on the side of the head by an unidentified knee. He was instantly concussed, and, after five minutes, carried from the field with his head in a red brace. Newlands hushed, almost eerily, as the World Cup icon departed on a stretcher.

Someone handed me the captain's armband.

Was I captain now?

The matter had never been formally discussed.

Several weeks earlier in Australia, there had been doubt over François' fitness and André Markgraaff had asked me whether I would be able to captain the side if required. I told him I would do so, but nothing more had been said since that day. Now François had left the field, and people were looking at me, but nobody had told me I should take over the side.

In the event, I started to lead the forwards, making the line-out calls and trying to keep the guys going, while Joel Stransky ran the backs. There was no clear message or instruction from the bench and, somehow muddling along, we braced ourselves to defend our lead until the final whistle.

Perhaps sensing our lack of organisation, the All Blacks suddenly stormed back into contention and produced 20 minutes of truly devastating rugby. We did not score another point and were ultimately beaten 29-18. There are no words to describe the depths of my disappointment at the final whistle. We had had them on the hook, we had let them go and, there they were, celebrating again.

Our changing room was still afterwards, with André Markgraaff and Louis Luyt standing around. It did strike me at the time that neither of them had been to the medical room to enquire about François' state of health. That was odd, and it so happened that, when François returned to the dressing room, he found Luyt sitting in a vacant seat beside me. I was not talking to the SARFU president, and didn't have much to say to anyone at that particular time ... but he sat down next to me and, for some, this constituted a form of anointment.

People glanced around. Conclusions were reached. What was now clear to everyone in that changing room was that neither the coach nor president was overly concerned about the captain. Luyt's antipathy could be traced back to François' perceived victory in the World Cup contract negotiations, and perhaps Markgraaff regarded François as a threat to his authority. I don't know.

It is hard not to colour reflections of events that had not yet unfolded, but my own instinct that evening at Newlands was that François' future as captain was, at the very least, unclear and uncertain.

The following day, Sunday 11 August 1996, with François confirmed as suffering concussion and ruled out for an obligatory three weeks, I was officially appointed as the Springbok captain for the three-Test home series against New Zealand. I had reached the pinnacle of the game, but, in truth, I did not want the job. My mind was focused on securing my place in the team and I had been very happy playing under François. That was surely enough. Ever since school, I had not sought the responsibility of leadership. Once given the role, I embraced it, but captaincy had never been any kind of Holy Grail for me.

Now, Markgraaff was asking, and I had to accept. After some encouraging words from my father, I adjusted my mind to the new challenge.

However, within hours of my appointment, another crazy storm blew up and was soon crashing against the battered defences of the squad. Some New Zealand journalists had seen James Small at a Cape Town nightclub after one o'clock on the Friday morning before the Test against the All Blacks. The story came out, and it ran without reins for the next ten days.

Competent administration would have handled the matter internally and decisively. Instead, we were treated to the spectacle of *The Bold and the Beautiful* being temporarily displaced as South Africa's favourite soap opera. James was initially dropped from the squad, then reinstated, summoned to a disciplinary hearing, hauled over the coals and then dropped again. At least, I think that was the sequence of events. As with *The Bold and the Beautiful,* you know the saga is always gripping but you do forget what happened.

Again, time and energy were wasted. My first reaction had been that André Markgraaff was right to insist James be publicly disciplined; on the other hand, he had emerged as one of our most effective players at Newlands and the matter could perhaps have been handled in private.

The first Test of the series against the All Blacks was to be played at King's Park, raising the ideal prospect that I would lead South Africa on to the field for the first time on my home ground in front of my home supporters. These were momentous events in my life, but amid the continuing drama and controversy, I was simply trying to stay focused and survive from day to day.

From the outset, I resented the almost daily press conferences as an extra burden when I wanted to concentrate on the team. The experience did, however, give me a greater appreciation of politicians. It is not as easy as you might think to talk for hours and still say nothing at all. I have heard it said that journalists did not find me an easy interviewee, something for which I am sorry but I cannot say I especially regret. Their idea of a 'story' was me saying something that I would have preferred to say to the people concerned, privately.

Some coaches and captains like to conduct their team talks in the press, and a few are skilled enough to use the media for their own ends, but I was not that foxy. To me, they would always be necessary, but a distraction. Perhaps this meant I was failing in my obligation to market the game. At the time, my primary obligation – to the players – was proving a challenge in itself.

It was a path I had trodden many times before, but the floor from the home dressing room at King's Park out on to the field seemed to be trembling shortly after five o'clock on the evening of 17 August 1996. I remember closing my eyes and telling myself to calm down because this was just another game, and then I recall opening my eyes, and seeing the packed stadium and hearing the bloodcurdling roar, and mocking myself for thinking this was just another game.

Where does that noise come from … the roar that seems to hail from the depths of the earth when a Springbok team takes the field in South Africa? It is different to anything else I have heard. Even if we score a magnificent try, even if the final whistle confirms a great victory, the crowd's reaction is not the same as the noise that greets the arrival of the team. It is soulful, emotional and timeless, and I know it will stay in my memory so long as I draw breath.

Out on the field, I started to wheel my arms, trying to settle down, to loosen up, calm the nerves and excitement, and focus on the task at hand. I allowed myself a glance at the All Blacks, warming up at the other end of the field. Wallowing in all our own problems, we had failed to acknowledge the strength of our opponents. They had retained the core of their 1995 team, but added the extravagant threat of Christian Cullen, the young sensation at full back, and they seemed driven by the twin desire of avenging the World Cup final defeat and becoming the first New Zealand team to win a full Test series on South African soil. I never doubted our ability to win the series, but I knew it would be tough.

Another mighty contest ensued. We trailed 18-9 at half time but fought back strongly in the second half and, with a little luck and a couple of penalties passing between the uprights rather than narrowly past, might have won. In the end, we suffered another huge disappointment, beaten 23-19.

I congratulated Sean Fitzpatrick after the game, and was impressed by his demeanour. We had met for the very first time at the toss before the match, and the sheer weight of his experience and presence set me back. As a hooker, he is often found in the dark corners of a match, but he has always played the game with respect and earned the admiration of friend and foe alike.

His disposition was never especially friendly, and he was sometimes hard to read. Was he angry? Was he bored? Was he shy? We never knew and, such is the selfish nature of professional sport, we never much cared either. Through an entire month of playing Test matches against each other, the Springboks and the All Blacks never once socialised and relaxed as a group. That was a pity, but Nick Mallett and John Hart would address the issue in 1998.

Defeat in Durban brought new pressures – one more defeat and the series was lost. I discussed the issue of team spirit with Morné du Plessis. He was evidently concerned about morale and, I sensed, still demoralised by what had happened with the flags in Bloemfontein. The smooth and united administration of 1995 was now a distant memory, and he appeared uneasy both in his relations with SARFU and André Markgraaff – although he never said so.

Morné is, first and last, a man of honour, and it was sad that he had been placed in such an invidious position. I was not surprised when he resigned after the All Black tour, but I was profoundly disappointed. He would be sorely missed until sound, proactive management was restored in late 1997.

The series moved to Pretoria, where we were now portrayed as standing on the brink of ignominy, the first team in Springbok history to lose a home series against the All Blacks. Our backs were pinned to the wall.

I tried to focus on doing my job as efficiently and effectively as possible, and actively ignoring all other matters. Team selection was not my province, so I was not concerned by what some might have regarded as panic selections. The public relations of the team, and the sport, were appalling, but that was not my area of responsibility either and I ignored that malaise as well.

My task was to motivate the players selected, to implement the game plan as laid down by the coach, and to maintain my personal performance on the field. Hopefully, I enjoyed some success in all these areas.

Even amid the sense of desperation and despair that had

enveloped our squad, there were lighter moments. We were training at B field at Loftus Versfeld on the Wednesday before the second Test, when someone walked over to hand André Markgraaff a message scribbled on a piece of paper.

'I am a farmer from the far Northern Transvaal, and I watched the Durban Test on television,' the message read. 'The problem is that you're not scrumming properly. I have travelled for three hours this morning and I would like the chance to show you what you're doing wrong, and put things right for Saturday. You will see me standing on the west side of the field. I'll wait for your call.'

André looked up and saw what can only be described as a portly, if not downright overweight, gentleman in his rugby kit, waving at us. A few of us had read the message over the manager's shoulder, and we implored him to give this rugby angel a chance to deliver his wisdom. In honesty, we applauded the depth of support but we also felt in need of a decent laugh.

So the manager beckoned the farmer to join us, and asked him what he wanted us to do. The man replied that we should go to the scrumming machine, and he would pack down in the front row to show us what he meant. André took one look at his physique and courteously asked whether he felt he was physically fit enough to survive the rigours of a Springbok scrum.

'Of course,' he replied indignantly.

'Well, I would feel a great deal more comfortable about all this if you would just run around the field once to prove your fitness.'

The man agreed, and the entire Springbok squad watched as he set off at a brisk pace, slowed to a jog after 50 metres, was walking after 120 metres and finally ground to an undignified halt at the opposite end of the field. As he stood, head bowed, hands on hips, the players laughed for the first time in weeks, and, with some relief, André cancelled the extra scrum session.

FOR THE RECORD

The farmer was not alone in his enthusiasm. The record of never having lost a home series to the All Blacks was cherished by the rugby public, and almost everyone had their own opinion of who should be playing or how we should be playing. Our supporters were desperate for a victory at Loftus, and so were we. Our preparations were intense and, for once, smooth.

Time and again, I told the guys we could beat the All Blacks. We had been unlucky in Auckland, had thrown the match away at Newlands and would have won in Durban with more consistent goal kicking. Yes, I knew that we had lost three times out of three, but the reality was that we could have won three out of three. Each of the Tests had been incredibly close; the margins between triumph and defeat had been infinitesimal.

Our scrums had been solid and our lineout was coming right. I made the point that we had actually been playing pretty well against the strongest team in the world. That was nothing of which to be ashamed. The players listened, and, as Saturday approached, I sensed we were getting somewhere. Training had been more player-friendly, and, as a result, successful. Our victory was not guaranteed, but my team would give everything. That was certain.

And they did give everything, in another intense match of high quality rugby played with courage and skill. It is hard to convey the brutality of the big hits around the fringes of the scrum and the midfield. It is hard to convey the degree of planning before an international, the level of concentration required to be in the right place at the right time, the kind of courage required to place your body in the path of a muscular, charging opponent – all to be executed under the kind of pressure that meant one error could condemn you to a place in history as the individual who lost the series against the All Blacks.

I sometimes wonder whether spectators appreciate the depth and impact of such pressure, whether they can conceive of a situation that could brand them for the rest of their lives, and beyond. Jack van der Schyff once missed a kick at goal that would have beaten the British Lions. No matter what else he achieved in his life, no matter what else he might have achieved, his name is synonymous with his team's failure that afternoon. That is pressure. That is what it was like to be wearing green and gold at Loftus on 25 May 1996.

With ten minutes remaining, we trailed 33-27. I can remember shouting at the forwards that there was still time, that the All Blacks were finished, that this match was there for the taking, and we surged forward. Aware and desperate at the same time, we carried the ball forward and literally pitched camp on the New Zealanders' try line. If they won the ball, and kicked to touch, we won the lineout and thundered back upfield. If they tried to run clear, our defence moved up and crash-tackled them back on their heels.

We would not lose. We would not be defeated. Time after time, we drove for their line. Time after time, our path would be blocked, sometimes illegally, but there was little time left so penalties were always tapped and run. A try and a conversion would draw the match and give us an opportunity to square the series by winning the third Test at Ellis Park. We drove forward again.

I watched every minute tick down on the electric clock. I saw the number reach 0, and then start dipping into injury time: –1, –2. Surely we could not lose this match. We had not deserved to lose. We did not …

The final whistle.

Exhaustion flooded every cell of my body, disappointment overwhelmed me … and, for perhaps the only time in my career, I literally slumped to the turf and lay on my back, eyes closed, racked with pain. I heard nothing, and saw nothing. Everything was screaming: my legs, my arms, my knees and the history books that had just been rewritten. This was agony.

After some time (it felt like hours, may have been seconds), I struggled to my feet and managed to congratulate a group of ecstatic All Blacks. I could see the joy in their eyes. And I looked around the stadium, at people scurrying to the exits. What would they be saying on the way home? What would they be thinking about the first team to have lost a home series to the All Blacks? What would be said about the first captain to have lost at home to the All Blacks?

I took the defeat personally, and, I hope, with dignity. Morné, André and I walked down the corridor and congratulated John Hart and Sean Fitzpatrick on their success, but I felt so desperately sad for my team who had given so much and come away with nothing except infamy and failure. Amid the battered limbs and quiet desolation, I saw some players had tears in their eyes.

As captain, I held my own emotions in check, at least until I met up with Nicky after the game, and I was able finally to share my disappointment.

Sleepy Sundays soothe, and cold Monday mornings bring harsh analysis of what went wrong and a distribution of responsibility. We watched the video, and concluded that the team had played well but had simply lacked that elusive ability to wrap up the game, to land the knockout punch. We might so easily have won by a reasonable margin, but we had lost 33-27.

Why?

'Bad luck,' somebody said.

'Nonsense,' I replied. 'That is a pretty lame excuse for anything.'

I didn't shout at anyone. That would have been counterproductive, but I was angry. We had lost four successive matches against the All Blacks, and we wanted to put everything down to bad luck? It wasn't good enough. We had to accept responsibility for what happened. No sportsman or sportswoman should ever summon 'bad luck' to rationalise a disappointing performance. It is weak, it is inadequate, and it demonstrates a lack of candour and courage.

In my view, we had lost because, despite all our enthusiasm

and effort, we did not truly believe we could beat the All Blacks. Our inadequate administration, the World Cup contracts and the climate of controversy that had dogged us since we gathered had all sown seeds of doubt and confusion in our team. As a result, we lacked the conviction and arrogance that sets winners apart.

We lacked the ruthless edge required to crush opposition, to convert long periods of possession into points on the scoreboard.

We were still performing like gung-ho amateurs, while the All Blacks, well handled off the field and sanely contracted by their union, performed with a focus that embodied everything excellent about professionalism. We had performed as if starring in *The Charge of the Light Brigade:* death or glory with a flourish. By contrast, the All Blacks were stars of *The Day of the Jackal:* calm and collected as they gently pulled the trigger and neatly bisected the target.

Others expressed their views as well. Some said we were not physically fit because we had tended to fade in the final quarter, but this was not the case. An experienced journalist described us as one of 'the worst Springbok teams ever'. Of course, he had toured with Paul Roos' side back in 1908.

We headed for Ellis Park, talking up the opportunity to win lost pride and take something out of the series. But this was purely for media consumption. The rubber was dead, and the series was lost. I could not pretend otherwise, and the players would have laughed if I had tried to convince them to the contrary. We would give our very best at Ellis Park, but we knew very well the result would only be significant in so far as it would determine our mood when we gathered again.

I was pleased to see François Pienaar just after the official photograph session at the team hotel in Johannesburg, and he walked over to wish me luck in the match on Saturday. Since being concussed, he had steered clear of the squad, diplomatically following the tradition that injured players slip away leaving those who must play to concentrate on the task at hand.

But he seemed agitated. I would later learn that he had arrived at the hotel personally to confront André Markgraaff with rumours that the coach had insisted to a group of people that François had not been seriously injured in Cape Town and had used the injury as an excuse to get out of the series. The coach denied the rumours. I don't know where the truth lies. It was not my business.

Even then, in the week before the third Test, I assumed, perhaps naïvely, that François would be recalled as captain for the end-of-year tour to Argentina, France and Wales. I was surely only the caretaker captain.

Henry Honiball was recalled at flyhalf, and we duly won at Ellis Park. We had not played much better than in any of the preceding Tests, but I sensed the edge was missing from the All Black performance. The tackles didn't seem to thud into my rib cage as they had done at Loftus the week before.

We had mercifully avoided a whitewash, and duly dedicated the victory to Morné du Plessis, who had announced his retirement as manager. In often difficult situations, he had always maintained his calm and his dignity. When the same was said of me, I would think I learned well from Morné.

I returned to the Natal ranks, and we maintained steady progress towards a second successive Currie Cup final, this time against Transvaal at Ellis Park. By then, South African rugby was aflame with public outrage on a scale seen neither before nor since. The game lived on the front page, on everyone's lips.

The Springbok squad to tour Argentina, France and Wales was to be announced on the Saturday evening after Natal had played a Currie Cup match against Eastern Province in Port Elizabeth. I had no knowledge of what would happen although, like almost everyone else, I had heard rumours that François Pienaar's place was in jeopardy. I found that difficult to believe and, given my last rand to wager that afternoon, I would have bet that he would be named as captain of the touring squad. Aged 29, he was hardly history.

We defeated Eastern Province comfortably and were standing around at the post-match cocktail party when George Davids, the genial EPRU president, cleared his throat and declared he was able to announce the Springbok touring squad. He moved through the positions, just as they had on the radio when I was first named in a Springbok squad three years previously.

There was no mention of François Pienaar among the loose forwards and, when he completed the list with 'Gary Teichmann, captain', there was a round of applause in the room. Players and officials from all sides moved to congratulate me on my appointment, but I felt no overwhelming sense of joy.

Up in Johannesburg, François had led Transvaal to an important Currie Cup victory over Western Province, and there he was informed of his omission. At a press conference soon afterwards, he voiced his support for the players and wished us well on tour.

Just 16 months after leading the Springboks to victory in the Rugby World Cup final, he had been omitted from a national squad of 36 players, including one unheralded, veteran flanker named Theo Oosthuizen, from Griquas, Markgraaff's own province. The coach had dropped a bombshell on South African rugby and, within hours, radio talk shows were crackling with outrage.

The *Sunday Times* subsequently held a telephone poll, asking whether Pienaar or Markgraaff should be dropped from the tour party. More than 60 000 people called, and 95% of them supported the former captain. The coach was broadly branded a small-minded fool who had dismissed one of the great Bok captains in his prime, all because the coach wanted to feel in control.

I said nothing. Again I had not sought the captaincy, but was not in any position to decline the responsibility. André Markgraaff was the coach, and he would have to take responsibility for the decision.

With hindsight, I believe it was a mistake to drop François. His form was nowhere near as poor as some people believed, as he amply demonstrated in producing a storming Man-of-the-Match performance in a Currie Cup semi-final against Northerns just a week later. He retained the respect of the squad, and he remained an outstanding leader of men.

Throughout the year, I had stated that Springbok teams should always be picked on form and not past glories. It would have been wrong to retain the World Cup winning captain just because he was the World Cup winning captain. He would have to earn his place, just like everyone else, and my view is that he had done enough to secure a place in the squad.

Under enormous pressure, André Markgraaff eventually explained to the media that he had dropped François because he was not in his Test side and he would not have imposed on the former captain the indignity of playing in the midweek team. I believe this was another mistake.

An arrangement whereby François was the tour captain, handling each of the media conferences and continuing to work as an outstanding ambassador for South Africa, and I led the Test team, would have worked spectacularly well, and I know François agrees. I was surprised that André had apparently ruled this neat option out before even asking an opinion from either of us.

I was even more surprised, in fact taken aback, to learn the coach had not even managed to contact François and personally inform him. Again he maintained he had tried to call twice, but if so, it seems curious that he opted not to leave a message and have François call back.

The whole affair had been a shoddy business, but it was not my concern. My task was to lead the squad, as selected, to the best of my ability. Soon after the touring squad gathered, I arranged to address the players.

'Look, everyone knows there has been a lot of controversy surrounding the selection of this squad,' I said, 'and I am not going to express my opinion, because it is the coach's job to select the squad, not mine.

'But we have a long and difficult tour ahead of us, and I am determined that we should leave this country as a happy and united group. So, I would like you all to be honest in answering the question I am going to ask.

'Is there anyone here who is unhappy with the squad, or with me as the captain? If there is, I would like you to raise your hand …'

I looked around the room, and looked hard. No-one raised their hand, and I hoped that, within the squad at least, the exercise had drawn a line beneath the furore. As the tour gathered pace, this seemed to be the case.

By the end of 1996, I was setting down my own footsteps.

7

André Markgraaff's Captain

André Markgraaff had made the decision to omit François Pienaar from the Springbok squad, but it soon became abundantly clear that both of us would suffer any consequences. Our fates were joined at the hip.

If the Springbok tour to Argentina, France and Wales unfolded as a great success, we would survive. If we failed on tour, we would not. The coach had raised the stakes, but we were both staring anxiously at the roulette wheel, waiting to see where the white ball would land.

Our 1996 record to date did not inspire confidence. We had lost four matches out of six, a ratio that was unacceptable to the South African rugby public. Neither André nor I needed to be reminded that previous Springbok coaches and captains with better results had been sacked.

Perhaps it was these circumstances that then enabled me to see André Markgraaff in a much kinder light. Where he had appeared dogmatic during the All Black series, now he would listen and discuss. Where he had seemed rash and callous in his selection policy, I now found him to be knowledgeable and sympathetic towards the players. He recognised the problems caused by the World Cup Springbok contracts, and he did not shrink from the task of trying to find a solution. He seemed clearly on our side.

ANDRÉ MARKGRAAFF'S CAPTAIN

I was more comfortable with this approach, and the players enjoyed being treated like adults. Of course, we might still behave like children on the odd Saturday night, but the reality was that rugby had become our job, our entire lives, and we knew better than most what kind of training and preparation would help us perform to our potential on Saturday afternoon.

We spoke. André listened. The result was that, before the tour was even two days old, team spirit had been transformed. The anxious, pressure-laden expressions of August were replaced by smiles and enthusiasm.

There is also no doubt that the coach and most of the players were able to relax on tour to a degree they found impossible at home. At stages of the series against the All Blacks, I sensed André was taking the intense media criticism too personally, becoming angry and agitated by what he read in the papers or heard on television. To me, this was a waste of energy.

Former Springboks, let alone journalists, sitting in the stand or watching the match on television, cannot truly understand the circumstances or flow of the game. Their opinions might appear in print the next morning, but they are always by definition second hand and bear little relation to reality. They have a job to do, and they do it as well as they can. I don't let it affect me.

On tour, of course, there are no South African newspapers at breakfast; on tour to Argentina and France, there were not even any newspapers in English at breakfast – so there was no criticism, and everyone relaxed.

It was even better than that: there were no well-meaning supporters in the hotel foyer, trying to explain that they had spotted a weakness in our back row defensive patterns, and there were not even any friends constantly calling to wish you well, and unearth one or other tactical gem. At home, we felt imprisoned by the pressure. On tour, it felt as if we were liberated.

André had personally crafted the tour management team,

disposing of a manager altogether and taking on a new role of supremo for himself. He brought in a high-powered coaching team, who would report to him and handle almost all the work on the training field. Nick Mallett, the Boland coach, would take the pack and Hugh Reece-Edwards, my recently retired team-mate at Natal, would direct the backs. Carel du Plessis, the former Springbok wing, was the third member of the coaching staff, taking on a general role as Technical Director.

This was a different structure, supposedly more appropriate to the rigours of the professional era. With hindsight, we still lacked a capable person uniquely concerned with ensuring smooth and seamless administration, but I was happy to embrace new ideas. André was always thinking, always trying to do things in a different, better way. No-one could accuse him of being cautious.

A tour to Argentina provided welcome respite to the 1993 Springboks, and it offered the same prospect to the 1996 squad ... although this time the local referees blew fair, the rugby was generally clean and the squad settled after the traumas of the home international season. People were smiling again, even sitting next to players from other provinces at breakfast. We enjoyed ourselves and played reasonably well, winning the two Tests against the Pumas, the first 46-15 and, a week later in the same Buenos Aires stadium, the second 44-21.

Henry Honiball was emerging as a key player in the team and, after playing well in the second Test, he allowed himself the quiet luxury of a few beers in the changing room. By the time he finally reached the team bus, André Markgraaff and I were already sitting side by side in the front seat.

Grinning from ear to ear, Henry saw me and swung a playful punch in the direction of my face. Unfortunately, his sense of direction was not all that it might have been, and his fist swung dangerously towards the coach's face. He must have avoided punching André's nose by the tiniest of margins.

In August, I suspect everyone would have frowned and considered the event to have been a major breach of discipline. In Argentina, I hesitated for a nervous second ... and then saw the coach smile broadly.

'Ja, Henry. Well played.'

We were getting somewhere.

The business end of the tour was represented by two Test matches in France. No Springbok side had ever won a series in France, but André and I were in no doubt that, given the pressures and expectations back home, this would be an excellent time to make some history. We simply could not afford to arrive home with more Test match defeats to explain away.

Our strategy before the first Test in Bordeaux was to set the French back on their heels with an early physical onslaught. We needed to make them feel every tackle, every scrum. To give the French any chance to run and express themselves would be to invite disaster. More than any side in the world, maybe in any sporting code, the French rugby team thrives on confidence.

With their spirits high, their supporters at their shoulders and the wind in their sails, they can defeat any team in the world, as the All Blacks would learn once again in the 1999 Rugby World Cup semi-final at Twickenham. The trick in any Test against France is to make absolutely certain their first step is backwards, and to squeeze the spirit out of them.

On this wet afternoon in Bordeaux, Kobus Wiese memorably personified our physical approach as he led a rampant charge. Kobus had played club rugby in France, understood the Gallic mentality and clearly relished every opportunity to storm at the blue jerseys. Rugby is first and foremost a team game, but I have always enjoyed the sight of a team-mate on the charge. That was Kobus on this day: thundering into every maul, demanding the ball.

Another South African hero this day was André Joubert, who kicked the ball so cleanly out of the hand that, time and again, I would wearily raise my head from the scrum and watch as one of his spiralling punts pushed play back to the French 22-metre line. Such kicking refreshes the legs.

I had played so much rugby with 'Jouba', for Natal and South Africa, that I might have started to take his exceptional talents for granted. First and foremost, he is the most relaxed person I have ever met. Nothing seems to irritate him, and nothing seems to upset him. He maintains that same familiar serene expression whether he is just arriving for breakfast on a Wednesday morning, or playing in a World Cup semi-final with his right hand broken in two places.

And as a player, everything he did was executed with a touch of class, something that can never be coached, something the overwhelming majority of us have to accept is granted at birth. Of course, he was not perfect. He made awful errors, and had off-days, but even the top-of-the-range Rolls Royce can clip the kerb once in a while. 'Jouba', however, even looked good when he was shocking.

In pure rugby terms, his positional sense was outstanding: the sight of him scurrying back to collect the ball is not something I can remember. He appeared to read the game so well that the ball simply came to him. And he was quick, even as advancing years added thousands of rands on the premium of his insurance contract. Few would catch him on the burst.

Perhaps the neatest measure of his ability is that, throughout his career, spanning 11 seasons from his Springbok debut in 1989 to his retirement in 1999, he gave confidence to everyone around him. There were critics who claimed he was erratic, and he was in and out of the Bok side at one stage, but I never saw a team with him at No. 15 that needed to look over its shoulder.

If André Joubert was at the back, then all was well. Could he have played in the 1999 Rugby World Cup? Of course he could.

By half-time in Bordeaux, the French players were checking their ribs and staring at a 19-6 deficit. We maintained the defen-

Left: Deep in thought, growing up in Gwelo (now Gweru, Zimbabwe).

Below: My pet bush baby 'Stinks' provided hours of entertainment for me as a child.

Bottom left: The highlight of my cricket career was selection for the Partridges, virtually a Rhodesian primary schools side. My father, Jack Teichmann, *left*, is in conversation with Ian Smith on the occasion in Salisbury when the then Rhodesian Prime Minister awarded caps to the team.

Bottom right: Cricket was certainly my sport of choice until the age of 12.

Left: Playing for Hilton College against Michaelhouse, I was lucky to finish on the winning side of the traditional derby three times in a row.

Below: Posing in uniform with my father, after which I was sent to pass away two years of uneventful national service in South West Africa.

Bottom: My first team Hilton days! I suppose you could say the start of things to come.

Top: The Teichmann family: *(back row)* David, Gary and Ross; *(front row)* Robyn, my father Jack, mother Mickey and Lindsay.

Bottom: Nicky and I on our wedding day, 10 February 1996.

Opposite page
Top: There is something noble about the Springbok No 8 jersey, something that makes every opportunity to wear it feel like a privilege.

Bottom: Playing rugby against Argentina was always enjoyable; keeping it tight on the drive with André Venter.

Above: In Currie Cup conflict with Tiaan Strauss of Western Province, the brave eighthman who blocked my Springbok ambitions until 1995.

Right: Western Province arrived at King's Park as favourites in the 1995 Currie Cup final, but we managed to prevail in the wet conditions and claim the golden trophy for the third time in six seasons.

5

Opposite page
Top: On the charge against the All Blacks, and looking to get rid of the ball with Walter Little, Zinzan Brooke and Justin Marshall in pursuit.

Bottom: A moment's peace on tour, but I'm not writing poetry!

Above: Changing of the guard: François Pienaar has just spoken what turned out to be his last words to André Markgraaff, but he still came over to wish me all the best before the third Test against New Zealand in 1996.

Right: Hand on my heart. We were supremely motivated before the consolation Test win over New Zealand at Ellis Park in 1996.

7

Opposite page
Top: Victories in France were hard earned and richly savoured; driving on with Joost van der Westhuizen, Ruben Kruger and André Venter in support.

Bottom: The glow of victory celebrated with, from left, André Venter, James Dalton and Krynauw Otto.

Top: On tour in France, pounding the pavements with Mark Andrews, (*middle*), and Hennie le Roux, (*right*).

Bottom: Plotting victory in France with André Markgraaff in 1996, but his sudden resignation early the following year took us back to square one.

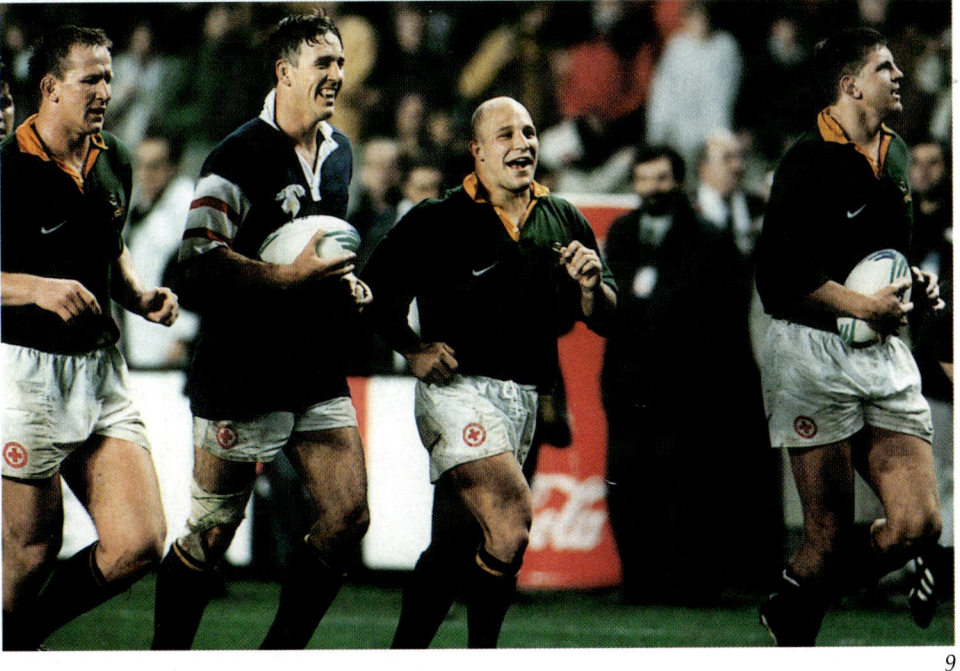

9

10

Opposite page
Top: First Test of the Lions tour to South Africa at Newlands 1997.

Bottom: Victory in the 1998 Tri-Nations championship returned South Africa to the pinnacle of world rugby. After two difficult years, triumph tasted sweet.

Left: Delight in Wellington – Joost van der Westhuizen, Henry Honiball and I celebrate our long-awaited Tri-Nations victory over the All Blacks in Wellington in 1996.

Below: Lifting the Tri-Nations trophy in 1998 was vindication after all the near misses of the previous two years.

11

Opposite page Top: Breaking down barriers with Nick Mallett on Robben Island, and we did serve with pride.

Bottom: I was fortunate enough to meet former President Nelson Mandela – pictured here with Nick Mallett and Arthob Petersen.

Right: Wayne Fyvie gives me a lift at the back of the lineout.

WELCOME
ROBBENEILAND
WE SERVE
WITH PRIDE
ONS DIEN MET TROTS
WELKOM

Opposite page
My wife, Nicky with our daughter, Danielle, who has already grasped her Dad's career firmly in her hands.

Bottom: A new beginning – Franco Smith, Tony Brown (CEO Newport) and I at the media announcement of my Newport contract.

Right: Taking a breather to plan more success with Natal, the team of the 1990s.

Below: Mac, André and I bidding farewell at King's Park – September 1999.

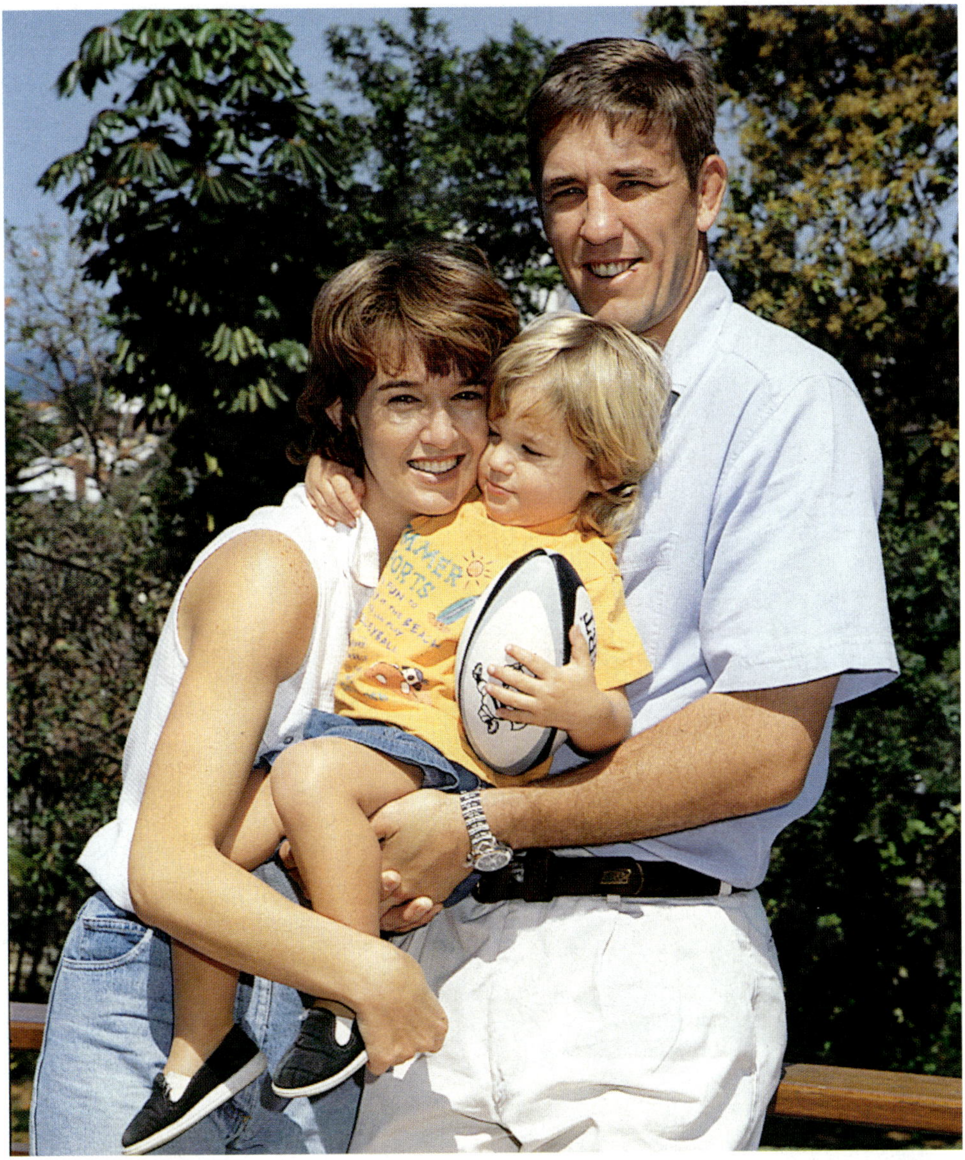

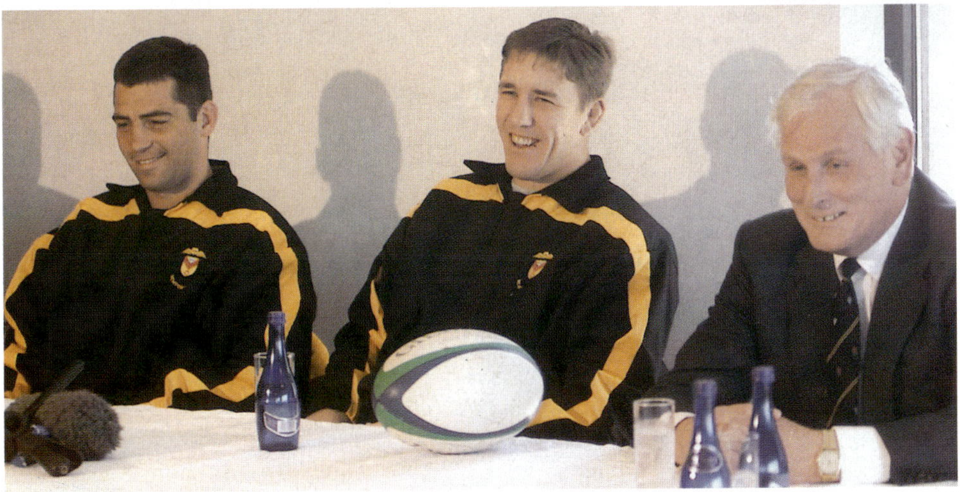

Below: Wearing my new jersey with pride.

Right: Playing conditions are a lot tougher in Wales and the rugby more physical.

Bottom: In action on my debut against Pontypridd county, Newport.

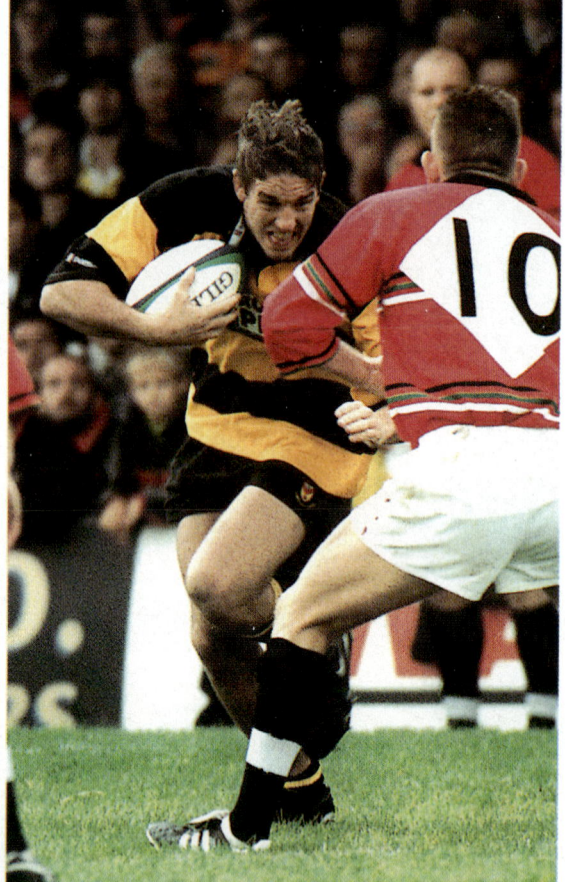

sive pattern into the second half and cantered off the field with an excellent 22-12 victory.

As we arrived in the changing room, André Joubert put his arm around me and asked if I had enjoyed the game. He obviously had. We all had. As we all bound arms in the post-match huddle, I thanked the guys for carrying out the game plan so professionally. In wet, difficult conditions, we had cooked. I glanced across at Kobus Wiese. He seemed ready for another half.

The contrast between the Springbok changing room at the Parc Lescure, and that at Loftus Versfeld 11 weeks before, was truly startling. Our spirits and our outlook had been completely transformed but the difference was nothing as nebulous as a change in fortune; it was confidence, that was all.

We anticipated a French revival in the second Test, to be played in Paris a week later, but we looked forward to the challenge with excitement, not fear. A team that couldn't win in August now believed it could not lose.

James Dalton, our feisty hooker, scored a try that would become familiar in television advertisements for years to come, surging to the try line with French defenders clinging to various parts of his body and, with ten minutes remaining, we were clinging to a precarious 13-12 lead. The French had improved vastly on their first Test performance and were mounting a grandstand finish. The crowd became involved, and the famous passion soared again.

Under the most intense pressure, we stuck together and made the tackles. Wherever they surged, we blocked. Wherever they ran, we covered. Wherever they rucked, we rucked too. We were brave, but we were also disciplined in our concentration. One error, one penalty conceded, and all would be lost.

'No penalties! No penalties!' Joost van der Westhuizen was screaming incessantly at the forwards. He was right. No penalties!

It is in times such as that last ten minutes at the Parc des Princes that – for a moment – I do not envy the world's leading tennis players and golfers their many millions, for, in their individual sports, they never know the experience of a shared triumph. They may smell the glory in a Ryder Cup or Davis Cup, but the spirit within a team under threat, a team drawing on its last ounce of energy and commitment, a team helping each other, is life and soul enriching.

At the climax of one brief surge upfield, I exposed my inexperience as a captain by screaming at Joost to run the ball when we won a penalty near their posts. We obviously should have kicked for the posts, and extended the lead to four points, but I was so pumped up by the circumstances, the adrenalin and the buzz that I thought we should go for the try.

As time ticked away, somehow we held our lead. With one minute left, Ruben Kruger managed to reach out and deflect with his outstretched fingers a drop goal attempt by Christophe Lamaison that seemed to be heading for the target. We had identified the threat, and detailed Ruben to charge the kick. Against all odds, he exploded off the mark, dashed six metres and touched his target. The ball flew wide. The margin between victory and defeat is often tiny, but that does not mean it is impossible to control.

The final whistle saw us crowned as the first Springbok team ever to win a series in France. I dashed across the field to congratulate André Markgraaff. I wanted him to know that we appreciated his role in the success. Whatever the rights and wrongs of his selection decisions, I don't believe anyone should ever suffer the sort of abuse he had endured back home. During the course of the tour, he had endeared himself to the players to a point where his knowledge was respected without exception, and his empathy had inspired genuine affection among many.

The 2-0 series win was his response to the critics; it was also the players' response. Not for the last time in my career, wreathed in smiles as I walked off the field at the end of a major match, I allowed myself the luxury of a prolonged glance in the direction of the press benches, thinking to myself, OK fellas, what are you going to write about that then.

So there we sat in the visitors' changing room at the Parc des Princes: André Markgraaff, the head coach feeling vindicated; Nick Mallett, Carel du Plessis and Hugh Reece-Edwards, the coaching staff who had produced the results, and me, the captain, exhausted, relieved and proud of my team. That happy night in Paris, in late 1996, we might have believed we were witnessing a new dawn for Springbok rugby. The 1995 World Cup was history. We were real, the new deal. As each individual among us was to discover during the highs and lows of the next three years, life is not so straightforward.

During the course of the celebrations, the coach offered to buy beer for the players all night. He had not bargained on Parisian prices, and discovered the next morning that the bar bill on his room account was R12 000. I hope SARFU approved his expenses; to be honest, he had earned them.

At the outset, the management team had promised the players that, if the Tests against France were won, the last week of the tour leading up to the Test against Wales in Cardiff would be gentle and full of golf; they kept their side of the bargain, even if some members of the Welsh media identified an element of arrogance in our apparently casual approach to the match.

They may not have been aware that we had started training in the second week of January, just when Cardiff shopkeepers were putting away the 1995 Christmas decorations, that we had then played through the inaugural Super 12, the first Tri-Nations series, three arduous Tests against the All Blacks, an intense Currie Cup campaign and, after all that, embarked on a globe-trotting tour that started in Argentina, moved through France and was ending in Cardiff, where the Christmas decorations were back in the shop windows.

We had arrived emphatically in the professional era, but the rich syrup of victory kept fatigue at bay, and we were able to defeat Wales 37-20, producing a neat, expressive performance. Everyone was evidently enjoying their rugby, and Joost van der Westhuizen seized his chances to score three tries. His incredible hunger for the game had remained intact throughout the year.

The squad flew home, riding the crest of six successive Test victories and already looking forward to the twin challenges of 1997, defeating the Lions and mounting a serious campaign in the Tri-Nations series.

All was not, however, as happy as it seemed. Somewhere in the home of André Bester, the Griqualand West hooker, lay a cassette tape that would have devastating consequences for André Markgraaff, and would take the Springbok squad back to square one again. We would have to start all over.

The storm was unleashed in February 1997. I was at home, enjoying a quiet night with Nicky, relishing some calm before the rugby season, when the main evening news bulletin left me stunned. It relayed a tape recording of a private conversation between André Markgraaff and Bester, during which the Springbok coach had used racist and abusive language.

I was appalled that someone could seek to trap another person in such a way. There had obviously been some disagreement, but this was an underhand method of exacting revenge. I have no time for people who indulge in such conduct. Nevertheless, the racist terminology could never be condoned, particularly from the mouth of the coach of a national team that was supposed to be uniting all South Africans.

My instinct, however, was to support André, both privately and publicly, and hope that an apology might enable him to survive the controversy. However, on the point of speaking in his defence, I was warned by Rian Oberholzer, chief executive of SARFU, not to become involved. In fact, he instructed me to make no comment at all. Several of the players telephoned me and asked what they could do to help André through, but there was nothing. The coach, who had proved himself to his squad, had become too hot to handle, and he was forced to resign within a couple of days. I was bitterly disappointed.

It later transpired that André had first been informed of the tape during the tour to France, and I recalled there had been mornings when he had appeared at breakfast looking terrible and drawn, as though he had not slept at all. I don't know if this was related to the tape issue, but, amid the celebrations, he must have been enduring extraordinary levels of anxiety.

André Markgraaff's resignation robbed the squad of all the gains made on tour at the end of 1996. Just when it seemed as though we were getting back into tune, our conductor had been suddenly removed.

History will remember him as the coach who dropped François Pienaar. Right or wrong, that was a brave decision. I think everyone would agree that André was a Springbok coach who knew what he wanted, and had the courage to take the toughest decisions. At least, he knew where he was going and, at the very least, he had the guts to take the measures required to get there.

I have respect for him as a coach, and a man, and always enjoy seeing him in and around the rugby world. Each time I meet him, I can't help but wonder what we might have achieved if that fateful tape had never been made. My view is that we would have sustained the progress of late 1996.

Among the players, the consensus was that Nick Mallett would be named as the new Springbok coach. He had been the dominant personality among the assistant coaches on tour, and appeared ready for the challenge.

We were wrong.

The Carel du Plessis era was about to begin.

8

Carel du Plessis' Captain

When the South African Rugby Football Union announced Carel du Plessis as Springbok coach, they appointed the man, not the coach.

In the aftermath of the André Markgraaff controversy, it almost seemed as if SARFU was more focused on finding a national figurehead with the right profile and manner rather than on simply securing the finest available coach. Desperate to avoid further controversy, they sought a safe pair of hands.

Carel du Plessis could not have looked safer. He had earned widespread admiration during a distinguished playing career for Western Province, Transvaal and South Africa, and even established a global reputation in the years of isolation, scoring a 75-metre solo try for a Southern Hemisphere XV at Twickenham in 1986. Neatly turned out, perfectly mannered, he cut an impeccable figure.

Quiet, thoughtful and intelligent, he seemed assured and confident at his opening press conference. SARFU expressed the hope that the 'prince of wings' would become the 'prince of coaches', and bring stability.

His coaching credentials, however, were less secure. He had been on the Springbok tour to Argentina, France and Wales, but had not said much during meetings and played a minor role during training sessions, and he had assisted in coaching at the University of the Western Cape Rugby Football Club.

There was no doubting the depth of his knowledge and integrity, but the challenge of coaching requires more than this. He hadn't been exposed to either the pressures or responsibility at either provincial or senior club level, and it is hard to believe such an appointment would have been made in New Zealand. In that country, great players return to grass roots and work their way up the ladder of coaching. No-one jumps from top rung player to top rung coach.

I am aware similarly swift promotions have been successful. In 1988, the West German soccer authorities appointed Franz Beckenbauer, a playing legend with no basic coaching qualifications, to be national coach and, within the space of two years, he was coaching the new world champions. There have also been many examples where the result has not been so happy.

None of these reservations reflect badly on Carel du Plessis. He had been part of the coaching staff on tour the previous year and certainly felt well placed to sustain the progress achieved under André Markgraaff. Once offered the job, he was not the sort of man to shrink from the challenge. His nature was to seize the opportunity and commit himself completely to the task.

Several days after his appointment, I was pleased to receive a call from him. He wanted to see me and, together with Gert Smal, named as his assistant coach, he flew from Cape Town to Durban to see me. I was flattered, and eager to give him every possible support from the outset.

Over breakfast at the Elangeni Hotel on Durban's beachfront, Carel said he would like me to remain as Springbok captain and was eager to hear what I believed were priorities for the squad. I talked about the advantages of holding training sessions that were shorter and more intense, but I was very much more intrigued to know which direction he wanted to take.

My impression was that he wanted to carry on where we left

off in Wales. He seemed completely sincere and honest, young and enthusiastic, and I left the meeting thinking that we could work successfully together. The fact that he had not served his coaching dues remained at the back of my mind, a concern that the Springboks were moving forward on a wing and a prayer.

The Super 12 again put the international calendar on pause and, after another successful campaign with the Natal Sharks, but ending in semi-final defeat against eventual champions Auckland, I turned towards the Springbok challenge with some confidence, on the back of decent personal form.

Our first major opponents of the year were the British Lions, touring South Africa for the first time since 1980. The appalling record of northern hemisphere teams against the three southern giants in recent years kindled speculation that we would cruise to a 3-0 series win, and, to be honest, we expected nothing less. Perhaps an element of complacency did creep in.

I recall reading articles about the Lions' preparation, where they trained with the Royal Marines, and the various measures being taken by manager Fran Cotton and coach Ian McGeechan, but my conviction remained we would have too much quality in our team. They would be well prepared, well managed and well coached, but they surely lacked the talent to beat us.

Our preparation for the Lions series was a friendly Test against Tonga at Newlands, and this unfolded as a comfortable victory that proved very little. We had loosened our limbs, but the competition had not been good enough to provide a serious trial to any of our key combinations or tactics. It was not as if anyone was overly concerned: we were playing the Lions, not the All Blacks.

Through early training sessions, I could almost see the players standing back and forming opinions on Carel and Gert as coaches. Sportsmen at the top level can be ruthless judges of the people appointed to work around them; if they sense weakness or hesitation, they can be unforgiving. I am not suggesting this was the case but, at the very least, this period of getting to know each other prohibited any flow of confidence from the victories over France.

We were all feeling our way again, trying to develop relationships. There were no shortcuts. A change in coach meant a change in gear.

In one particular training session, we spent time being taught how to pass the ball at speed and I sensed several senior players wincing at the drills, looking around, and exchanging quizzical glances. These were international players: if they couldn't pass the ball at speed at this stage of their careers, then they should not be in the Springbok squad. As we moved back to the changing rooms, two or three guys walked beside me and asked what on earth was going on. I told them quite firmly to stay positive and concentrate on their own jobs.

But they had not asked a completely stupid question, and their boldness did reflect players' reservations from an early stage. The coaching challenge at Test level is not so much to rehearse the basic elements and skills of the game, as to select the right team, to develop a game plan that the players understand and support, and to motivate the squad.

Carel did approach these broader issues and, at stages, the entire squad would be summoned to attend long meetings where we discussed the coach's vision for how rugby union should be played. He spoke passionately about the importance of skills, and movement, and versatility, of releasing players from all restrictions, freeing them to play their natural game, but before long players were looking at the floor, or playing with their fingers, whatever.

I would sense his frustration that players did not immediately understand what he was talking about, and embrace the challenge of taking rugby to what he regarded as a new level. He was genuinely excited about the prospect, but the communication channel between coach and squad was blocked.

His message was not getting through. I am not saying the

message was wrong, and certainly no-one was to blame, but the coach might have thought the players were not listening, the players may have thought the coach did not know what he wanted ... and everyone became increasingly frustrated.

To be absolutely honest, I did not completely comprehend what the coach wanted either. The vision sounded fine, but it was undeniably fuzzy and difficult to put into practice on the training field. I have always been a Philistine in terms of rugby strategies, believing the game is about winning possession, retaining possession and converting possession into points. I see rugby as a wonderfully simple game, and tend to steer clear of analysis paralysis.

Again players approached me, asking me to intervene and suggest to the coach that the meetings should be much shorter and that the players should be told precisely what was expected of them. I did speak to Carel, but sensed only his disappointment that I failed to understand his position.

Some years before, I had spoken to a Natal cricketer about the problems faced by their team when Barry Richards, one of the greatest batsman ever, had taken over as coach. Barry had a brilliant mind and visualised how he wanted the team to play, but he struggled to convey precisely what the players should do to get there. 'Barry was a genius,' this player said. 'We were just an ordinary bunch of guys, and we couldn't get on the same level as him.'

I have often wondered whether Carel du Plessis and the Bok players were not experiencing similar difficulties during the 1997 season. He seemed to be on a different level.

The coach was determined to change our underlying approach to the game, and he resolved to be patient until his message got home, but rugby players generally operate on instinct. We simply wanted to play. We would have battled to spell the word 'philosophy', let alone discuss its merits with regard to our game.

The vision thing was taking up too much of our time. When

CAREL DU PLESSIS' CAPTAIN

would we work on set moves? When were we going to rehearse our defensive pattern?

While confusion and concern started to fester in our camp, the Lions were earning new respect around the country. Their forwards were organised, drilled and physical, they had several creative and dangerous backs, and perhaps the world's most reliable goal-kicker in Neil Jenkins. Their match schedule had been daunting, taking in all the major provincial teams without respite, but their colours were only lowered in a narrow defeat to Northerns.

Decent victory followed decent victory, their confidence visibly increased and, as the first Test at Newlands approached, their performance curve seemed to be moving emphatically upwards. For our part, we didn't have a performance curve, probably because we were still busy in a team meeting.

In all this, again, I attach no blame to Carel du Plessis. He accepted the job and sought to implement his ideas. It is hard to say where the communication faults lay, perhaps with the coach, perhaps with the players, perhaps with some kind of combination of the two. It doesn't matter. The fact is we were in a muddle, and on the verge of facing a pack of increasingly confident Lions.

We trained hard before the crucial opening Test, and discovered that Gert Smal, coaching the forwards, was another disciple of setting scrum after scrum to build up fitness. André Markgraaff had introduced the same measures when he took over as coach in 1996, but amended his training schedules later in the year. Now Gert was in charge and reverting to the same failed methods. It seemed as if we had taken two steps forward, and now took three steps back.

It was frustrating, and I decided to speak to Carel and Gert about the real dangers of over-training the guys, leaving them leg weary on Saturday, but there was little response. This was what they wanted to do. I was becoming concerned about the Lions threat, and increasingly despondent.

When I looked around our changing room, I saw players of world class but I knew we would not produce world-class performances until we were provided with effective management, until we were able to settle with a coaching staff who had confidence in us, and in whom we had grown confident.

And yet, despite all our problems, I still believed there was enough talent in our team to pull through and overcome the Lions, and I tried to convey this conviction to the players, but you can sense when the guys are taking in what you say, and you can sense when they are not. They were not.

In 1996, we had played the All Blacks with no confidence and lost. At the end of that year, we had rediscovered confidence and beaten France. Now, in 1997, the uncertainty created by the change in coach and the ongoing absence of skilful management eroded our confidence once again. As a result, our shared mental state ahead of the first Test was not one of believing we would win, but one of being desperate not to lose. It was a significant difference.

The first Test of a three-match series is always pivotal. I don't know how many sides in history have lost the first and recovered to win the next two, but I don't think it is very many. In my view, the first Test distributes pressure, taking it away from the winners who must then win just one from two to secure their goal and loading it on to the losers, who cannot afford another error.

Carel du Plessis knew this, I knew this, the players knew it and, as we advanced through our final preparations at the Cape Sun Hotel on the morning of the game, I recall a particular tension among the guys. It arose from the knowledge that, as a team, we were not well prepared for the challenge.

We started well enough. Os du Randt scored a first-half try, but we gave away too many penalties and Jenkins' goalkicking kept the Lions in the game. At half-time, we were trailing 9-8 but I told the guys I was satisfied with the overall performance and said we should press on and the points would come. I was not concerned that we would not win. We were in control.

There was a period after half-time when we could have ended the contest but we let a couple of chances slip by, a couple of passes didn't go to hand, and, all of a sudden, it started to rain at Newlands and we found ourselves involved in a dog-fight. We had displayed the classic signs of a team lacking the confidence to make opportunities count and finish off the opposition.

We led 16-15 with eight minutes left, but I purchased a dummy from Matt Dawson following a lack of communication between the flanker, the fullback and me, and the Lions scrumhalf scrambled clear to score in the corner; in injury time their centre, Alan Tait, scored again. In a blur, we had lost 27-16.

The result absolutely shocked me, maybe because I had never considered it possible. It felt far worse than defeats against the All Blacks or Wallabies. I could see our guys were genuinely stunned, left almost speechless.

As captain, I felt exposed by the lack of assistance and support from the team management. Carel and Gert were both quiet by nature, and our team manager, Arthob Petersen, was not the type of man to take hold of such a difficult situation. SARFU officials were conspicuous by their absence.

When I recall the management team during the 1995 World Cup, I have to say it was in a different mould. Morné du Plessis was a clear leader who oversaw all arrangements and disciplinary issues, a man of stature and integrity. The SARFU assistance was so hands-on and constructive that the Chief Executive worked as the team's media liaison officer. This solid structure enabled Kitch Christie to concentrate purely on the rugby, and François Pienaar to focus solely on his key responsibilities as captain, motivating the players and planning.

I am not making excuses, and I am certainly not suggesting the problems were everyone else's fault but mine. It is, however, important to make clear that professional sports teams lean heavily on their management to create the right mood within the camp and, as I have said before, to allow each individual player to fix his mind solely on playing the game. I simply believe the Springbok teams of 1996 and 1997 were not afforded these circumstances.

Sleep did not come easy in the week before the second Test against the Lions in Durban. I would lie in bed, wondering over and over how on earth we had got ourselves back into this crisis mentality. Had not the victories against France been hailed as the new dawn for South African rugby? What now? Where had we gone wrong? What had I done wrong?

The 1996 Tests at home had been a nightmare, and now it was all happening again. Just as we had arrived at Loftus 12 months earlier to stay alive against the All Blacks, so we arrived at King's Park to play the Lions, desperate for a victory to give us a chance of coming from behind to win the series.

We trained hard again in Durban, and I spent a great deal of time during the week, sitting down with players on a one-to-one basis and ensuring they all understood exactly what was expected of them on Saturday. We could afford no misunderstanding, no uncertainty, and I told every one of them the Lions were a strong side, but, in terms of talent, not in our class.

Again, I didn't rant and I didn't rave at anyone. That has never been my style, but, this particular week, I did enlist the help of two senior players, Mark Andrews and Joost van der Westhuizen, in motivating certain members of the squad. It may have been a word in jest over a meal, or just an aside as the players jogged around the field at training, but things needed to be said to certain people. We needed to restore confidence, self-belief, even a bit of arrogance, to the team. I was determined that we would not lose to the Lions. The thought was intolerable.

At one stage during the week, I bumped into Ian McIntosh at King's Park. He could see we had problems, and he understood what was happening within the side. He told me to keep going, keep trying to get things right. I appreciated his support, and his positive attitude. He said we would pull through. We had to play well at King's Park, and we did play well, dominating long periods of the game and scoring three tries without reply. Each player met his personal targets. Yes, we missed a few try-scoring chances. Yes, we might have been more physical in the opening stages, but, by the end, I had no cause to complain that anyone had let us down on the day.

Yet, on the most disappointing day of my entire rugby career, we lost 18-15, victims of a late, late drop goal. The series was lost.

Even now, I find it hard to understand how we failed to win the Durban Test. The atrocious goalkicking obviously didn't help our cause but, on the balance of play, we deserved to win by 20 points. That is not an exaggeration. We had been the better side in every phase of the game ... but we lost.

I held myself partially responsible for the goalkicking shambles. In total, we missed six out of six goalable attempts. Just two out of six would have been enough to win the match. Henry Honiball tried twice, and missed twice. Percy Montgomery tried twice, and missed twice. André Joubert tried twice, and missed twice. People said afterwards we should not have gone into a Test without a top goalkicker, but all three players were recognised goalkickers and, either before or since, each of them has won Test matches with his boot.

My mistake may have been a reluctance to name any one of the three as our nominated goalkicker. With such richness of talent, I had not even considered goalkicking would be a problem. If one of them was struggling, then I had thought there were still two safe options to step into the breach. But I should have given one man the responsibility, enabling him to concentrate on the role.

Instead, all three players took the field, unsure if and when they would be required to kick for goal. Uncertainty clouded performance and, time after time, the ball was propelled narrowly wide of the upright.

'Ja, but we had no luck against the Lions,' people would say for years afterwards, and it was true that the French referee had not been kind on the day, and it was true that our goal-kicking had often failed by centimetres, but it is simply not enough to rationalise this stunning series defeat by citing luck. In the first place, such a judgement doesn't acknowledge the Lions' achievement, and, second, we should have been so far ahead that fortune was irrelevant.

The decisive drop goal is one of those rugby moments etched deep in my memory. We had been pressing well inside the Lions' half, when the ball popped clear and was fly-hacked upfield. Their flankers led the chase, and a loose maul formed in front of our posts. The Lions had the ball. I shouted to somebody to mark Neil Jenkins and beware a drop goal. The flyhalf had moved to a deep position but I recall thinking we had him covered.

In the event, the ball was passed to Jeremy Guscott, the centre, and it was he who launched the drop goal attempt for glory. The ball squirted over the crossbar like a deflating balloon. It was not majestic like Joel Stransky's drop goal in the 1995 World Cup final, but it counted three points and, for the very first time in the entire match, the Lions had taken the lead. 'Stay calm, stay calm,' I implored the players as we ran back to half-way. The referee told me two minutes remained to play. We kicked off, and earned a lineout between half-way and the Lions' 22-metre line. This represented our last chance to keep the series alive, and I called a throw to the back of the line, with the intention that we would drive strongly off the tail.

The throw was good, but the Lions didn't even contest the ball. Yet again, they were thinking intelligently. By not contesting the throw, they reduced the risk of conceding a penalty to zero. The 1997 Lions will be remembered as a squad who made the absolute most of the players at their disposal. Their management and coaching were exceptional, and the team clearly developed a spirit that was remarkable.

They had done their very best, and it was enough.

At the final whistle, I felt instantly drained. I found it so hard to accept we had lost the match that we had so comprehensively dominated. A stone-silent Springbok changing room had become a familiar experience for all of us over the past two years, and here we were again, coping with defeat.

Lions' tours to South Africa are only scheduled once every six years, so a player can only expect to play them once in his career. For me, this was the most devastating thought after losing the series: there would be no opportunity to take revenge. This had been a one-off, and we had failed.

In the wake of defeat in Durban, the mood in the Springbok camp started to deteriorate. I sensed the players retreating to the old provincial groups, and I overheard players blaming specific team-mates for the series defeat. The series had become a disaster for South African rugby, and people had started to run for cover, concerned only with salvaging their own reputations.

It was deeply depressing. Yes, people might say, but why didn't you do something about it? You were the captain. It was your team.

I have often considered my own role, envisaging a scenario where I call the entire squad together, deliver a bloodcurdling address that restores a sense of purpose and morale. Players who were negative and selfish suddenly become open and constructive, coaches who were quiet and hesitant become strong and confident, managers who were ineffective become inspirational, and the entire squad leaves the room, emboldened and excited.

Then I wake up ... it only happens in the movies.

People can look back and blame me for the Lions defeat if they want. As captain, I accept responsibility, but, in all sincerity, I cannot look back and say I could have done this or I could have done that, and we would have won. I had tried everything I knew and given everything I could. In those circumstances, at this particular time, I was comfortable with my own efforts.

The Lions were kind enough to say publicly afterwards that I had been the Springbok player of the series, and the maintenance of my form on the field has always been an important element of my captaincy, but such accolades offered no consolation in the context of the team's overall defeat.

We headed to Ellis Park for the third Test, trying desperately to persuade ourselves that there was something at stake. We performed creditably in stages, and did enough to defeat a Lions team that had clearly achieved its goal, and, mentally at least, was still celebrating a historic series win.

I suffered a cut above my eye, and was compelled to leave the field seven minutes from time to have the wound stitched. It didn't seem to matter that I was not playing at the end of the Test match, and I doubt whether anyone saw any significance in the fact I had failed to see the series through to its conclusion. Joost van der Westhuizen took the captain's armband, and gave a post-match interview in which he said the 35-16 'klap' showed we were the better side.

Back in the changing room, however, I was frustrated. As the Springbok captain during 1996 and 1997, two desperately difficult seasons, I had wanted to be a leader who never shirked his responsibility, who always saw it through and who always supported his players. After we had run the penalty with moments left to play, leading by a single point in Paris, I had taken public responsibility for the decision. When we had neglected to appoint a designated kicker in Durban, I took the blame ... and I wanted to be on the field when the final whistle sounded on this desperately disappointing series against the Lions.

My pride and stitches healed swiftly. Other battles lay ahead.

To his great credit, Carel du Plessis did not abandon his core strategies in the wake of defeat. It would have been easy for him to forsake his ideals ahead of the Tri-Nations series, to retreat to some kind of safety-first approach against New Zealand and Australia, to embark on a damage limitation exercise with the aim of saving his own skin. He is not that type of man.

We gathered for the opening Tri-Nations Test, against the All Blacks at Ellis Park, and Carel opened the meeting by saying we had all made mistakes against the Lions, and we now shared the responsibility for putting things right against New Zealand. He reaffirmed his views on how we should play, taking a more pragmatic approach than earlier in the year, and stated his conviction that this Springbok side had the potential to beat anyone.

He spoke well. Hurled in at the deep end of international rugby, this thoroughly decent man appeared to be rising to the challenge, and his team reflected the coach's renewed sense of confidence and ambition. We trained efficiently during the week and produced an outstanding performance of courage and skill against an All Black team at the peak of its powers.

The Ellis Park crowd rose to the occasion as well. To my mind there is no better atmosphere in the world of rugby than that provided by a full house at the Johannesburg stadium, and I could feel the depth of their support when I led the Springboks onto the field that day. Maybe naïvely, I sensed a bond between players and supporters. We had suffered together against the Lions, we would advance together against the All Blacks. It never appeared as though they were sitting back to judge and condemn. Maybe I was wrong, but it seemed to me the Ellis Park crowd remained with us. We were lifted.

And the players responded. After 30 minutes, we were leading 23-7. The forwards performed as a unit, with purpose and discipline, and the backs ran strong and hard. The All Blacks appeared to be on their knees.

We should have kept them there but, once again, we lacked the belief to nail down the opposition when we had the chance. They broke clear to score two soft tries before the interval, and we reached half-time disappointed to be leading by no more than 23-19. But we were in the game, suddenly playing at a level far beyond anything we had remotely realised against the Lions.

Jannie de Beer had retained the flyhalf berth from the third Test against the Lions and, throughout an unbearably tense second half, kept us strongly in contention. We matched the All Blacks tackle for tackle, burst for burst as the contest came down to the wire. If they had expected an easy game against the side beaten by the Lions, they were being emphatically disappointed.

Carlos Spencer kicked a penalty late in the game. Jannie swiftly kicked a penalty in reply. With 12 minutes left, both teams had run themselves to a virtual standstill, and yet were still locked together at 32-32.

Whose nerve would hold?

The visitors' nerve held. Spencer kicked a further penalty, awarding the All Blacks a tiny lead and, with a minute remaining, Jannie pulled what would have been the equalising penalty strike narrowly past the left upright. I could scarcely believe my own eyes. After such a Herculean effort by every member of the side, there was absolutely no shame in our defeat. There was, however, once again a crushing sense of disappointment in our changing room.

Players sat and stared into the middle distance, wondering what on earth might have been done to give South Africa an opening victory in the Tri-Nations campaign. We had worked so hard and played so well, and still lost. I sat and watched any remnant of confidence drain from the vanquished squad. No word or deed could have stemmed the flow on that sad evening.

People were kind, saying we had contributed in full to a genuinely great game of rugby, but we were professionals who had desperately wanted to win at Ellis Park. Anything less had to be regarded as failure.

CAREL DU PLESSIS' CAPTAIN

The reaction to this disappointment unfolded in an appalling performance against Australia in Brisbane two weeks later, without doubt the worst Springbok display I have seen. We had travelled east in hope, and trained diligently, but the heart and soul was inexcusably missing. We scarcely competed for the ball in the first 30 minutes, appearing lethargic and disinterested, and might have suffered a much more emphatic defeat than the 33-22 scoreline suggests. We were trailing 19-3 after half an hour and never looked anything but losers.

Such performances were embarrassing and unacceptable. When I heard from home that Carel du Plessis was being quoted attacking unnamed senior players for failing to play the way he wanted, I confronted him.

'No, I've been misquoted,' the coach replied. 'I never said that.'

The wheels were starting to come off, and I began to feel increasingly impotent as captain. When players asked me to raise an issue with the team coaching staff, and I did raise it, and was ignored, I sensed those same players starting to lose faith in me. I was desperate.

Amid a torrent of abusive faxes that arrived at the team hotel, one was addressed to me and featured one word, written large: 'Resign!' Others featured far more abusive language. I resolutely read through an entire pile.

Resignation appeared the only reasonable course of action and, in my Brisbane hotel room, I decided that I would step down as the Bok captain at the end of the Tri-Nations series. Someone had to take the flak for our poor performances, and I accepted it should be me.

I had resolved not to be a quitter, fervently wanting to be someone who saw the battle through to the last, but the situation within the squad appeared so hopeless and confused that I was being rendered ineffective. The All Blacks were waiting at Eden Park, Auckland, literally chomping at the bit to take full and merciless advantage of a South African side in trouble.

The team management had settled on a new travel plan, staying four days in Brisbane and only travelling across the Tasman Sea to Auckland on the Thursday before the Test. I did not know whether this would work well, but the thought struck me as innovative and I raised no objection.

Upon our eventual arrival in New Zealand, however, we were subjected to a standard of management and administration that would have had most social teams raising their voices in complaint. We were supposed to be one of the top three teams in the world, but we had become a laughing stock.

First, the entire squad was firmly instructed to attend the opening press conference in Auckland, and I could see the guys becoming embarrassed as they stood like rows of stuffed dummies, saying nothing, as they listened to the media asking cynical questions and writing off our chances. There was no good reason at all why the players were forced to attend, and no-one could give me a reason afterwards. Was anyone thinking at all?

That Thursday evening, we duly arrived at Eden Park for the captain's practice. It was getting dark, so I asked for the floodlights to be switched on, only to be told there were no floodlights and, in point of fact, there was no more than 15 minutes of daylight remaining for practice. It had been the responsibility of our own management team to schedule the training sessions.

As locals sniggered, I felt acutely foolish and embarrassed. Making the shambles even worse, various suite holders had been allowed into the stadium and they started shouting abuse at us. This was supposed to have been our one and only private practice at the stadium, and it degenerated into a rushed, abbreviated session marked by abusive heckling.

Worse was to follow on match day. Again it was the responsibility of our own management team to arrange the time of departure from the hotel, and the time did strike me as being a little late when I read the daily schedule early that morning.

But, for goodness sake, this was not my responsibility. I was too busy trying to motivate the players to worry about our travel plans.

In the event, we left the hotel too late and arrived at Eden Park no more than 25 minutes before kick-off. This was inexcusable, farcical and totally unacceptable. Flustered and anxious, the players virtually sprinted off the bus to our changing room. I had to drop my bag and proceed immediately to the toss of the coin. There was no time for any team talk or contemplation. We were supposed to be the world champions, and we couldn't even arrive for the match on time.

And yet, once again, I was left to marvel at the tenacity and resilience of the Springbok team. Despite our low morale, despite our poor preparation, we focused and started the match powerfully, surging to an early 10-0 lead. By the interval, however, we had lost both our flankers: Ruben Kruger with a broken ankle and André Venter, most controversially sent off after what seemed to have been a minor incident, expertly exaggerated by Sean Fitzpatrick.

The All Blacks were finding their momentum and, after leading only 23-21 at half-time, they ran rampant as the game wore on. Our players never stopped trying, never stopped tackling, never stopped chasing, but New Zealand had scored no fewer than eight tries by the end of the afternoon.

And, for the first time in 107 years of rugby, South Africa had conceded more than 50 points in a full international. We had been thrashed 55-35, hurled involuntarily into the record books once again.

A squad meeting was held later that night and it was James Small who showed the courage to say what every player was thinking. In the intimidating presence of Louis Luyt, the SARFU president, James stood up and said the players had been seriously let down by the management.

That was a fact.

We had.

Luyt interrupted him. 'You should be more careful when you talk about the people who are paying the mortgage on your house,' the president said, sharp and threatening. The meeting instantly turned sour.

I had to intervene. As captain, it was my duty.

'Dr Luyt, you should know James is not expressing his personal view. I believe that is the opinion of the entire squad.'

The president mumbled on, and, amid the worst imaginable atmosphere, the meeting ended abruptly. I returned to my room, called Nicky and told her in no uncertain terms that I would resign as Springbok captain after the concluding Tri-Nations match. She listened and urged me not to make any hasty decisions, but my situation was becoming intolerable.

This dismal evening in Auckland turned out to be the darkest hour before the dawn for Springbok rugby. Unbeknown to any of us, feeling battered on one side by the All Blacks and bruised on the other by our own administrators, we were poised to embark on a run of 17 successive Test wins.

We returned to South Africa and, with the Tri-Nations series already won by New Zealand, cast caution and concern aside in playing the last match of the series, against Australia in Pretoria. Under no pressure and less expectation, we galloped to an impressive and entertaining 61-22 victory. This was the first time the Wallabies had conceded more than 50 points in an international match; a week after accepting precisely the same medicine, we handed it out ourselves.

The consensus amid the celebrations at Loftus Versfeld was that, at the end of a traumatic home international season, the players had finally fastened on to what coach Carel du Plessis had been relentlessly outlining all year, with the result that we had pushed back the boundaries of the sport and annihilated one of the top teams in the world in devastating fashion.

This was the vision, the new brand of rugby.

Led to believe that this enthusiastic, decent young coach would remain in his position, I was surprised several weeks later to hear on the television news that Carel du Plessis had been summarily sacked only six months into a contract which initially extended to the 1999 Rugby World Cup.

On a personal level, I felt genuinely sorry for him. He had struggled to get his ideas across to the players, but this might have been different if he had been given more time and weaker opposition. The fates granted him a well motivated Lions squad and the Tri-Nations series instead, and ultimately these tough circumstances proved barren ground for his bold plans.

Elements of his team selection had seemed bizarre at various stages of the season, and Carel was widely criticised for his persistence with the young Western Province utility back, Percy Montgomery. One newspaper cartoonist depicted the coach choosing the Bok side by throwing darts, with the dartboard having a massively outsized central area marked 'Percy'. Such criticism must have been hard for a promising player to accept, but Percy emerged to become an outstanding Springbok, completely justifying the faith of the coach who brought him so quickly to international level.

Some time later, Carel and Gert Smal would contest the terms of their dismissal as Springbok coaches, eventually taking SARFU to court. In the course of these proceedings, I was asked by senior SARFU officials to support their reasons for sacking the coach and give evidence against Carel.

I refused.

Whatever might have happened, whatever might have gone wrong, I had still been Carel du Plessis' captain. The coach deserved my loyalty, and he would receive nothing less.

9

Team of the Nineties

There were talented players, there was an experienced coach and there were many thousands of fervent supporters, but the single greatest factor in the huge success of Natal rugby during the 1990s was that we had fun.

That might sound trite, too frivolous to be truly significant set against the hours of planning and hard work required to be successful in provincial rugby, but this infectious and inherent ability to laugh at each other and enjoy ourselves was a major difference between Natal and many of our rivals.

In some parts of South Africa, rugby was taken so seriously that players and coaches wore a constant frown. They would arrive at matches, striding from the team coach like mourners at a funeral. Major defeats would prompt lengthy, agonised meetings, sackcloth and ashes, front page apologies, 12 changes for the next match, public disgrace, 200 scrums, 500 press-ups, etc.

Make no mistake, we wanted to win as keenly and ferociously as anyone, stood back for nobody in the physical exchanges, got stuck in when required, but the game was always a game. If we happened to lose, we would be disappointed but never devastated; someone would laugh, and life would go on.

The contrast in attitude can perhaps best be illustrated by the manner in which we approached our Super 12 tours to Australia and New Zealand. Most of the South African provincial teams would be so obsessed by the challenge, they would train twice a day, and spend any remaining time at their hotel. When Natal visited Brisbane to play Queensland, for example, we would check in to a hotel on the Gold Coast and essentially have a couple of days' holiday.

Each to his own. That's fine, but, of all the South African teams, the Natal Sharks have compiled by far the most impressive Super 12 record in Australia and New Zealand, and we have never failed to enjoy the ride as well.

The central personality within Natal rugby's structure was Ian McIntosh, the team coach during the ice-breaking Currie Cup triumphs of 1990 and 1992, who left to guide the Springboks for two years before returning to King's Park and inspiring further Currie Cup glory in 1995 and 1996.

The province had won nothing in 100 years but then celebrated four Currie Cup titles in seven seasons. That simple statistic illustrates the sheer scale of the golden era, but the true soul of our success was personified by that loyal, emotional, clever, diligent man known to all as 'Mac'.

His private office lay behind a door off the broad players' tunnel at King's Park; there, surrounded by wall charts and instructional posters, he would sit and plot the next training session, the next game plan. As long as I have known him, Mac has been consumed by the challenge of rugby, fascinated by the options of the game, intrigued by the possibilities. He has always given the impression of pursuing a beloved pastime rather than working for a living.

The happy flow of silverware has now enshrined Mac in the annals of Natal rugby, but – to be rigorously honest – there have also been times when he suffered the slings and arrows known to prophets in their own time.

Andy Keast, a bright and enthusiastic coach from England, had arrived in Durban as Noel Olivier's assistant in 1994, and had remained in that position when Mac returned as coach in 1995. The contrast between Keast and Mac was sometimes unflattering to the veteran South African. Keast brought new ideas, Mac offered only old routines; Keast was fresh, Mac was familiar.

As the season wore on, people started to whisper that Keast should be given an opportunity to coach the side on his own. It was darkly rumoured that Mac's days were numbered and, at the time, to be quite candid, I started to accept the logic of what was being said. Maybe it was time for a change ...

Then we went out and won the Currie Cup again. McIntosh was triumphant once again, and all the treacherous talk of change disappeared under the celebrating fountain of champagne.

I feel guilty now for having even contemplated a future without Mac, but it is important to recognise he has not always been carried shoulder high by the people in and around Natal rugby, although that is what he deserved. At stages, he has felt intense pressure, fought his corner and survived.

The primary challenge of any coach who thrives for so long at the highest level of the game is constantly to reinvent himself in the minds of his players. I believe Mac was able to do this because he was humble enough to seek and to take on board the views of other people in the game. Not for one moment did he believe he knew everything. Every minute, he craved learning.

In the late 1980s, when South African rugby was still imprisoned by the international sporting boycott, and most South Africans arrogantly supposed the rest of the world could teach us nothing, Mac took the trouble to visit Australia, attend top coaching conferences and develop lasting friendships with thinkers on the game such as Rod McQueen, who would coach Queensland for many years, and become the World Cup winning Wallaby coach in 1999.

He would talk but, more importantly, he would listen and

the product of this rugby education was South Africa's Team of the Nineties. Mac was the first South African coach to recognise we did not have all the answers, and he reaped the benefits of his humility. For many years, his training methods and approach bore the distinctive hallmarks of Australia's leading sides.

I was privileged to be one of the players around whom Mac built his Natal side. If there were times when he relied on me (and I hope there were!), then the fact is I relied on him and my provincial team much more.

Time upon time, Natal rugby provided me with a warm and happy home away from the crisis and controversy of the Springbok team. In many ways the provincial squad, where I was accepted and appreciated, comfortable and able to express myself, proved my saviour during 1996 and 1997.

People have asked me how I managed to remain relatively calm during the series defeats against the All Blacks and Lions, and the Tri-Nations losses of those two seasons, and my reply has always been because I was always able to fall back on the security and success of the Natal team. No matter how wild the Springbok storm became, no matter how battered and bruised I may have been, there was always a hot meal and warm bed at King's Park.

And there was always Mac, steadfastly loyal to the players around whom he constructed the Team of the Nineties. He would see no wrong in those upon whom he relied.

On one occasion, Henry Honiball arrived for training at King's Park, scarcely able to walk. Our flyhalf lived near Bergville and, on that particular day, had taken part in a 30-kilometre walk for charity before climbing in his car and driving his regular two-hour trip to training in Durban.

'What on earth has he done?' asked Hugh Reece-Edwards, our assistant coach, standing beside Mac as Henry staggered out onto the training field.

'No,' replied Mac. 'He's fine, he always walks like that.'

Such was his unshakeable belief in his players and, year after year, match after match, they would perform for their Coach of the Nineties.

I vividly recall one particular training session soon after the 1995 Rugby World Cup. The players were ambling around King's Park, limbering up, while I had joined a group of forwards indulging in a goal-kicking competition. I looked up and saw Mac striding towards me from some 50 metres away.

He was staring at me, walking directly at me. I began to wonder what on earth he wanted, what he was going to say. In an instant, I concluded he was going to tell me I had been dropped. That was it! Mark Andrews had been moved to eighthman during the World Cup final and I became convinced that he would now play in that position, my position, for Natal.

Mac kept walking. I stopped kicking, braced for the bad news.

'Teich, can I have a word?'

It was OK. I could take it. We pulled away to one side. Mac looked me straight in the eye. I returned his gaze. I knew this would happen ...

'Teich, I want you to take over as captain. Can you handle that?'

'Er, yes, sure,' I stammered.

'Great,' he said, slapping me briefly on the shoulder.

That was that. Mark Andrews would remain in the second row, and I was installed as captain of South Africa's strongest provincial team. My heart was pounding when, moments afterwards, the coach announced his decision to the rest of the squad, but another great adventure had begun.

Nine weeks later, we were preparing for the 1995 Currie Cup final, to be played against Western Province at King's Park. Province's status as the clear favourites had been earned by a powerful pack of forwards constructed on the celebrated ability of their prop, Tommie Laubscher, a broad farmer from the West

TEAM OF THE NINETIES

Coast whose strength had assumed mythical proportions. We read newspaper stories of how his father was known as 'Groot Tommie', and his son was 'Klein Tommie', but he was called just Tommie. I don't know if this was true or not, and he was certainly an impressive player, but I recall someone in our side saying, thank goodness, we're playing only the middle Tommie.

Our challenge in 1995 included a French dimension. To their credit, the Natal Rugby Union had that year demonstrated their ambition by drawing two of France's most admired World Cup players to the Natal squad. Olivier Roumat, the former international captain and stylish lock forward, and Thierry Lacroix, a flyhalf of genuine quality, had performed consistently well all season; and, on a wet day in Durban, they again made outstanding contributions.

We had struggled to get them to train during the week before the final, because the French standard is to take things easy before a major match, but it was exhilarating for the rest of our squad to see how these two veterans, giants of world rugby, recognised wherever the game was played, were excited by the prospect of playing in a Currie Cup final at King's Park.

In driving rain, we maintained our game plan. Adrian Garvey and Robbie Kempson, our prop forwards, responded heroically to the challenge of standing firm in the scrums and, to a man, we held the famed Province pack in place and laid the foundation for a narrow but deserved victory.

I was thrilled to be raising the Currie Cup at the conclusion of my first year as captain, but my delight appeared insignificant alongside the sheer joy beamed across the faces of our two Frenchmen.

Arm in arm, tears of joy streaming down their faces, they saluted the crowd at the final whistle and later reflected on one of the great moments of their careers. Four months earlier, Roumat and Lacroix had stood similarly drenched at the same ground, narrowly defeated by the Springboks in the semi-final of the Rugby World Cup, weeping tears of disappointment. At least they had secured a small measure of compensation in the colours of Natal.

The 1996 season brought the launch of the Super 12 competition, the much hyped successor to the Super 10, bringing the leading provincial teams in the southern hemisphere together in three months of intense rugby. I relished the event, and enjoyed the physical scale of the challenge.

Mac had planned meticulously, and Natal started to produce a powerful challenge. We were winning our matches at home, playing particularly well in the match against Canterbury on the day when both John Allan and I celebrated our 100th appearance for the province, and we were undaunted playing away.

We powered through the group matches, secured a place in the last four and produced perhaps the outstanding performance of the competition to defeat Queensland in Brisbane and secure a place in the inaugural final, to be played a week later in New Zealand, against the mighty Auckland team.

Mac savoured the post-game celebrations in Brisbane as much as anyone. As the coach of Springbok touring squads, he had been unlucky to lose Test series against Australia in 1993 and New Zealand in 1994, and I was pleased that his success with Natal so emphatically restored his reputation.

Auckland proved too streetwise and powerful in the final, employing a series of tactics that could be described as consummately professional within the laws of the game. When Henry Honiball made a burst, the home defenders made their runs in such a way that our support players were cut off. There was nothing illegal in their tactics, but we appeared naïve in comparison.

Sean Fitzpatrick, the Auckland captain, raised the trophy, but we had been encouraged by our efforts in the inaugural Super 12 and carried our outstanding form into the Currie Cup competition. By October, we were reflecting on a fine season in which we had won no fewer than 23 of 29 matches.

And then there was only one game left – the 1996 Currie Cup final against Transvaal at Ellis Park. The match was played amid hysteria in Johannesburg, at the epicentre of the controversy surrounding André Markgraaff's decision to drop François Pienaar from the Springbok squad to tour Argentina, France and Wales at the end of the season. François was leading Transvaal, I was captaining Natal, and the stage was set for the most perfect drama.

On reflection, I can perfectly understand François' emotions on that sunny, warm day: he had been painfully dropped as Springbok captain and earned this opportunity to humiliate the architect of his downfall by leading his team to glory on the showpiece day of the South African season. The match would prove his last before leaving the country to pursue his career in Britain. Strangely, I would find myself in precisely the same position three years later.

In 1996, however, we spoiled François' occasion. The match crackled with tension for most of the first half, and Transvaal occasionally threatened to ride the wave of emotional support to our tryline, but we were focused and organised, bright and confident in our set moves and our strategy.

André Joubert scored two tries, both from moves rigorously rehearsed in training, and we emerged the stronger team – comfortable winners. We looked every inch a champion side, slick and efficient. We didn't give possession away cheaply, and we didn't concede unnecessary penalties; we performed the basic elements of the game with economy and honed skill, and we fielded players with natural flair to provide moments of genius and inspiration.

I was the lucky captain of this team, fortunate and proud to be raising the Currie Cup for the second time in only my second year as captain. By now named Springbok captain as well, I was still learning the ropes of leadership, growing in an ability to read the game, to refine elements of strategy during play and to get the most out of both the other 14 players in the team and myself.

In my view, the central challenge of captaincy is to stand apart from the side and its circumstances, and always keep sight of the larger picture. This was a difficult enough task when composing a last minute teamtalk as the team bus was making its way through milling crowds to the stadium, but it represented an immense trial when contemplating changes to the team strategy during the heat and bustle of the game. I had never sought the captaincy but, as time passed, I grew to enjoy the role and more gladly accept the responsibility.

The Natal team of the mid-1990s was, of course, easy to lead. I do not believe our achievements have been fully appreciated outside our own province. For example, how many rugby people in Cape Town, Pretoria or Johannesburg are aware that Natal won 27 successive Currie Cup matches from the middle of 1994 to early 1997, setting a new record for the competition?

At a time when Transvaal were powerful, when Northerns and Western Province expected to win every match at home and when a flood of money into the game had spread playing talent across 14 provinces, this was a remarkable record, the product of a settled team and a great coach.

Other teams in other eras established their own marks. Through the late 1970s, when provincial teams played no more than eight matches per season, Buurman van Zyl coached a Northern Transvaal side that lost only three matches in the space of three seasons. Those Blue Bulls have been rightly hailed as one of the great provincial teams. Our side stands comparison with them.

Everyone would expect me, as the eighthman, to maintain the core of this Natal team lay among the pack, so I won't disappoint anyone. I do not remember a single match through 1995 or 1996 when we were outplayed up front, and the primary factor in this consistency was a sympathetic training regime that owed nothing to prehistoric edicts of the past but everything to Ian McIntosh's ability to keep his team in pace with modern advances and research.

Nothing ever stands still, least of all a fast-evolving sport like rugby. It is almost possible to say that if a team is employing the same fitness and training drills as they did through the previous season, they are missing an opportunity. Yes, we must always learn from the past but in sport, I believe the challenge is to keep driving into the future, to keep pushing back the frontiers.

The scrum is 'the alpha and the omega of rugby', declared Buurman van Zyl, and Ian McIntosh proved as innovative in this area as any other, effectively using substitutes long before they were formally legalised and recognised by the International Rugby Board. Again, Mac blazed the trail.

We had three international prop forwards in our squad – Adrian Garvey, Robbie Kempson and Ollie le Roux, and our strategy was that one would leave the field with 'an injury' after around 60 minutes, enabling a third prop to bring fresh legs to our performance in the scrum and the loose. More often than not, Garvey and Kempson would start, with Le Roux to follow but the time and nature of the substitution depended on the match situation. Appropriately, Mac would convey his instructions to the field via the medical man.

The players did not particularly enjoy the 'injuries', and I am certain they would all have preferred to play the full 80 minutes every game. Anyone would. I understood the frustration of being rotated in and out of the side because that is precisely what happened to me and John Plumtree in the 1993 season, but, after some time, everyone could see the front row substitutions worked, and the three men involved settled down to perform their roles for the team.

Garvey had arrived from Zimbabwe, providing an amiable, light-hearted presence in the team. His mobility around the field offered a new dimension in a province that had grown accustomed to large prop forwards, although Garvs did make a manful attempt to fit in with the tradition.

Mac always weighed the forwards on a regular basis and, on the first occasion, Garvey was noted as 108 kg. Three weeks later, he was on the scales again, and the coach was thrilled to see him weigh in at 120 kg. It only emerged later that the prop had placed weights in his pockets.

Kempson reflected a surprisingly softer side through his skill in playing the piano, and the larger-than-life Le Roux would become one of the distinctive characters of his rugby generation.

Taking any two from three, they sandwiched John Allan, the combustible Scottish hooker, whose loyalty, courage and determination proved so crucial to our team for so long. Federico Mendez helped fill the gap at No. 2 when John retired, and performed so effectively that André Markgraaff, as Springbok coach, suggested the Argentinean should remain in the country for four years, qualify by residence and then claim a place in the South African side.

Unfortunately, the plan failed when Federico moved to England, because the lure of very many pounds sterling then proved substantially greater than the prospect of a possible Springbok cap in three years time.

The scrum was locked by Mark Andrews and Steve Atherton, two modern forwards who eagerly accepted their responsibilities extended far beyond taking their own ball in the lineout and adding their bulk to the scrum.

Mark was perhaps the complete footballer, bringing class and immense natural talent to the heart of our pack. Initially capped by South Africa as a loose forward, he became recognised through the mid-1990s as one of the outstanding locks in world rugby.

I had known Steve Atherton since we played together at Craven Week, and knew him to be an immense talent. As captain, I recognised him as one of those players who occasionally needed to be inspired. Steve was the type of player who would not respond if you brashly told him to do something. The way to get the most out of him was to let him know how much he was contributing to the side and how much the other players needed him to perform.

John Slade provided depth in the second row, an uncomplaining player who could come into the side and prompt not a moment's concern.

A variety of players accompanied me around the fringes of the scrum, in the rucks and mauls, but the latter part of the decade brought a consistent loose trio of Wayne Fyvie, Wickus van Heerden and Teichmann. I think we were strong and I believe we were mobile; we seemed to get the work done.

Like me, Wayne had emerged at Hilton College and worked through the age groups of Natal rugby, albeit at a somewhat faster pace. Naturally talented and absolutely honest, he advanced swiftly to the Springbok squad and seemed destined for an outstanding future in the game. In 1998, however, he suffered a serious knee injury and was ruled out of action for a year.

Many would not have recovered from such a setback, but Wayne refused to be beaten, recovered full fitness and has now resumed his career. I recall the time and place of his injury, during a Currie Cup match against Eastern Province, with particular pain because I believe I was partially to blame.

We had won a throw-in close to the EP line, and I selected a move where, following a short lineout, Kevin Putt, our scrumhalf, whipped the ball flat and hard to Wayne charging through at pace. My mistake was not to take into account that our proximity to the EP try line would mean the defenders were close at hand, and I can hear even now the sickening thud as bone crashed into bone. Wayne's studs snared in the turf, and his knee was wrenched asunder.

The third member of our loose trio claimed an entirely different pedigree, providing a bizarre link between our side and the Northern Transvaal team of the late 1970s. Wickus van

Heerden, younger brother of Moaner van Heerden, the Blue Bull legend, brought height and strength to our cause. He produced season after season of consistent rugby, but never claimed the headlines he deserved until the unfortunate and frankly unfair manner of his retirement.

During a Super 12 match against New South Wales, Wickus found himself being held around the neck by Phil Harry, an Australian prop. Desperate to break the grip, he bit the hand that was choking him and was eventually banned for the ridiculous period of two years by an Australian disciplinary committee. In the first place, there was scarcely a mark on Harry's hand; secondly, while Wickus should not have bitten, his opponent was effectively strangling him.

Wickus never returned to first class rugby, but his reputation as a talented and brave loose forward will certainly outlast the Harry incident.

If these were the forwards who won possession, then it was generally put to good use by a backline that worked hard to develop innovative moves, defended steadfastly and earned the pack's quiet respect.

The primary link between forwards and backs was a New Zealander who invariably managed to keep talking for most of the 80 minutes' play, occasionally too much to the referee, but never too much to team-mates grateful for the stream of instruction and encouragement. In every aspect of his game, Kevin Putt was an outstanding scrumhalf, but his communication was peerless. When he decides to retire, I have no doubt he will become an excellent coach.

He had played provincial rugby in New Zealand, representing Waikato and Otago, before deciding to travel the world. We were initially wary of him, wearied by a succession of itinerant New Zealanders who turned up in Durban, claimed to be All Black trialists but ultimately battled to make a club XV. Putt was different, a player of genuine class and a huge asset to the side.

His verbal jousting with the referees of South Africa prompted amusement in our dressing room, but these were never too serious. At the start of the 1990s, too many local referees failed to communicate decisions, behaving like a bunch of tinpot dictators unwilling and unable to justify themselves. However, standards have risen steadily through the decade to a point where I would now agree South African officials compare favourably with any in the world.

The finest referee in my experience, so far, has been a New Zealander, Paddy O'Brien, primarily because he always gave the impression of wanting the game to flow. Locally, a generation of players appreciated the knowledge and generous support of the late Ian Rogers. As a Natalian himself, he was unable to handle any of our provincial matches but he often attended our training sessions to convey recent law changes, and was highly respected.

Natal's No. 10 jersey became the personal property of Henry Honiball during the latter half of the 1990s, and this quiet, dedicated man delivered a consistency of performance, in attack and defence, that earned the absolute respect of all his teammates. Henry must rate among the very finest flyhalves I have seen: he may not be flashy, but his vision is superb, and his tackling so lethal that he is widely nicknamed 'Blade' (in Afrikaans, 'Lem').

I have rarely seen Henry lose his temper, although he did come close to a frown once when he was late-tackled in a Super 12 match. His calm demeanour is as unchanged in victory as in defeat. He gives the impression of giving everything for rugby during the 80 minutes on the field, but manages to keep sport firmly in its place within the broader scheme of things on this planet. Whisper it, but Henry seems to recognise rugby is not a matter of life and death.

There has only been one occasion when I have witnessed him show any extreme emotion at all, and it was far from the rugby field. The Natal squad was staying in Dunedin, New

Zealand, spending two days at leisure before returning home after a Super 12 tour, and we were all gathered in a restaurant.

The guys were playing a game in which each player puts between one and five matchsticks in his hand, everyone guesses the total number of matches held and the player who guesses right opts out. It was agreed that the forfeit for the player left at the end was to strip down to his underpants, run out of the restaurant, sprint across the main road and stand on a rubbish bin posing like a bodybuilder while the local traffic passed by.

Amid great excitement, player after player opted out until only Cabous van der Westhuizen and Henry remained. As they each placed matches in their hands, the one who guessed wrong would have to strip. This was a prospect that horrified, maybe even terrified, our decent and upstanding flyhalf.

Both players thrust their hands forward.

'Eight,' guessed Henry, all nerves.

Cabous opened his hand to reveal three matches.

Henry opened his hand to show five and, as he did so, he leaped a metre off the ground and started punching the air. Relief prompted ecstasy. Henry went berserk, whooping and hollering like a teenager at a boy band concert. Meanwhile Cabous accepted his penalty and started to strip. It soon became very clear that our flamboyant wing would enjoy every minute of his show.

Dick Muir was another key player in the team, the type of centre who gave direction and shape to the backline, who read the game, spotted the gaps and, in many cases, did the spadework to send the wings galloping clear. A great team man in every respect, Dick lived and breathed Natal rugby.

It was, therefore, Natal rugby's greatest blunder of the decade when, at the end of 1996, the union allowed Dick to leave for Cape Town where, instantly appointed as captain, he led Western Province to Currie Cup glory. Our success had almost completely stopped the traditional talent drain away from King's Park, and it was difficult to watch one of our own succeeding in a rival jersey.

The reasons behind Dick's departure were purely political and unrelated to rugby. Relations between players and the NRU had been sound through most of the decade, with the exception of a tiny spat in 1994 when the players refused to attend an official function because we wanted more respect.

In 1996, small differences began to fester, such as the quantity and quality of tickets made available to the players' friends and family for matches played at King's Park. We wanted more, were given less. The union did not appreciate our approach and, in the players' view, earmarked Dick and John Allan as the ringleaders of our resistance. The two stalwarts became disposable.

John eventually accepted an opportunity to play for London Scottish in England and, in the absence of a new contract being offered at the end of 1996, Dick accepted a move to Cape Town and seized his chance with Western Province. At a time when the NRU should, at the very least, have rewarded his efforts with a one-year contract, they dithered and prevaricated because of his age. As captain, I implored Ian McIntosh to intervene on Dick's behalf, but it was too late. The centre justifiably felt let down by a province to which he had committed his entire career; so he packed his bags and left. We missed him.

Dick Muir's most regular midfield partners both established themselves in the Natal team, left the province but eventually returned home. Jeremy Thomson spent some time with Transvaal, and Pieter Muller enjoyed a couple of seasons in Australia, but the black-and-white colours did not run.

Jeremy brought a touch of class to everything he did, whether it was drifting through a gap or delivering a perfectly timed pass. A typically happy and relaxed Natalian, he did everything with style, and a smile.

Pieter emerged from a different mould, becoming one of the

first so-called 'fast props' that began to proliferate in the midfield. Broad and strong, he took the responsibility of physically dominating the opposition, making the sort of big hits that seemed to rock the entire opposition back on their heels.

Either midfield combination proved successful in providing possession for our wingers, James Small, Cabous van der Westhuizen and, until his career was cut short by injury, Joos Joubert. Each player was a natural finisher who reliably and consistently delivered tries to the cause year after year.

James was a rare natural talent, competitive and brave in so many ways. The consensus holds that he proved difficult to handle throughout his career, but I never found this to be the case. He was no problem at all. On the contrary, his passion for the game proved infectious within the squad, and his knowledge was such that he often took a key role in developing tactics.

South African rugby has sometimes been too strait-laced and inflexible to make the most of its assets, and I believe this was occasionally the case with James Small. His different approach should have been celebrated and utilised to the benefit of the game, instead of sometimes souring into conflict.

Of course, there were times when his emotions ran away from him on the field. During one match against Otago, he dashed in from the wing and delivered such a volley of abuse at the forwards that an enraged John Allan threatened to exact grievous bodily harm on his team-mate. But, if these were crimes, then they were crimes of passion. James Small remained a huge asset.

Cabous was another player who broke the mould. His flamboyant locks of hair and surfer's appearance prompted unkind suggestions in conservative cities such as Pretoria that this beach boy did not belong on the rugby field, and it may have been true that Cabous did not enjoy the physical aspects of the game.

However, he laughed last, scoring try upon try upon try. Perhaps the most effective finisher of his generation, the sight of Cabous high-stepping over the try line became one of the enduring images of the decade. And he would smile, and the entire Natal team would smile with him. Central to team spirit, central to our scoring strategy, Cabous was an essential element in our mix.

With the impeccable and peerless André Joubert anchoring the team at fullback through most of the 1990s, Natal was able to field a team that included between eight and 12 Springboks at any one time.

There were other people, who worked far from the public gaze, but even so contributed importantly to our efforts, most notably Kevin Stephenson, our fitness expert. Arriving from a soccer background, he succeeded in making the task of maintaining peak physical condition seem fun. Whether we were running through the waves on Durban's North Beach or sweating through sit-ups, he took trouble to study other codes and introduce new drills, new options.

Kevin was also clever enough to confine his contributions to the area of physical fitness. South African rugby has developed an unfortunate tradition of enthusiastic fitness experts who foolishly become involved in the rugby and start instructing players how to pass and execute moves. Players become irritated, the fitness adviser allows himself to be drawn into some physical exchanges and, by the end, it is much more than a lycra ego that is bruised.

Following on the successive Currie Cup triumphs of 1995 and 1996, Natal continued to emerge as South Africa's strongest representatives in the Super 12 and to be a dominant force in the Currie Cup, but we also developed a profoundly frustrating tendency of losing major semi-finals.

In 1997, another strong Super 12 campaign ended in a semi-final defeat against Auckland, the eventual champions, at Eden Park. Five months later, we fell in the last four of the Currie

Cup, losing a frantic semi-final at King's Park to Free State. We had been close, but smoked no cigar.

To our intense frustration, we suffered the same fate in 1998. Competing in the Super 12 as the Coastal Sharks, a new brand based on a Natal core but drawing new depth from the Eastern Province and Border squads, we reached the semi-final for the third successive year and, also for the third time, were only knocked out of the competition by the eventual winners: in this case, it was the free-running Canterbury Crusaders who doused our hopes.

Again we powered through the Currie Cup schedule, playing a semi-final against a resurgent Northern Transvaal team at Loftus Versfeld. Determined to reach another final, we raced to a 17-3 lead but, to my horror, wilted in the face of a dramatic Blue Bull fightback. Joost van der Westhuizen and Franco Smith led a remarkable surge, and we lost yet another semi-final.

Two seasons of outstanding but trophy-less rugby provoked disappointed outbursts in Natal that the South African season had become lop-sided, starting with 12 weeks of intense, physical, demanding Super 12 rugby, moving through the Tri-Nations series and ending with a diluted Currie Cup system in which the 14 provinces were divided into two groups of seven and the top four teams in each section advanced to the quarter-finals of a knock-out phase.

I did not accept these criticisms.

To my mind, the Super 12 is an outstanding competition, where the level of play is so high that, if you're not on top of your game, any team could beat you by 40 or 50 points. The standard of play is equivalent to that of international rugby, with the difference that longer lead-in times tend to mean Test matches are played under greater pressure and scrutiny.

No South African needs reminding that the Super 12 title has remained in New Zealand ever since its inception in 1996, although I think the disappointing results of the Western

TEAM OF THE NINETIES

Stormers, Golden Cats, Coastal Sharks and Northern Bulls can be largely explained by an inability to win away.

It is an unavoidable fact of the competition that South African teams must tour for a month in Australia and New Zealand, while teams from those countries travel in the opposite direction for only a fortnight, but the apparent mental block that affects South Africans on the road needs to be addressed.

Do our players sincerely believe they can win regularly in places such as Sydney, Auckland, Wellington, Brisbane and the rest? Until they do, our teams will not realise their potential and claim the title. The Super 12, nonetheless, is growing from strength to strength. Many northern hemisphere players have told me of their burning ambition simply to take part in the event.

It is popularly agreed that the rise of the Super 12 has contributed to a parallel fall in status of the Currie Cup competition. Many people favour a return to a strength-versus-strength format in which the top provinces play in a round-robin league with the top two contesting a final. They say the expanded format, embracing 14 provinces, has lowered standards.

A compromise solution might be to introduce a two-tier system where all 14 provincial teams start in one league but with the top six sides then advancing to an intensive, strength-versus-strength format in the second half of the year. It should be possible to develop a structure that provides both a broad base for the game and the highest possible playing standards.

And no-one should underestimate the enduring appeal of the Currie Cup among South Africa's leading players. The tradition and status still carry weight in the professional era; and, given the choice between winning the Super 12 and the Currie Cup, I believe most would choose the Currie Cup. I would, because Currie Cup glory sustains a team though November,

FOR THE RECORD

December and into the New Year while a Super 12 triumph is submerged in mid-season.

As the Team of the Nineties will confirm after four sips at the Golden Cup in the space of seven seasons, the Currie Cup still stands apart.

10

Nick Mallett's Captain

By August 1997, everyone agreed Springbok rugby needed to break free from the rollercoaster of crisis and controversy; we needed a strong man to take hold of the entire structure, shake it down, shake it up, put it right.

Cometh the hour, cometh the man. Nick Mallett, the outspoken Boland coach, considered by the South African Rugby Football Union as being 'too hot to handle' just six months earlier, was invited to interview at the SARFU offices. By all accounts, Nick ended up interviewing the SARFU panel.

He set out his basic requirements, and, finding themselves with no other serious candidate for the position, the union was forced to appoint Mallett on his own terms. He had had to wait for the opportunity to coach the national side, but the delay ensured he took the job from a position of strength.

I was pleased. Nick was the obvious candidate and I had appreciated his coaching as an assistant to André Markgraaff during the 1996 tour to Argentina, France and Wales. He was blunt and frank, appearing every ruddy inch the ideal antidote to snide, sly rugby politics, even if he was widely reputed to be a rough hothead who flew off the handle whenever his team lost.

Free State players told me how he arrived in their dressing room after they had defeated his Boland team in the 1997

Currie Cup quarter-final, congratulated them on the win and then made new enemies by telling them they had no chance of beating Natal in the semi-final (unfortunately, they did!).

I had heard other tales of his competitive spirit on the cricket and rugby fields, of swearing at his players, of his overwhelming desire to win every match he played. None of this troubled me at all. This was what we required, someone who would march in, sweep clean and get the Boks winning again. If he did ruffle a few feathers along the way, I thought, so much the better.

He called me soon after his appointment and assured me of his intention that I should remain as captain of the team. I was obviously pleased, and a little relieved, although my general form during 1997 had been sound. This was the third successive Springbok coach asking me to be his captain. It did not occur to me at the time, but this was an exceptional honour. Three separate men had arrived in the hot seat and they had all turned to me as their captain.

Nick continued the conversation, outlining the management team he had handpicked to put things right within the Springbok squad.

'And I have been asked to include one Coloured coach in the set-up, to give opportunities as part of development,' he told me on the 'phone, 'so I have chosen two assistant coaches, Alan Solomons and Peter de Villiers.'

I had never met either man before and, from his phrasing, assumed Alan Solomons was the Coloured coach. The surname was common among the Cape Coloured community and it was only a day or two after the squad had gathered ahead of the tour to Europe that I realised my mistake. Alan had been coaching the University of Cape Town side, but I didn't know him at all.

In fact, as the Springbok squad to tour Italy, France, England and Scotland assembled under the new regime, and we were all introduced to a new structure and a new code of conduct, it was Alan Solomons who first seemed to notice my depression. I was not myself, was struggling to motivate myself for the tour. This was strange for me. I had never felt this way before. Everything seemed such a trial, everything seemed such an effort. I hardly spoke to anyone, hardly showed any enthusiasm for anything. I was drifting downstream.

Soon after we arrived in Bologna ahead of the Test against Italy, Nick called me to one side and asked what was wrong. His tone was sympathetic, not in the least aggressive; he was understanding, not brash.

'I don't know,' I said. 'I think it's just that I'm tired of having to adapt to a new coach, I'm tired of starting all over again. It's nothing personal but you are the third Springbok coach most of us have had in three years. We just want to settle down and play decent rugby, but, instead, we are always being asked to change the way we play. It's depressing and draining.'

It cannot have been easy for a new coach, pumped full of enthusiasm, to hear his captain talking in such terms. On reflection, I am surprised he didn't tell me to stop moaning or go home, but he was extremely sympathetic, and said he understood how I felt but that he wanted to get things right.

He recognised management and administration functions had not been properly fulfilled, and said he had appointed Rob van der Valk, a highly effective Cape Town businessman, to resolve all these issues. They would no longer be our concern. We would be consulted regularly, but we would no longer have to worry about anything other than playing the game. He said he knew what had happened within the squad before and said, under the same circumstances, he could imagine himself feeling exactly the way I was feeling.

I was not simply pleased to hear him speak like this; I was at once thrilled and immediately inspired. Here was a straight-talking, sincere man who not only understood the problems faced by players, but had also paid his coaching dues in France, at the False Bay club and latterly with Boland.

My mood improved dramatically. I felt confident in Nick Mallett's capacity to create the right environment for us to realise our potential. Most of the players were similarly impressed. In a matter of two weeks, the new coach had made a great start. Positive vibes immersed us all.

The coach was not all cheese and kisses. If he did not like something, he said so. If he wanted a prop to make ten tackles in a match, he said so, and he would climb all over him if he fell short. In my experience, such crystal clear discipline works well with rugby players. Everyone knows where they stand, and everyone knows what is expected of them. Nobody whispers, nobody mutters.

Some of the Afrikaans-speaking players were initially uncertain of Nick's forthright manner. Accustomed to a more regimented, austere style of coach in centres like Pretoria and Bloemfontein, they would wince at his blunt manner, at the way he spoke to players, alternately matey and robust. Within a few weeks, however, this infectiously eager man had won them over as well.

There were other rough edges to wear down. The players had not taken long to recognise most of the coaching staff came from Cape Town, and I sensed hackles being raised when we were asked to learn training drills that 'had worked really well for Western Province this season'. Temperatures rose further when a Province player would be asked to demonstrate the drill.

Province had not won the Currie Cup for 9 seasons. How could they be held up as an example to players from successful provincial teams? I am certain Nick intended no offence, and he was probably not overly concerned that offence was taken, but sporadic mumbling against a Province bias would remain audible within his Springbok squad throughout the next three years.

Relaxed and beautiful Italy was an ideal location for the first period of the tour and the general mood was so laid-back that, during a squad visit to the Ferrari factory, I felt sufficiently assured to peer inside one of the gleaming red machines and remark, 'these are only for World Cup players'. Such a comment may have provoked outrage in 1996 but, two years on and within sight of the expiry date of those contracts, people laughed. There was still no security available to the other players in the squad, but, at least, we were moving on.

Italy were comfortably defeated in Bologna, but this was more significant than just another international win against inferior opposition. Nick had clearly set out the way he wanted us to play, and we had immediately understood what he required. In essence, he wanted us to score try upon try.

'You must score four tries to win a Test match,' he said, 'and, on the basis that we will convert half our chances, then our goal must be to create at least eight scoring opportunities per match.

'If we get a penalty kick in their half and we are absolutely certain of being able to kick the penalty, then we'll take the three points. But, if there is any doubt at all, then we should kick for touch, preferably close to the corner flag and aim to drive through from the lineout and get over for the try.'

Go for the try: this became Mallett's mantra. Kick down the touchline, win the lineout and crash over. Seven points is better than three.

If his strategy was crystal clear, then the coach's selection policy also bore the hallmark of common sense. Percy Montgomery had endured a testing year, appearing occasionally brilliant, then error prone. He was smartly returned to his preferred position at fullback, and told to enjoy himself. André Snyman had been playing on the wing, now he was returned to the midfield. Players would not be selected out of position, Mallett proclaimed emphatically.

Out of Italy, we embarked on a second tour of France in two years. Nick had previously coached two French club sides, and his knowledge both of local conditions and the language successfully eliminated the uncertainty and brooding suspicion that affects English-speaking tour squads in France.

It is hard to exaggerate the sense of general relief and excitement that, by now, was developing among the Springbok players. Where before we had been concerned and uncertain, now we accepted this constant flow of positive energy from a coach who always seemed to be bounding into breakfast with a plan, who would listen to anyone with a problem but who would not hesitate to tell you if he thought you were wrong, who evidently believed in his team.

We were contemplating a tough tour of Europe at the end of yet another exceptionally arduous year of professional rugby, but the squad was starting to play excellent rugby and we were winning. I do believe there is such a concept as too much rugby, but in my experience, winning teams rarely complain about feeling tired, physically or mentally, at the end of the year.

Krynauw Otto, the talented lock forward from Pretoria, was a classic example of how a coach's attitude can transform a player. For the past three seasons, Krynauw had been hovering around the Springbok squad but always seemed to be standing in for someone. Nick sat him down and told him in no uncertain terms that he was the first choice lock forward. The result was a new player, charged with positive emotions, playing great rugby.

The coach had not said: 'Go out and prove yourself – this is your chance to secure a place.' That would have loaded pressure on the player. He had told him simply: 'You are my first choice – go out there and play.'

Mallett again demonstrated his pragmatism by naming Dick Muir, at the age of 32, in the team for the first Test against France in Lyon. Some coaches would have baulked at selecting such an experienced player, but Nick was only concerned with winning the match. One year after the Natal Rugby Union had not even been prepared to offer Dick a contract, Mallett turned him into a Bok; and the decision worked, bringing the Muir order and direction to our midfield.

Still buoyed by the memory of our series victory in 1996, we set about the French with an amazing appetite in Lyon. The forwards combined a raw physical presence with outstanding discipline, and the backs rasped out moves that tore the defence to shreds. France were not playing badly, but we were on top of our game and had established a 20-point lead by half-time.

Into the second half, the home side raised their performance, pushing us deeper and deeper into our own half; and, as penalty upon penalty chipped away at our lead, French supporters began to sense a dramatic comeback. With the wind in their sails, the home side began to attack at will.

'Just concentrate,' I told our players. 'Make the tackles!'

This was our task: to block out the cacophony of noise in the stadium, to cut ourselves off from the seething atmosphere, to focus on our basic task, to get our positioning right, to make our tackles, to give nothing away. The procession of the first half had become a desperate tussle in the second.

With order and discipline, we withstood the French charge and trooped off the field, relieved to have clung to a 36-32 victory. It had been a titanic game of rugby. We had been tested, and we had prevailed. It was, in many senses, a triumph of our new-found spirit and direction. We had needed to be strong, and much of that strength originated in the personality of our coach.

There was sadness among the celebrations. Joost van der Westhuizen, our scrumhalf, had suffered a serious injury and would spend the night in a Lyon hospital before returning home to South Africa. He had become an important part of the side, but his misfortune created an opportunity for Werner Swanepoel, the young Free Stater. Every negative had to become a positive.

Waves of emotion appeared to be rolling over French rugby as the second Test approached. The match would be the last rugby international played at the old Parc des Princes, the neat 45 000-capacity national stadium straddled over the circular motorway that encircles the city of Paris.

The magnificent new venue for international rugby and soccer, the Stade de France, was nearing completion to the north in Saint-Denis, but the sense of a grand era drawing to a close arose not only from the stadium, but also the team. Heroes like Laurent Cabannes, Thierry Lacroix, Phillippe Saint-André seemed to be nearing the finale of their distinguished careers … and, like gallant old soldiers, they donned their suits of armour one last time to defend French honour against the raiding visitors in the last match at their old home.

There are occasions in sport when even the most hardened competitor is sensitive to the mood of opponents and, as we lined up for the two national anthems in Paris, this was such a moment for me. Defeated in the first Test, it was possible to feel the French resolve to square the series. The honour of the Parc des Princes, the great matches and players, of all the memories of sizzling backline moves on sunny afternoons, required one last win. It was impossible not to be moved by the crowd's singing of 'La Marseillaise'.

We set to work, producing probably the finest 80 minutes of rugby I have ever seen played by the Springboks. Every move was impeccably executed and every pass went to hand. We moved around the field with the swagger of a calm and controlled executioner, lethal in every aspect of the game.

One early try set France back on their heels, and others followed. Rassie Erasmus enjoyed a magnificent afternoon, voracious in the loose, and it was he who provided the image that endures in my mind: intercepting deep in our half and gloriously outpacing the home defenders, passing to Pieter Rossouw, who stretched his legs and dashed through to score an exhilarating try.

Montgomery at the back, Small and Rossouw on the wings, Snyman and Muir in the midfield, Honiball and Swanepoel at half back; Du Randt, Dalton and Garvey in the front row, Otto and Andrews at lock, Erasmus, Venter and myself the loose forwards. This was a powerful combination and, remarkably, no more than two and a half years on, the side included only three members of the Springbok side that won the Rugby World Cup in 1995.

Watching this team play with such passion and power, I found it almost impossible to understand how essentially the same group of players had seemed so abject and abysmal in losing to the Lions earlier in the year. We had effected a truly remarkable transformation and, on this memorable afternoon in Paris, we began to express ourselves, enjoy ourselves, run rampant.

And as the score mounted, the partisan French crowd progressed from a predictable phase of whistling their own players to an entirely unpredicted period when they actually applauded us. At one point, I looked around the stadium, and wondered whether I was hallucinating. Was this possible?

Swanepoel passed to Honiball … 'Ole!' the crowd roared.

Honiball to Muir … 'Ole!'

Muir to Snyman … 'Ole!'

Every time a pass was held, the crowd cheered; every time the ball was recycled from a ruck, the crowd cheered. It is a great feeling to be supported by your own fans, but to arrive in Paris in the full expectation of a hostile reception and to be hailed as heroes was a bizarre, incredible experience.

Returning to the changing room after our staggering 52-10 victory, I told the guys no Springbok captain could ever ask for more than they had given. Nick was as breathless and wide-eyed as the rest of us. Had this really happened? Had we put 50 on the French and been cheered in Paris?

'Guys, whatever happens with this team, whatever we may or may not go on to achieve, I can tell you that we will always look back on this day with special affection,' the coach told the arm-linked circle of smiling Springboks. 'If any two of us happen to run into each other in 20 or 25 years' time, no matter where we will be or what we are doing then, we will be able to look back on this match and, suddenly, there will be a very powerful bond between us. We have shared something very important today. You must all enjoy it.'

It was a wonderful sentiment. I suppose we must wait for 20 or 25 years to find out whether it proves accurate or not. I hope it does.

While the Test team was relishing its Saturdays, the midweek team was enduring a punishing schedule of matches against powerful French teams, and a couple of matches were lost. To his credit, the coach did not cut himself off with the Test team and turn his back on the dirt-trackers. He coached them, shared in their complaints about the referee and empathised with them. He also turned on them if he sensed their conduct or performance was not proper.

After one defeat, Nick climbed aboard the team bus, looked up and saw one of the players laughing and joking with the guys. It happened that this player had performed particularly badly during the match, and it appeared incongruous that he should be enjoying himself under such circumstances.

'Heh!' the coach snapped.

The player looked up.

'I don't know what you have to be smiling about.'

Silence.

Such abrupt interventions were absolutely correct. This was Nick Mallett at his best, whipping a player back into line in such a way that the entire squad was able to hear and receive the message: losing is not a laughing matter. If anyone had doubted the coach's resolve, they doubted no longer. He was determined his players would learn to loathe losing every bit as much as he did.

At the end of a long evening, many coaches may have let the incident go, preferring a less confrontational end to the day. Not this coach. He had set out to build a great Springbok team, and he would not rest in that challenge. Ever alert and aware, he would make his point whenever, wherever necessary.

The coach instructed us to score tries, and the team had touched down no fewer than 21 times in the first three Tests under his charge, building confidence ahead of our arrival in London for the third leg of the tour. The opportunity to beat England at Twickenham proved especially exciting to every player. There seems to be something about the white kit, and the talk of HQ, and the patrician style of management that particularly motivates visiting players.

Throughout the week, the British media had portrayed the match as a kind of revenge fixture following the series against the Lions, and the sheer number of Lions in the England team had not escaped my attention. Nothing could change what had happened in June, but at least we would feel better.

England started well, and scored a soft try, and we even trailed at half-time, but the match was moving in our direction and I was not concerned. We were stronger in the pack, and more direct among the backs.

One of our tactics, specific to this match, was to get our backs running at their forwards and, midway through the second half, André Snyman was able to set off at pace from 30 metres out, tie Jason Leonard, the England prop, in knots and touch down a truly magnificent try beneath the posts.

Twickenham was quiet; and the chariot stopped swinging as we ran out winners by 29-11. The great and the good of English rugby were left to ponder another defeat, and the travelling Bok fans celebrated a sixth win in a row.

Just as the 1996 tour management had promised the last week of the tour in Wales would be gentle if we defeated France, so the 1997 management pledged a quiet final week in Scotland if we beat France and England. We duly earned the prize and, settled in Edinburgh, we headed for St Andrews, in search of some golf, only to find the Old Course closed for the day.

The coach and I spent a considerable amount of time together during that concluding week of a tremendously successful tour, working out where we had made progress and where we needed to concentrate our efforts. We appeared to be getting along extremely well, understanding each other.

Nick would generally run selection issues past me before reaching a final decision, although there were relatively few points of contention when the team was playing so well and winning. Our meetings were not forced and formal, but casual though sincere: Henry Honiball and I might meet Nick and Alan Solomons in the foyer, and we would wander off for a quiet beer in the bar.

I believed I could raise any matter with Nick, and speak with total openness, free from affectation or concern, and it was this open nature of our relationship that was so important to me. I assumed the sentiment was mutual.

Our prime challenge against Scotland at Murrayfield was, regardless of the strength of the opposition, to maintain the same standards of discipline and skill that we had set at the Parc des Princes and Twickenham. We wanted to be a consistently powerful international team, rigorous and ruthless as we set about our business, getting the basics right ... and being able to produce performance peaks when confronted by the All Blacks or Wallabies.

The result of our cold efficiency was a one-sided match in which the Scots collapsed after half-time, enabling us to win 68-10 and once again demonstrate the growing gulf between the northern and southern hemispheres.

The gap would gradually close but, in 1997, we believed that, so long as we picked a decent side and kept reasonably well organised, there was no way we would ever be defeated by opponents from the north. This knowledge made our series defeat against the Lions all the harder to accept.

Within the context of our overwhelming victory, there were moments when the developing morale within the squad shone through. Percy Montgomery, now emerging as a fullback of exceptional vision and quality, was running clear to the Scottish line when he became aware of James Small on his inside. The veteran wing was within one try of establishing a new Springbok try-scoring record and, on the spur of the moment, Percy passed the ball inside and gift-wrapped the try for James. Such incidents spread morale through the squad.

We received a heroes' welcome upon our return to South Africa, although it is hard not to yield to cynicism on such occasions. The people slapping you on the back when you win are usually the same people who were stabbing the same back six months before when you were losing. But it would be ungracious to make that point amid the enthusiasm and celebrations, so you just smile and thank the people and move on homewards as quickly as possible.

Fame and fortune are such fickle friends to professional sports people that it is not long before you reach the stage where the only people whose views you respect in any way at all are those of your coach and team-mates, your family and friends. The rest are a blur, mere background for the passing show.

On this occasion, however, we were invited to join President Mandela for lunch at the Presidential Guest House near the Union Buildings in Pretoria. I had never met the greatest living South African before and was impressed not only by his presence, but also by the way in which he took control of proceedings. Even Nick was briefly reduced to just another face in the crowd.

Watching Nelson Mandela at close quarters prompted me to wonder about the essence of authority. He seems to command that quality so naturally, without raising his voice, even without raising an eyebrow. Real authority appears to be less about the power to scream and shout at subordinates than the product of a manner and level of conduct that brings people into line.

The Springbok squad effectively disbanded for six months from the middle of December 1997, but Nick Mallett appeared to take a more active interest in the Super 12 than his predecessors. His main concern was that the top players in the country should all be competing at the highest level and, in this respect, he was looking for a degree of co-operation from the Super 12 coaches. For example, if there were three potential Springbok wings in one Super 12 team, he would have liked to move one of them to a side with no top wings.

It is a measure of the continuing, historic and maybe even genetic disunity within South African rugby that this co-operation was not always forthcoming. In New Zealand, by contrast, every individual or provincial need is considered totally insignificant when set alongside the interests and demands of the All Blacks. There is a unity of purpose in establishing the national side that is enviable.

Nonetheless, making the best of the situation, the Springbok coach took the trouble to watch Super 12 matches in Australia and New Zealand, as he put together his squad for 1998 and chose his strategy to mount a serious challenge in the Tri-Nations series. Through these weeks, Nick and I met a couple of times and spoke on the telephone every other week, comparing notes, keeping in touch. The captain-coach association was warm and constructive.

Our preparation for the Tri-Nations series in 1998 was ideal: four home Test matches against northern hemisphere opponents represented the perfect opportunity to regain the winning momentum last seen at Murrayfield.

Ireland were the first in line, scheduled to play two Tests, in Bloemfontein and then in Pretoria a week later. These gave us the rare opportunity to wear the elegant white Springbok jerseys. That, however, was where the fun stopped.

The Irish approached the matches with the plain aim of playing overtly physical, spoiling rugby, of simply keeping the score down. I have no doubt they enjoyed themselves hugely off the field, but their strategy on it did little for the profile of rugby, either among the mediocre crowds inside the stadiums or in the minds of the millions watching at home, on television.

Keith Wood and Paddy John were never far from the heat of the action, and I have always respected them as fair, hard players, but the barrage of stiff-arm tackles and flying fists was difficult to accept. In the end, our challenge was to maintain our discipline, and put points on the board.

In Bloemfontein, we probably failed in this respect, and it was only the fine try-scoring ability of Stefan Terblanche that enabled us to secure a 37-13 victory, but we performed more efficiently at Loftus Versfeld a week later, scoring 33 points without reply, and emerged from the two-match series with the sense that something constructive had been achieved. We had regrouped as a squad, and were working out the rust.

An under-strength England team, fresh from a 90-point thrashing by the Wallabies, had flown halfway across the world to be our next opponents, although they hardly seemed excited by the challenge and spent much of the week before the Test moving from one hotel to another in Cape Town.

It seemed as if several leading England players had taken one look at the scheduled end-of-season tour to the southern hemisphere, and quickly decided they would rather be lying on a Spanish beach. Again, the entire exercise was a poor reflection on the ways and means of professional rugby.

Whoever controls the Cape Town weather was also un-impressed, and a dour Test match was played in appalling conditions. The driving rain and sodden mud compelled us to kick more than we would have liked, but we maintained our discipline and emerged, dirty, with a solid 18-0 victory.

Our final opponents in this preparation were a Wales touring squad missing even more regular players than the England party. At full strength, they would have battled to withstand the Springbok side and the act of turning up in Pretoria with what amounted to a 'B' side was an insult to the proud heritage of Welsh rugby, to the game and, frankly, to South Africa.

Once again, Nick implored the players to forget about the opposition and to concentrate on ruthlessly maintaining our own standards. After 80 minutes, we had scored 15 tries, conceded just three points and finished only four points short of the century against a 'major' rugby nation. I remember feeling quite irritated as we left the field at Loftus because I had desperately wanted to put 100 points on the board. In truth, the Welsh Rugby Union deserved nothing less.

The South African media were generally dismissive of our four victories, but we knew they had left us in a better position to challenge for the Tri-Nations title than was the case in either 1996 or 1997. At last, after two years of messing around, I felt we were in a position to realise our potential.

At the end of June, we were packing for Perth. Our opening match of the series would be played against the Wallabies at the Subiaco Oval, another stage in the Australian Rugby Union's campaign to encourage public support for rugby union in all parts of the country, even in Western Australia.

We didn't mind where the match was played. Aware that we had not won an away match in either of the first two Tri-Nations series, we braced ourselves for an almighty challenge. It was all very well winning our way through Europe, and demolishing northern hemisphere teams at home, but this was the ultimate Test. We were worth nothing until we had won in Australia and New Zealand. We knew that, accepted it and looked forward to the challenge.

And, it's worth restating, our minds were focused solely on the rugby. All the management functions were being carried out with such calm efficiency that we hardly noticed they were being done. Rob van der Valk was applying his mind to the issue of contracts and payments, and the players were happy.

We trained all week in warm Perth sunshine, and were surprised to find match day dawn grey and wet. The experience of playing England in the Cape Town rain proved useful and we adapted our strategy accordingly, but the fuss and bluster may have set us slightly out of our stride.

Whatever the reason, we showed the Wallabies far too much respect on this occasion. We had played so often against weaker teams, and we were so determined to prove ourselves against the best opposition, that we hesitated in the face of the challenge, almost waiting for them to take the initiative. Perhaps it was the case that real confidence could only be reaped from defeating Australia and New Zealand ... and we still lacked that confidence.

At any rate, the match was tight and only decided by a moment of gutsy inspiration from Joost van der Westhuizen. We won a penalty close to their try line and, not waiting for my call, the scrumhalf instinctively tapped and wriggled his way over the line under challenge from John Eales.

We held on to win 13-12, and again had cause to be grateful for the game-breaking qualities of our world-class scrumhalf from Pretoria.

His greatest quality is his appetite for the game. Irrespective of the game, of the opposition, of how many people are in the stands, of how much he is being paid, Joost wants to score tries and desperately wants to win. Added to his physical strength and natural talent, this has made him a player who, in any given moment, can completely change the course of a game.

Playing for Natal against Northerns, my strategy would always be to give Wayne Fyvie the task of policing Joost. Wayne was clever enough to know that, as a flanker, you could not afford to take an extra yard and put pressure on the flyhalf because Joost would spot the gap and be gone, exploding out of the blocks, sprinting clear and dotting down beneath the posts.

Certain players constantly cause concern and occupy the opposition's thoughts. As one of them, Joost was a huge asset to the Springbok cause, and it was his opportunism that enabled us to smile in Perth, 1998.

Nick Mallett, however, was not smiling. There was absolutely no euphoria in our changing room after the game at the Subiaco Oval because he knew we had performed poorly, and that we might easily have lost the game if Matt Burke's goal-kicking had been less indifferent.

The following Monday night, the coach left us in no doubt of where we had under-performed during a rigorous and meticulously researched video session. It had become standard practice after every match for each player to be handed a typed report indicating what they had done right and done wrong. Such blunt and clear communication was much appreciated by the squad.

At the end of the session, having chastened most of us, Nick placed his notes on the table and, a broad smile creasing his face, said: 'And, by the way, you have just become the first Springbok squad to win an away match in the Tri-Nations series. Congratulations.'

We headed for Wellington, and the ultimate rugby challenge. The victory in Perth was equivalent to winning the first Test of a series in so far as it relieved the pressure on the squad. We would start favourites in our two home matches, all of which made the away match against New Zealand feel like something of a bonus. Our psychological status could not have been better.

Throughout the past 10 months, Nick had stressed the need to develop consistency of performance, to eliminate errors and execute moves regardless of the strength or form of our opponents. This approach had worked at Murrayfield, and now it would be implemented at Athletic Park in Wellington.

There was no master plan to defeat the All Blacks. As always, we would seek the ball, retain the ball and translate possession into points ... and, on this day above all, we would defend with every sinew and muscle.

I sensed urgency, and perhaps even a lack of control, in the contorted All Black faces as they performed the *haka*. For some

NICK MALLETT'S CAPTAIN

years, Springbok teams have simply lined up opposite while the men in black indulged their custom. Most of us were not fazed by the show, staring blankly into the middle distance; a few of the guys stared back, a couple of them shouted something back.

All Black *hakas* used to be moments of great significance for Springbok teams, but that was in an age when the teams played Test series against each other perhaps once every three or four seasons. We were playing them at least twice every season and the dramatic impact was wearing thin.

The match unfolded as precisely the bruising, intensely physical contest that both sides had come to expect. Margins of victory are almost always small and, in my view, are determined not so much by luck as by which team gets the mental preparation right on the day. In Wellington, that was us.

New Zealand attacked with the anticipated power and fluency, but our defence was remarkable, and was perhaps best epitomised by Pieter Muller in the midfield. The powerhouse centre executed no fewer than 22 tackles during the match, more than one every four minutes. As the All Blacks huffed and puffed, we held firm and started to exert a measure of control.

There were, of course, occasional shocks to our system, sharp reminders that we should take nothing for granted. At the start of the second half, I asked Henry Honiball to kick off long and deep. The ball was collected by Jonah Lomu, and the giant All Black icon gleefully charged upfield, picking up pace with every stride. I confronted him, but was reduced to the level of a speed bump as Lomu ran over my challenge. Mercifully, he did not score.

The minutes ticked by. The score was 8-3 in our favour with ten minutes to play. There was still only one converted try between the teams. I told the guys we needed to keep the ball in the All Black half, to make no errors, to concede no more penalties. There was no panic at all in my voice. All afternoon, we had played tough, disciplined rugby. We were in control.

We were calm, focused, concentrating for dear life.

Then we won the ball outside the New Zealand 22-metre line, to the left of the posts. It was clean ball, whipped wide from Joost to Henry. The flyhalf shaped to feed the ball on, but brilliantly switched inside and popped the ball up for our left wing, Pieter Rossouw, bursting on the loop at full pace.

He was through!

Clear!

The defence hardly laid a finger on him!

I have rarely felt such delight on a rugby field. Pieter scored beneath the posts and, in an instant, I recognised that, after all the defeats and pain we had suffered against the All Blacks, we were beating them. I threw my arms around Pieter and glanced towards the New Zealanders as they gathered in a huddle behind their own line, awaiting the conversion.

And they were arguing! These giants of the game, for so long apparently unbeatable on their own grounds, were debating who had been to blame for the missed tackle, for letting Pieter breach their defence. I felt justified in enjoying the moment because I had been behind that line so often myself.

The 13-3 victory was followed by euphoria in our dressing room. Bottles of champagne appeared by magic (as they do on such occasions), and 31 thrilled South Africans sat back, resolved to share the moment. The changing rooms at Athletic Park are in need of some major redecoration, but we didn't mind, and we must have stayed there for at least two hours after the match. Perhaps we just wanted the mood and sensation of that day to last forever.

Once again, we were hailed as national heroes upon our arrival back at Johannesburg airport. Past experience enabled the senior players, at least, to maintain perspective, but the hero worship wasn't bad. It was more welcoming than the letters demanding my resignation just 12 months earlier.

When Australia defeated the All Blacks the following

Saturday, we faced the unexpected prospect of a home match against New Zealand in Durban that was irrelevant in terms of the Tri-Nations title. That would only be claimed if we defeated the Wallabies at Ellis Park seven days later.

Those were statistics for the brain, but the facts of the heart are that every match between the Springboks and the All Blacks is a battle and, within moments of the start, we were thrown back on our heels by New Zealanders desperate to salvage some honour from what was unfolding as one of the most catastrophic seasons in their history. Amid all the rivalry, I have total respect for the men in black.

By half-time, the All Blacks led 17-5, and I had begun to accept the real possibility of defeat. I was disappointed. A capacity crowd had packed King's Park in anticipation of a rout. Well, they were seeing a rout, all right, just not the one they had expected. I felt we had let them down.

Nick was angry, saying he did not expect us to win every match but that he did expect us never to lose without a struggle. I walked back to the field for the second half with Mark Andrews, and the thoughtful lock casually remarked that he felt we could still turn the Test around.

With 15 minutes remaining, we trailed 23-5. I was starting to doubt the wise head on Mark's young shoulders. Surely there was no way back. Then, out of nothing, Joost van der Westhuizen lit the fuse, scampering through a gap on the fringe of a ruck 25 metres out and dashing through to score.

Belief flooded through the team, and the spectators in the stands. Amid a crescendo of noise and excitement, of Springboks rampant, the entire world seemed to come crashing down around the All Blacks.

We hurled everything into attack. With five minutes left, Bobby Skinstad, the emerging Western Province flanker who had been brought on as a substitute, scored after a move that passed through seven phases of recycled possession and, in the dying seconds, amid bedlam, James Dalton crashed over following a drive at the back of the lineout. Out of the jaws of certain defeat ...

We were not jubilant afterwards, rather relieved and perhaps somewhat surprised that we had managed to pull the game out of the fire. But this was the nature of the team. There was no such thing as a lost cause. Nick Mallett was obviously thrilled by our comeback, although I suspect he would have preferred us to play for the full 80 minutes, rather than only the last ten.

To a man, Taine Randall's side collapsed to the turf at the final whistle, shattered by the dramatic manner of the 24-23 defeat, but I would be dishonest if I said I felt much sympathy for them. I had not noticed too much comfort from the All Blacks when we were trounced in Auckland the previous year.

They had been unlucky to lose at King's Park in 1998, just as we had not deserved to lose in Christchurch in 1996, at Newlands in 1996, at King's Park in 1996, at Loftus in 1996, at Ellis Park in 1997 ... such is rugby.

Earlier in the year, the two coaches, John Hart and Nick Mallett, had been discussing the fact that the Springbok and All Black teams so rarely mixed with each other, despite the fact we played so often, and so a golf day was arranged for the two squads on the day after the Test in Durban.

Nick and I played a four-ball match against John Hart and the former All Black captain, Sean Fitzpatrick, and managed to secure a narrow victory even if, when all the scores were in, the New Zealanders won the match.

Hart was evidently under enormous pressure as All Black coach, but he has always appeared a knowledgeable and decent person to me, someone who knew how to behave. When François Pienaar was concussed at Newlands in 1996, Hart was among the first to enquire after him; and when Ruben Kruger broke his leg in Auckland, Hart visited him in hospital.

At one point of our match, Fitzpatrick three-putted from

three metres, prompting the coach to declare: 'Come on, Sean, I've got four million New Zealanders on my back, and now I must carry you around the course as well.'

Never mind on which side of the fence you operate, the pressures and expectations in New Zealand and South Africa are the same.

As the All Blacks returned home, we turned our attention to what would be the most important match played by South Africa since the 1995 World Cup final. A victory over the Wallabies at Ellis Park, or even a draw, would secure the Tri-Nations title. It was that simple, that straightforward, that tough.

Australia would send out a backline that relied heavily on Tim Horan, and a pack of forwards built around John Eales. They would always win a respectable share of possession, and they had the skills to be dangerous. They would give nothing away; every point would be hard earned; and they would pounce on any moment of weakness. As we prepared for a match that was effectively the Tri-Nations final, our paramount aim was to eliminate unnecessary mistakes.

There was something else on my mind as well. I had picked up a neck injury against the All Blacks in Wellington, and it had deteriorated in Durban. Under normal circumstances, I would not have played against Australia, but these were not normal circumstances. This was one of the biggest rugby days of my life. I requested an injection to numb the pain, and played.

Nobody was aware of the problem with my neck, and I am sure doctors will assert that I was foolish and taking an unnecessary risk, and I am sure they are right, but I wanted to play in this match. It was important. I wanted to make sure that we won, and I wanted to share in that victory.

The buzz at Ellis Park on another warm and sunny afternoon was quite magnificent and we managed to produce the kind of disciplined and controlled performance that Nick and his coaching staff had so carefully planned. It was never easy, it was never comfortable, but there was not a single moment during the game when I ever thought we would not emerge victorious.

Our spirits were raised in the opening exchanges when Pieter Muller produced a tackle on Horan that knocked the Wallaby genius back five metres. As the crowd hailed the big hit, each of us began to believe.

The match would produce an enduring image when Bobby Skinstad, the talented young Western Province flanker, was brought on as an impact player for the last quarter of the match. Gifted and able to pick up the pace of the game almost immediately, Bobby grabbed possession and burst through to score beneath the Wallaby posts. His swallow dive was captured by the photographers, and instantly enshrined in Springbok history.

South Africa 29 Australia 15 ... and so the Tri-Nations was won.

After two seasons of pain, we had emerged in triumph. Four wins out of four matches left us as undisputed champions in 1998, and had taken the side's winning streak to 14 matches, three short of the world record established by the All Black team of the late 1960s. That milestone lay ahead of us.

It was Joost van der Westhuizen who said after the triumph at Ellis Park that winning the Tri-Nations compared favourably with winning the World Cup. I did not know, because I had never played in a Rugby World Cup.

As we all sipped Tri-Nations champagne that night in Johannesburg, that experience, I felt certain, would also lie ahead ... in Wales, in 1999.

11

The Record

There was enthusiasm and confidence on every smiling face. Two months after its Tri-Nations triumph, an excited Springbok squad gathered for a training camp in Johannesburg prior to departure on tour to Britain.

We were assured in our ability, confident in the coaching staff and secure in the team management. An onerous match schedule was built around Tests against Wales, Scotland, Ireland and England on successive Saturdays, but we looked forward to the opportunity of winning the Grand Slam. We were on top. Rugby was not a chore. This was fun. People liked us.

And there, at the back of our minds, was the record, the chance for our side to stand apart from all the international teams that had taken the field anywhere in the world in more than 120 years of rugby.

Towards the end of the 1960s, the New Zealand team recorded no fewer than 17 successive Test wins; we were leaving for Britain on the back of 14 Test victories in a row, meaning we would be in position to stand alone in the history books if we won all four international matches on tour.

Players are not supposed to be concerned about records: we concentrate on one match at a time, focus on our own game, etc. etc. … But this opportunity had crept up on us. It was being trumpeted in the media and I could see it had started to mean a lot to the squad. It certainly meant a lot to me.

So we were happy and intensely motivated ... completely unprepared for what would be our first jarring experience with Nick Mallett. Until this moment, so far as most of us were concerned, the coach had not put a foot wrong. Bright and bold, eager and knowledgeable, inside 14 months he had transformed the Boks from a confused rabble to the strongest team in the world. In my view, he was the best thing since sliced bread, maybe even better than that.

On the first day of the training camp, the coach gathered the shadow Test team to one side, and began to tell us how we would need to keep our playing standards high because there were other players in the squad who were performing exceptionally well and staking powerful claims for a place.

This was odd. He was addressing the team that had won the Tri-Nations series. Maybe he was trying to bring us down to earth, but most of us had been through the traumas of 1997 – we actually needed such undisguised threats like a hole in the head. On the contrary, we didn't want him to shift the pressure to us, we craved his confidence, we wanted him to believe in us and grow with us. If we didn't perform, then he could talk about changes. But not now ...

He went on ...

And the hole got deeper ...

'There are some great players on the fringe of this squad, like Bobby Skinstad ...' The coach reeled off other names, but it was the mention of a player who, through absolutely no fault of his own would prove the catalyst for divisions within the Springbok squad for the next year, that resonated longest.

The young Western Province flanker had been brought on as a second-half substitute in the home matches against the All Blacks and Wallabies, and he scored celebrated tries on both occasions. His smiling face was soon to be seen on the newsstalls, and the phenomenon of 'Bobbymania' erupted. Posters were breathlessly pinned on the walls of teenagers' bedrooms nationwide, and it seemed as if Nick Mallett was relatively keen on him as well.

I was as excited as anyone by the emergence of a fine young talent, even one who, it was already very clear, would eventually challenge for my position in the team. I had never worried about competition, and would not start now. On the contrary, I would always welcome strength in depth.

However, it was generally accepted that the incumbent Springbok loose trio of Rassie Erasmus, André Venter and myself ranked alongside any in the world at the time. We had clicked, and thrived at the highest level; and Skinstad was still young, still learning and, most experts accepted, still used to best advantage as a clever impact player in the last quarter. The system was working well.

Yet Nick seemed desperate to find a place for Skinstad in the starting XV as soon as possible, even at the cost of breaking up a successful loose trio and rupturing our hard-won team morale. His words at that very first training session before leaving on tour stayed with a few players, dampened their enthusiasm and blurred their focus.

Never mind, I told them quietly, let's get on with the job at hand. Erasmus, Venter and Teichmann were named as the loose forwards for the opening Test of the tour, against Wales at Wembley stadium, and we played an important role in withstanding what unfolded as an almighty Welsh effort.

Graham Henry, a former Auckland coach, had been appointed to prepare Wales for the 1999 Rugby World Cup, and the New Zealander swiftly restored fire and brimstone to the red jerseys. It required only a couple of drives by either of the Quinnell brothers for us to realise this was a different team to the one thrashed 96-3 at Loftus Versfeld seven months before.

In contrast, we appeared complacent and lethargic, unable to find any kind of rhythm or momentum. Wales bounced into a

14-0 lead within 25 minutes, but a Joost van der Westhuizen strike and a penalty try pulled us back into the game before the interval. Nick made a couple of familiar changes at half-time, bringing Ollie le Roux into the front row for Adrian Garvey and calling Bobby Skinstad into the fray, moving André Venter to lock and taking off Mark Andrews.

Still we were unable to stoke the fire, unable to kick-start the engine that, in full flow, would surely have powered us to an emphatic win. The minutes ticked away and our situation become more and more serious. We were not at all focused, not at all clinical, not at all ruthless. We were poor.

'Concentrate, concentrate.'

I must have yelled the word every minute of an increasingly frantic second half. With three minutes of normal time left, we trailed 20-17.

Close enough to smell the looming disaster, however, we did not panic, maintained our discipline and set about the salvage operation. Eventually, our pressure on the Welsh line prompted the defence to creep offside, and Franco Smith's calm penalty goal brought the scores level, but it was still not enough. Our assault on the record required victory, not a draw.

Again we surged forward, winning a lineout close to the Wales 22-metre line. The rebuilding of their national stadium in Cardiff may have forced the team in red to temporary lodgings at Wembley, but the atmosphere within the soccer stadium in London was outstanding. 'Concentrate,' I urged.

As we formed the lineout, I called a set move where we would take the ball forward into a ruck situation, Joost would attack the blind side, pass inside to Rassie Erasmus, who would set André Venter clear. Happily, the move was executed to perfection, we scored and another Franco Smith penalty fully seven minutes into injury time gave us a fortunate 27-20 victory.

We were relieved to escape, but, as Nick pointed out afterwards, we had shown outstanding mental strength in the closing stages. This was the winning habit in all its glory. Our ambitions had survived intact.

The following morning, I arrived at breakfast and someone mentioned the match report in the *Sunday Times,* a British newspaper. Stephen Jones, rugby correspondent, had written that my reputation as the world's best eighthman had 'collapsed in flames' the previous afternoon. This would be the first in a series of personal attacks that peppered his coverage of the tour.

I had been around long enough to brush aside sniping criticism, but Nick Mallett and Alan Solomons could not have been more supportive, suggesting to me that this particular journalist always picked on eighthmen, and assuring me that they were satisfied with my form. It was a heartening response, and absolutely typical of their sympathetic and constructive approach at the time.

The tour moved north to Scotland, and our coach chose this moment to announce his most significant decision of the tour. André Venter was dropped from the Test side, replaced by Bobby Skinstad in the starting line-up. The players had known the change was likely ever since the opening training session and, to his credit, André accepted the decision with great dignity.

Nick was evidently eager to bring the young prodigy into the team, but I thought at the time that André's physical presence and unselfish work rate would bring more to the side than Bobby's undoubted natural talent. I don't believe it would be inaccurate to say many leading players shared this opinion, but I said nothing to anyone. As captain, I publicly supported the coach's decision.

But I was frustrated. We were effectively using Bobby as a substitute, and we were winning. Why was there an overpowering need to change the system, to disrupt the loose trio combination that had won the Tri-Nations title? No adequate explanation has ever been offered and, it seems to me, a measure of discontent within the squad can be traced back to André's omission.

In spite of the glamour of winning a Grand Slam, in spite of our proximity to a new world record, it proved difficult to motivate the team ahead of the Test at Murrayfield, where we had posted 60 points the previous year, doubly so when we arrived to find the famous stadium barely half full.

In another surprising change from the side that may not have played well but had still defeated Wales, Christian Stewart replaced Franco Smith at inside centre and the goal-kicking responsibility passed to Percy Montgomery. He struck two early penalties but, once again, our efforts lacked the ruthless dimension that we had hoped to demonstrate.

I felt our physical presence in the forward exchanges was not as strong and commanding as it might have been, but nobody could have failed to be impressed by the explosive impact of Bobby Skinstad. At one point in the second half, he made an electric outside break, sprinted up to the last Scottish tackler but, with Stefan Terblanche outside him and unmarked, he held on to the ball and the move came to nothing. Then, at the end, he appeared at outside centre, and ran in an impressive try beneath the Scottish posts.

This was the issue: we were a successful, winning team but the coach, and his closest advisers, believed we needed to accommodate this exceptional emerging talent in the starting side as soon as possible. The timing and manner of his accommodation would affect our morale, our performance, everything that had been so effectively developed during the previous year.

Scotland were ultimately defeated 35-10, but once again the Test team had not played particularly well and, as we travelled to Ireland, I sensed divisions starting to emerge within the touring squad.

While the Test side spluttered against Wales and Scotland, the midweek team were cruising to high-scoring victories. In

THE RECORD

their minds, these results should have prompted more changes, but in our view, it was impossible to compare their matches with ours because we were playing highly motivated Test teams and the standard of their midweek opposition was poor.

A traditional tour itinerary would have resolved these debates because the Saturday matches between Tests usually presented ideal opportunities to experiment with new combinations, but our schedule was so compressed, featuring Tests on four successive weekends, that it almost started to feel as if we were playing two separate tours in the same country at the same time.

The midweek players started to feel excluded, and we, as the Test team, began to resent the occasional darkly whispered remarks. Spirits were sagging.

Our next appointment was with Ireland at Lansdowne Road, Dublin, and the Venter-Skinstad debate appeared to take a decisive turn when the youngster produced two moments of genius to bury the Irish team. There is no other word to describe his quality. His gifts were not coached, they were inherent.

It needs to be stressed once again that, throughout this period, the team regarded his emergence as entirely positive. It was the manner in which the coaching staff was handling his talent that was causing concern.

Ireland started the match with astonishing vigour, and we hardly ventured beyond our own half during the opening half hour. Ireland had recently conceded 35 points to Romania, but they found a talisman again in Keith Wood, the hooker, who stampeded over James Dalton early in the game, visibly charging the spirit of his compatriots both on the field and among the capacity crowd.

But we weathered the storm, were settled by Rassie Erasmus' try before half-time and were leading 10-6 five minutes into the second half.

Enter Bobby.

First, he collected the ball from a lineout, simply galloped downfield and sidestepped Conor O'Shea to score a fine individual try. Two minutes later, he found another gap, raced clear, spread utter mayhem in the Irish defence and created the chance for Joost van der Westhuizen to dart over.

The game was over, and, in the aftermath, I sensed Nick felt the manner of our 27-13 victory had entirely justified his decision. André Venter emerged as a replacement for Mark Andrews at lock, but we will never know if his physical presence and work rate in the loose exchanges would have enabled us to build a much stronger forward platform much earlier in the game. Selection tends to be driven by instinct, rather than science. Nobody is ever 100% right.

We headed to Twickenham with three wins out of three, but the general level of confidence of the team had dropped during the tour. We appeared to have lost momentum since the Tri-Nation series, and were relying far too much on individuals to pull us clear from potentially difficult situations. The rhythm, the drills, the pattern, the confidence had gradually ebbed away.

And the toughest Test lay ahead. While we were winning in Dublin, coach Clive Woodward's England side had been unlucky to lose by a point to Australia. They had prepared carefully and were coming to the boil. I told the guys anything less than a 50% improvement in our performance thus far would not suffice. We had now equalled the All Blacks' record of 17 successive wins, but we had to rise again if we were to secure a place in history all on our own.

We started well, with Pieter Rossouw barely cantering past the England defence to score from 40 metres out after only seven minutes, but the home side rallied and drew level when Mike Catt's chip was collected by Dan Luger, and fed on to Jeremy Guscott. As the match wore on, we struggled to subdue the England forwards, struggled to subdue the brewing excitement in the stands and struggled to exert any kind of control over the match.

Nick was animated at half-time, taken at 7-7, urging us to be more clinical among the forwards, and André Venter was yet again summoned from the bench to replace Mark Andrews for the second half, but against England particularly, we were missing his powerful presence in the loose. This was rugby as tough, harsh attrition, and it was proving to be infertile ground for Bobby Skinstad's free-flowing talents.

Matt Dawson kicked two penalties for England midway through the second half and a sisappointing penalty miss by us from directly in front of the posts sapped our self-belief.

Yet again the clock was running down, again we trailed and I implored the side for one last effort to claim the Grand Slam and secure the record. Just as we had fought back against New Zealand in Durban, and versus Wales at Wembley, I believed we could still snatch the single converted try required. One pass, one moment of inspiration, one burst of speed: these were all that separated us from a place in history, as the most successful team ever to play the game.

André Venter launched the last charge, bursting upfield, driving through tackles. The ball passed through six pairs of hands as we drove forward, in search of the gap through which we could reach immortality … but Luger stuck out a hand to deflect what might have been a scoring chance and, somewhere in the grey London gloom, Paddy O'Brien blew his final whistle.

We had fallen at the last hurdle.

Defeated 13-7 by England, we would have to be content with a place in the record books alongside the 1969 All Blacks as the only international teams to win 17 Test matches in succession. That would have to do.

I was more disappointed in the changing room afterwards than I ever expected to be. Rugby is about winning Test matches; records are by-products of success and should never become primary goals in themselves. I understood all this, but, as a group, we had been so close, and travelled so far, and I had desperately wanted us to reach the final destination.

To have recorded 17 successive victories, stretching from the consolation win over the Wallabies at Loftus Versfeld to the win over Ireland 16 months later, including home and away victories against Australia, New Zealand and England, was a remarkable and historic achievement by any standard. Given the pace and competitiveness of modern rugby, I doubt this feat will be matched.

We should stand back, and consider.

If anyone had stood up in our desolate changing room in Auckland, after we had conceded 50 points to the All Blacks, and declared that this same group of players would embark on a world record-equalling series of victories, they would have been ridiculed and instantly certified as insane.

Following the defeat at Twickenham, I was eager that the achievement of my team should not be lost and forgotten in short-term recriminations, and I took a much bolder line than usual at the post-match press conference.

'I believe we can still call ourselves the strongest team in the world,' I told the journalists. 'Our record speaks for itself. We won 17 games before today and this team still has to reach its full potential. There is no doubt in my mind the best is yet to come. We now have a six-month break from international rugby and we will be back stronger than ever for the World Cup next year.'

They were brave words, and I believed every one of them.

We may have had to share the record of most consecutive Test wins, but I hoped the greatest glory lay ahead. So did Nick Mallett.

The coach appeared to accept defeat at Twickenham in good grace, and he neatly thanked the players for their efforts during the tour.

'Now go home and have a decent rest,' he said, relaxed and

THE RECORD

assured in his authority. 'That is the most important thing. I do not want any of you to start playing in the Super 12 until you feel 100% fit and 100% rested. We all know that next year is World Cup year, and we must all be ready.'

At the end of a tour when he seemed occasionally to have lost touch with his players and acted purely on his own convictions, Nick had judged the mood impeccably. Rest for as long as necessary: that is what we needed to hear at the end of a punishing season. I was encouraged by his sensible approach, thanked him for his efforts and wished him and his family a happy Christmas.

12

Dream Denied

For me, the 1999 season was going to be prime time. It was my ninth full year of first class rugby and, all being well, it would culminate in an opportunity to lead the Springboks in defence of the Rugby World Cup.

All being well …

There seemed no reason why all should not go well. Physically, I felt very strong: the neck injury that had troubled me the previous season was completely healed and my knees were fine. The Grand Slam tour to Britain had been tough but, by the time I gathered with the Coastal Sharks for pre-season training ahead of the 1999 Super 12, I was genuinely well rested and raring to go.

As a rugby player, you typically roll through a career, taking every season and every match as it comes. This is not a sport where you can pick and choose your contest. It is a game that demands complete commitment each time you run onto the field, any field, against any opponents at any time.

So the matches come and go, and the seasons come and go, and, if you are fortunate, one or two golden Cups come and go as well, but you basically put your head down and play. There is no secret science to mapping out a career in this game. You play your guts out and accept whatever comes along.

At the start of 1999, however, I tried briefly to lift my head from the back of the scrum and consider the bigger picture, where I had been, where I was going. Just past my 32nd birthday, I could reflect upon three Currie Cup titles with Natal, 17 consecutive Test wins and a Tri-Nations triumph with the Springboks. In addition, I had made many friends in the game and never suffered a serious injury of any description. By any measure, I was in credit.

All that remained was to play in a Rugby World Cup. I have never been a player who sets specific goals and crosses them off as he goes along, preferring always to give 100% and see where that takes me. But this was different: even in my laid-back world, the William Webb Ellis trophy loomed large.

This would be the year. I was going to train harder, play harder than ever before. Yes, indeed, all being well, I was in the words of the song, to party like it's 1999.

The Super 12 soon gathered pace, and the Sharks were maintaining the form that had carried us at least to the semi-final stage in each of the three years since the competition started. Of South Africa's other Super 12 sides, the Golden Cats and the Northern Bulls were still struggling but the Western Stormers finally seemed to have come to terms with the pace of the competition.

In fact, when we travelled to Cape Town and lost to the Stormers, several journalists started to hail the Cape side as South Africa's strongest challengers in the Super 12. We had established our pedigree over three years, they had beaten us in one match, and, all of a sudden, we were being dismissed.

There was another article too, introducing a personal dimension to the debate. Bobby Skinstad had excelled at eighthman for the Stormers, and his performance was being compared to mine, the conclusion being that he was now ready to take over the Springbok No. 8 jersey. I was surprised, not least because I thought I had played well in the match, but the writer was entitled to his opinion.

That evening, following our defeat at Newlands, I was invited to attend a house-warming party for Robbie Kempson, the prop forward who had recently moved from Natal to pursue his career in Cape Town. Amid the drinks and snacks, I saw Alan Solomons, the Springbok assistant coach.

We greeted each other and spoke about the Super 12. I mentioned I had not spoken to Nick Mallett much recently and Alan seemed surprised, but not as surprised as I was hoping he would be. Maybe I was reading far too much into his response, but our conversation left me feeling strangely uneasy.

I was the Springbok captain, and all I wanted was for the Springbok coach to call and ask me how things were going. Was that too much to ask? Nick and I had spoken regularly during the 1998 Super 12, now we were not speaking at all. Should I call him? Would that be too forward? Maybe he did not want to speak to me? Maybe he agreed with the Skinstad article? I was uncertain.

Two days later, Nick telephoned me. We exchanged greetings. I wanted to know if everything was OK with him, and I believe he misunderstood what I was asking because he suddenly proclaimed: 'Look, Gary, please understand I can't give anyone any guarantees about anything.'

He seemed to think I had been asking him to confirm my place in the Bok team, but I would never have been so presumptuous. I just wanted to keep open the lines of communication, for us to speak freely as we had the previous year. But everything was suddenly different, everything felt strange.

'The Springbok team is going to be picked on form in the Super 12,' the coach continued, evidently irritated. 'That's the only way.'

Form in the Super 12?

Could this possibly be the same man who had stood in the changing room at Twickenham in December and told the guys to ensure they were 100% rested before they started playing in the Super 12? Now, he was saying they had to earn their places on the basis of form in the Super 12. He had changed his tune.

DREAM DENIED

It was so unlike the Nick Mallett that we knew and respected. When he repeated this statement on television, the players did not take long to understand the effect of his remarks was to shift the steadily increasing pressure from his shoulders onto ours. In December he was saying: 'I believe in you, have a good rest, see you next year'. Now he was saying: 'Get out there, prove yourself, I give no guarantees'.

Three years earlier, one of the 1995 World Cup squad had told me how their coach, Kitch Christie, had done everything in his power to shield his players from the external pressure. This had been an invaluable skill.

Within a fortnight, Nick was on the phone again. I was encouraged. Were we getting things back on track? I sincerely hoped so.

'Gary, how are you?'

'Fine, Nick, yourself.'

'Fine'.

He wanted to let me know that Jake White, our technical adviser, would be leaving the Springbok squad. I was disappointed. Jake had made a tremendous contribution to our success and earned the players' total respect. He came from Johannesburg, and therefore broke up the Western Province ranks on the coaching staff. I personally didn't care where anyone came from, but I knew that his presence was significant for the players from the north.

Nick went on to explain that Jake wanted to coach a side on his own, and added that, in any case, he and Alan could handle the coaching by themselves. I listened carefully, but I was not expressing enthusiasm and I began to sense Nick becoming irritated on the other end of the line.

'Nick, I think some of the guys will be upset if Jake goes.'

'Well, it's my job to select the coaching staff,' he replied abruptly, ' and I don't have to get approval from the players. The decision is made.'

'Fine,' I said.

FOR THE RECORD

That was that. Some weeks later, the rumour ran through the Springbok squad that Jake White had given a newspaper interview in which he was quoted as saying Bobby Skinstad tended not to make enough tackles. Nick Mallett and Alan Solomons were apparently angered by the remark and, ever since, Jake's days as part of the coaching staff had been numbered.

I recount this version of events not because I know it is true – I have never raised the issue with either Nick or Alan – but simply to demonstrate the growing perception among many players that Nick and Alan had elevated Skinstad to a position where he was treated differently, somehow set apart as an irreplaceable game breaker, protected from any criticism. Right or wrong, these were opinions that were being privately expressed when Boks gathered.

The cumulative effect of the newspaper talk, the meeting with Alan and my various telephone conversations with Nick was steadily to increase my sense of unease. There was no avoiding the fact that our relationship had changed. I channelled my energy into the Coastal Sharks' Super 12 campaign and took satisfaction from my contribution to our fine victory over Otago at King's Park.

Whatever was going on at Springbok level, whatever plots were hatching, I resolved to maintain my standards and plough on regardless. Several times, I called up Nick Mallett's telephone number on my cell phone, but then didn't push the green button. I wanted to talk, to get things straight, to feel assured again, but it was not right for me to call him; he had to contact me.

Still, the Super 12 rumbled on ...

The Sharks' campaign came to a halt when we lost to the Hurricanes in East London on a depressing day. Everything had seemed to go wrong from the moment the PA system reverberated with the Hurricanes' song when it should have been playing the Sharks' anthem. For the first time in four years, we would not be taking part in the semi-finals. It was disappointing after such a long successful streak.

Once again, the Springbok coach communicated with his captain through the headlines. He was quoted as saying some of the Sharks' squad seemed to have been coasting through the Super 12. This was an outrageous statement, and devoid of all truth. The criticism enraged several of our players but I calmed them down, saying Nick was probably misquoted. Maybe he was, maybe he wasn't; but, if the former was the case, it would have been clever of him to let us know.

Whatever the facts, the increasingly popular caricature of the coach was of a man besotted with Bobby Skinstad, preoccupied with Western Province (a team that was being coached by his assistant, Alan Solomons), and quick to pull the trigger at anyone or anything from any other province.

Personally, I don't think this perception was either fair or accurate. Nick picked the strongest team: full stop. And he appreciated Bobby in the same way that we all appreciated his talent. But the difference between the Nick Mallett of 1997 and the Nick Mallett of 1999 was that the 1997 model would have gone out of his way to put matters right, taken the time to explain what he meant if he had been misunderstood, especially by the players. In my view, the 1999 model was too busy and, with great respect, too confident that he was right.

Whatever the truth, these perceptions would sow the seeds of renewed provincialism within the national squad as the year wore on. Players from the north started to resent and suspect players from the south. Nobody seemed to care too much about the guys from Natal but the fact was we had been united as a squad in 1998; now we were drifting apart again in 1999.

The Sharks might have been eliminated, but the Stormers did succeed in reaching the semi-final, which they lost against Otago at Newlands. By then, the Cape team had already lost the services of Bobby Skinstad. He had crashed his car on the way home after a Super 12 match against the Canterbury

Crusaders. The vehicle was a write-off and the emerging superstar had seriously damaged his knee. I was sorry, and knew we would miss him later in the year.

Some people might read these words and suspect I am being less than sincere; they might think that, in reality, I would have celebrated an injury to a player who, it was clear, was threatening my place in the side. Well, if I must be absolutely honest … such people don't know me at all.

Bobby was a talented young player, doing his best. There had never, and has never, been a moment when I have ever wished him anything but the best in his rugby career. News of his accident was a huge disappointment.

There was further bad news for the Springbok coach. Among others, key players such as Henry Honiball and Joost van der Westhuizen were injured and would not be available for the Tri-Nations warm-up, which this year took the form of two home Tests against Italy and a Test against Wales in Cardiff.

Confronted by the first serious injury list of his term as Springbok coach, Nick introduced a squad system. His intentions were laudable: to keep key players fresh and to develop depth throughout the side. In practice, however, the system bred insecurity, uncertainty and ruined morale.

If you accept confidence is a crucial requisite for success, and that any sportsman or sportswoman at the highest level derives confidence from being selected in the team and playing well, then it follows logically that the squad system is not helpful in establishing a strong and successful team.

Squad systems might work in provincial teams, where a rest is sometimes welcome during a long and punishing schedule but, in a national squad, there are fewer matches and everyone wants to play all of them. Players want to play, not sit in the stands, or be replaced at half-time. They want to be involved and, more importantly, they want to feel the coach needs them. To my mind, the only policy for any national coach is to select the strongest possible side for every match.

DREAM DENIED

In the event, we could probably have selected a third team and still beaten Italy in the first Test at Telkom Park, Port Elizabeth. They looked indifferent in all phases of the game, and I was irritated to strain my hamstring.

My initial reaction was that I would recover in time for the second Test at King's Park a week later, but Nick wanted me to make a decision on my fitness by no later than the Tuesday, and, with a view to being fit for the Test in Cardiff, we agreed I would sit out the Durban Test against Italy.

I was disappointed. It was probably the right decision, but the fact was I had not missed a single Springbok Test since the start of 1996 and I was keen to keep that run going. Nonetheless, the hamstring triumphed and I watched Corné Krige lead the Springboks to a 100-point win against Italy.

The relationship between Nick and myself was never less than cordial during this period while the squad was assembled to play Italy, nor was it ever more than cordial. Once there had been complete honesty and openness between us, now there was nothing more than a professional relationship. Once I had felt able to say anything to him, now I was wary and anxious.

However, as the Springbok captain, I did require an open and transparent relationship with the Springbok coach. If we did not work together, the entire Bok squad would pick up the vibes and be unsettled. In 1998, he had consulted me in selection and management decisions; now he either told me firmly that it was his decision or he simply did not raise the subject. In 1998, he confided in me and was not afraid to reveal his hopes and fears regarding the team. Now, he appeared so much tougher, assured to the point of being arrogant.

It almost seemed as if phrases like 'I don't know' or 'I'm sorry' or 'that had not occurred to me' had been eliminated from his vocabulary, at least when he was talking to me. The empathy and humanity had disappeared.

Was I being over-sensitive?

I don't think so.

In fact, if Bobby Skinstad had not been injured in the car crash, I believe I would have been dropped before the matches against Italy. I am convinced that, by this time, Nick had already made his decision that I had served my purpose as captain of his Springbok side. Bobby's absence had just left him in embarrassing limbo. He couldn't say anything, and would have to tolerate me.

South Africa had played against Wales in Cardiff in 1994, in Johannesburg in 1995, in Cardiff in 1997, in Pretoria in June 1998, in Cardiff in November 1998 and now, again, to mark the opening of the Millennium stadium. Six Tests in four and a half years, and South Africa's all-time Test record against Wales stood at an impressive … Played 12, Won 12. We had never lost.

Our task was to preserve that record, but a seven-day overseas trip in the middle of our domestic season presented the players with unwanted disruption. It was not shaping as the happiest tour of all time when we gathered at the airport to catch the London flight. By the Thursday evening, it had become clearly the worst Springbok trip any of us could remember, ever.

The problem was unrelated to Nick Mallett. In fact, his authority within the structure and his strength of character emerged as our salvation. The burning issue that would scorch us all in Cardiff was 'affirmative action'.

Silas Nkanunu, the Port Elizabeth lawyer who had succeeded Louis Luyt as SARFU president, had addressed the matter during his speech after the Test against Italy in Durban, declaring that he could not understand how Deon Kayser and Breyton Paulse, two Coloured wingers, could ever have been left out of the Springbok side. Some of the players stood at the back of the room and muttered about what they saw as a blatantly provocative statement.

Nkanunu was only reflecting the prevailing mood. Politicians were openly demanding black faces in every

Springbok team that took the field, declaring that any national side should visibly represent the entire nation.

My own view was straightforward. Rugby did need to be transformed, but this could only be done from the grass roots up rather than from the Springboks down. SARFU should implement a development programme that, first, inspired interest in the game across all of South African society, and, second, identified talented youngsters and ensured they realised their potential.

Such a two-tiered programme might need several years to start bearing fruit but it is not possible to right the wrongs of 110 years in two hours. If we are serious about development as a means of transforming our sport, rather than a means for oiling political agendas, then it should be done properly. The concept of including a black player in the Springbok side regardless of merit was plainly ridiculous: unfair on the squad, the fans and the player himself.

Quotas and racial directives could play a role at the broader levels of the rugby pyramid, but the top team in the country needed to be exactly that: the top team in the country comprising the top players. So far as I was aware, Paulse and Kayser had been included in the Bok team on merit. They had both proven themselves to be outstanding players in provincial rugby, and it was on the basis of their form, not their skin colour, that they had been picked.

However, Nkanunu had spoken and, as waves of alarm rippled through the squad, we, the players, requested an urgent meeting with SARFU, at which the union could outline its affirmative action policy, once and for all. It was arranged that Rian Oberholzer, the CEO, would address the entire squad at a meeting in our Cardiff hotel on the Thursday evening before the Test. This was by no means ideal timing, but the matter needed to be addressed swiftly.

'This is a fact of life,' the CEO told us emphatically. 'You either accept the policy or you can find somewhere else to earn a living.' Several players started to shake their heads, others booed, a few even whistled. I had never seen such an angry group of players and, with each jeer, Oberholzer adopted a more inflexible and off-hand manner. The mood was appalling. I had not planned to speak, but there was a need to cool tempers and restore order.

I stood and spoke directly to the CEO: 'Please understand that the players would like every Springbok *team* to be selected on merit. Selection for a national team should be a mark of excellence, not race, and we are seeking assurances from SARFU that this will remain the case. However, we do understand that transformation must be seen to be happening, and we would suggest that places be earmarked for that purpose within the Springbok *squad*.'

Oberholzer listened intently, but he gave no assurances and set down no clear SARFU policy on affirmative action; his message was simply that this thing was happening and there was nothing we could do about it.

Nick stood unequivocally on our side. It was rumoured among the squad that the coach was not on speaking terms with the SARFU CEO at the time, but that was not our concern. We believed the coach wanted clearance to select his Springbok side on merit, and on merit alone. Some of the guys were saying Nick was insisting on a clause to this effect during the negotiations to extend his contract with SARFU beyond the 1999 World Cup.

The union obviously could not afford to risk losing their winning coach on this matter and, not for the first time, the players invested all their hopes in the strong character and firm resolve of their coach. If he stood firm, the principle of merit selection would survive. The more we relied on him, the more I regretted the apparent deterioration in our relationship. At heart, he was the top-class man that I had learned to admire so much. What was going wrong?

Notwithstanding their faith in Nick, most of the players left

DREAM DENIED

the meeting with Oberholzer in Cardiff feeling even more agitated than when they arrived. In terms of psychological preparation for what would be a rigorous Test match, now barely 40 hours away, it had been a disaster.

What could we do?

At a team meeting the next day, I implored the players to forget about the issue and focus on the game, but the impact of the CEO's statements was huge. Rugby was our profession, our lives, and he was effectively telling us that simply being good at our job would not mean we would keep it. I could see the guys were distracted, and there was nothing I could do about it.

Meanwhile, across the city, Graham Henry was motivating his Wales side to produce a performance worthy of the magnificent new stadium, even if it was only half finished and could accommodate only 27 000 supporters. As one of the local newspapers noted, Wales had never lost at the new venue …

By five o'clock on match day, that record was still intact. Wales had played somewhere near their potential; we had produced exactly the sort of lethargic and unfocused performance that our preparations deserved and duly became the first South African team ever to lose against Wales, 29-19.

We were in a mess, and Nick Mallett was feeling real pressure for the first time since taking over as Springbok coach. We had lost against England, not played impressively against Italy, lost to Wales and, having spent several days at home, were now heading off to play our first Tri-Nations match of the season, versus New Zealand in Dunedin. It was getting hot in the kitchen.

His most pressing problem was an inability to replace the injured halfback pairing of Henry Honiball and Joost van der Westhuizen. There seemed no plan or strategy in place. The coach had selected Braam van Straaten and Werner Swanepoel for the match in Cardiff but he pressed the panic button after defeat and chose a completely different combination to face the All Blacks.

Gaffie du Toit and David van Sloesslin were drafted. I don't know what Nick was planning, because he didn't confide in me, but I shuddered at the prospect of throwing these talented youngsters into a Test match of this intensity. In truth, they had not even cut their teeth in the Super 12.

Soon after the team was announced, I happened to walk past Nick in the foyer of the hotel. He looked up and was startled to see me.

'Oh well, you've got the team you wanted,' he blurted out, as he hurried away to the lifts. I had absolutely no idea what he meant but, upon reflection, supposed he was referring to the inclusion of Natal players, Mark Andrews and Pieter Muller. It was a bizarre remark. What had happened to make him regard me as some kind of opponent, even a contrary force?

I had played hard, and been praised for my second-half performance in Cardiff. Despite many misgivings, I continued to support Nick among the squad. I had been loyal to him. What on earth could have gone wrong? We had worked so closely the previous year. Our relationship was dissolving.

Nonetheless the team, as selected, was a fact in Dunedin and, with the youngsters at halfback, we had to make the best of the situation. I assumed long periods of the week's preparations would be spent reassuring Gaffie and David, introducing them to the moves, absorbing them into the game plan. I was wrong. That is what the 1998-brand Mallett would have done.

Instead, the 1999 model jumped on the youngsters' case at the start of the week, and remained there through every training session. Where he should have listened, he barked. Where he should have guided, he chided. Where he should have advised, he chastised. I was becoming increasingly angry.

At one point, Nick actually told Gaffie he had to tackle like Henry Honiball. It was amazing. Maybe he was supposed to kick like Naas Botha as well, and run the ball like Mark Ella. I could see the young Griquas flyhalf was bewildered and bemused. His confidence had effectively been shattered.

By Thursday afternoon, I had had enough and I told Alan Solomons that Nick had to start saying something positive about the players. I said he had been too critical of the guys, and they were starting to feel the strain. I didn't raise the issue with Nick directly. Why? I'm not sure. I don't think I was wary of him, but it seemed as if all communication had broken down. By now, 'Solly' appeared to be a more understanding and generally easier man to approach.

Dunedin was literally dressed up for an occasion that had been formally designated by the local authority as an 'All Black' day, when everyone was asked to wear black clothes. The impact was outstanding and the All Blacks rose to the challenge, cantering to an emphatic 28-0 victory.

In the circumstances, I had been more determined than ever to maintain my own standard of performance and, by full-time, I was saddened by what had been a deeply depressing defeat but I was satisfied with my own efforts. I had made the tackles, carried the ball, marshalled the team and was duly named as South Africa's Man of the Match in two newspapers the following day. This was no consolation but, in their view at least, my form was sound.

Nick said nothing to me after the game, but he was not short of words in the post-match media conference where he lambasted Gaffie du Toit and David van Sloesslin as being 'clearly not up to international standard'. If that was true, whose fault was that? Had they asked to be selected? No. Who had decided to throw the youngsters in against the All Blacks? Nick.

I was appalled by his statements and far from alone among the players in concluding that once again, when the pressure arrived, the coach had shifted the burden to his players. It is likely that even Nick Mallett, on reflection, would agree his comments in Dunedin were inappropriate and unfair.

There was worse.

Mark Andrews approached me in the changing room after the Test against the All Blacks. He appeared unusually concerned and preoccupied.

'Teich, look at this,' he said, showing me a match programme. There was some scribbling on the side of the centre page, and I immediately saw that the Springbok coaching staff had written their score predictions before the match. It was not unusual, probably just a game. Mark told me to look again.

The writing was unmistakable ...

'NM: NZ 32 SA 25'

Every member of our coaching staff had predicted a Springbok win, with the exception of Nick Mallett. What hope did we have if our own coach was so casual in predicting his own side would lose to New Zealand? I couldn't believe my eyes and merely shrugged at Mark. There was nothing to say.

The last element in what had now become a broadly desperate situation was the lump in my leg. Unbeknown to anyone, I had taken a knock on the thigh and suffered a haematoma. I had finished the match, but I understood the injury and knew I would not be fit to play Australia the following Saturday. That night, I discussed my situation with the team doctor, and he concurred.

Ruled out of the Test in Brisbane, people expected me to go home, but my instinct was to stay with the team. Morale was sinking fast, several other injured players were already booked on the next flight to South Africa and I sensed it was right for me to stay, not to quit and run.

If anyone had instructed me to go home, I would have left, but nobody said anything. So I stayed, and tried to encourage and assist the guys in any way I could. It wasn't easy. I had captained South Africa for three years, and yet the vibes from the management were making me feel sadly uncomfortable in a Springbok squad. The support of the players carried me through.

Rassie Erasmus was appointed to lead the team against

DREAM DENIED

Australia, and we spoke at various times during the week. I have always respected him, and I think the sentiment has been mutual. Industrious and brave on the field, he is every bit as loyal and decent away from the rucks and mauls. Even his magnificent efforts, however, could not deny the Wallabies an emphatic 32-6 victory in Brisbane.

I watched from the stands, frustrated and disappointed for my team-mates, increasingly angry towards the coach. I could not fathom why he could not simply sit down with me and tell me what was on his mind. Nick Mallett, the man I had admired so much, had become an inexplicable enigma.

We could not carry on like this. It was ridiculous. I saw Nick early during the evening after the game in Brisbane, and I asked if we could talk. We agreed to meet in his room at nine the next morning. Contrary to an impression given by Nick later, it was me who initiated the meeting.

I knocked on the door.

'Come in.'

Nick was sitting there, with Alan Solomons at his side.

'OK, Gary, what's the problem?' he asked.

'Well, there is clearly some sort of problem. You don't communicate with me any more. I would just like to know where I stand.'

There was a pause. Mallett gazed at me, his large round eyes fixed in my direction. He seemed to be considering his options.

'Look, I must tell you that Bobby is definitely going to the World Cup, and he will be going as the eighthman.'

'OK, that's your decision.'

'Yes, it is.'

He had given an extraordinary reply. I had asked where I stood and his response had been to inform me that he had already included in his World Cup squad a player who had not played any rugby for three months and appeared to be far from certain of being fit for the tournament. It was incredible. He didn't refer to me in any way at any stage of the conversation, didn't say I would be dropped out of the squad, didn't say he wanted to change the captaincy.

I was not going to leave the matter there.

'Nick, I think you make a mistake when you and Solly go overboard about Bobby. The guys notice these things. Every time he does anything, you just can't stop yourself telling everyone how brilliantly he played. But consider a player like André Venter. He might not be as flashy as some players, but he does the tough work. When was the last time you praised him?'

The coach nodded, seeming to take the point.

'OK, I understand,' he said. 'Is there anything else?'

A squad golf day had been arranged and the bus was due to leave for the course at quarter-past nine. Nick's mind was on the first tee; our meeting clearly would not continue. That was it. No thanks, no nothing.

Incredibly, Braam van Straaten and I were then drawn to play in a four-ball against Selborne Boome and, yes, the coach. On this particular day, Nick Mallett would probably have been my very last choice on the planet for a golfing partner. We did not exchange a word through 18 sombre holes.

We flew home the following day and I had barely taken my seat on the South African Airways jumbo jet when one of the players handed me a copy of the *Sunday Times* from home. It was speculating that Bobby would play eighthman at the World Cup. It was odd: I had not noticed any journalists in the room during my meeting with Mallett and Solomons.

Still nothing was said. During the flight, nothing; when we arrived back in South Africa, nothing. The Springboks had a weekend off before facing their next Tri-Nations match, against the All Blacks in Pretoria

On the Wednesday evening, I was telephoned at home by the rugby writer of the *Daily News,* Mike Greenway, and told that I was going to be dropped from the squad for the rest of the Tri-Nations series. Who told him?

My immediate response was to contact Ian McIntosh and ask him to put me in the Natal team for a Currie Cup match that Saturday. I wanted to play to prove I was fit. If Mallett was going to drop me, then I wanted to make sure he did not have an opportunity to pretend I was injured. This matter needed to come to a head, and I was not prepared to wait any longer.

Following Greenway's call, I telephoned Nick on his cell phone. There was no reply, but I left a message. He didn't return the call that day.

On Friday morning, I called again, left another message in his voice mail and, two hours later, around 11 o'clock, the Springbok coach came on the line. It was the first time he had called me in three months, and I happened to be lying in the physiotherapy room at King's Park, having treatment.

'Gary?'

'Yes.'

'I have decided to change the captain for the rest of the Tri-Nations series. I don't think you can hold down a place in the team any more, and I suggest you go back to the Natal team and play in the Currie Cup.'

'But Nick, if I may say so, I played pretty well in the second half against Wales and I was Man of the Match against the All Blacks.'

'Look, Gary, that's my decision.'

There was evidently no opportunity for discussion. The pragmatic coach of 1997 had become the absolute ruler of 1999. That was that.

We have never spoken since. Not one word.

Three years earlier, François Pienaar confronted André Markgraaff at the Sunnyside Park Hotel, and that Bok captain and that Bok coach have never spoken since either.

Why? What happens? What goes wrong? Some people say the coaches do not want to talk to the captains again, because they know they have treated the man badly and cannot face up to that fact. I don't know. But it does appear strange that successive captains have been so brutally dismissed.

In the physio's room at King's Park, I switched off my cell phone and told John Slade, who happened to be there with me, what had happened. I decided to drive straight home and tell Nicky, my wife, what Mallett had said. I won't pretend we were not very, very disappointed, but we dealt with the news together.

In the days and weeks that followed, the number of people who contacted me to express their support was overwhelming. The people of Durban, in shops and in the street, were incredible, and our telephone at home rang off the hook with people calling to express their good wishes.

John Hart and Sean Fitzpatrick took the trouble to telephone from New Zealand; Louis Luyt called and told me to 'hang in there'. Ian McIntosh went as far as calling Mallett and telling him he had made a mistake.

Joost van der Westhuizen assumed the captaincy, and soon telephoned me to say how he had been thinking of me. He is a decent man. If I had to hand on the honour of leading the Springboks to anyone, then I was pleased it was to someone like the absolutely dedicated and patriotic scrumhalf. His Bok side lost to the All Blacks, but rallied to beat the Wallabies only a week later, and started their final preparations to defend the Rugby World Cup.

I stayed at home in Durban, and focused on the challenge of leading Natal to the Currie Cup final. My World Cup dream had been denied.

As the weeks passed, various versions of what had happened between Nick Mallett and myself appeared in the media. At one stage, Nick suggested I had become more interested in playing golf than rugby. I do not believe he can seriously believe that: it is the most appalling nonsense.

I have generally tried to steer clear of discussing the matter in public, until now. In these pages, I have sought to set out an account of how what was a superb captain-coach relationship in 1997 and 1998 deteriorated so quickly. It is my account, not Nick's account, but it is the truth as I saw it. I have tried not to be self-serving or vindictive, but simply to let events speak for themselves. This has not been an easy task, and I hope I have achieved these goals.

My final reflection on the saga is this: I only wish Nick Mallett and I had sat down at some stage during 1999 and discussed the situation with mutual respect and civility, and I sincerely wish we were still friends today.

As I have written in the introduction to this book, the decision to drop me from the World Cup squad was neither the right decision, nor the wrong decision. Some people will say it was right, others would say it was wrong. All that matters is that it was Nick Mallett's decision, and he was doing his job.

That said, perhaps he could have done his job in a more decent manner.

13

New Dawn at Newport

Towards the end of 1996, I had been surprised when François Pienaar decided to leave South Africa and play club rugby in England. In his situation, I told myself, I would have remained with my province, continued to play in the Currie Cup and tried to regain my place in the Springbok side.

That was then.

By September 1999, I was wiser.

When I was also dropped as Springbok captain by a national coach who no longer spoke to me, I began to appreciate the logic of François' decision. It is a question of wanting to break from circumstances that have turned sour, to get away from the arena of controversy and make a fresh start.

As the storm surrounding my omission from the World Cup squad wore on, Nicky and I reached a decision that we should move overseas. It was not as if we were running away; we simply sought a fresh challenge. Nicky had been mentally strong throughout the saga, and she could see the benefits of spending a couple of years away from South Africa. It made sense.

Craig Livingstone, my business manager, happened to be in Wales at the time, concluding arrangements for the move of Andy Marinos, the former Natal and now Western Province centre, to the Newport club in Wales. I called him and suggested he keep his eyes open for an opportunity.

Within two days, Craig called to say Tony Brown, the businessman driving the revival of Newport RFC, was interested in signing me. The matter began to assume its own momentum, and a flying visit to Wales was arranged. I took Ian McIntosh into my confidence, and the veteran coach again responded superbly, allowing me to miss a couple of training sessions, saying nothing.

Craig and I flew to London, and emerged bleary-eyed into the revamped international arrivals hall at Terminal One, Heathrow Airport, to find Tony Brown himself, waiting to meet us. My initial impression of my future employer could not have been more impressive or encouraging. He could easily have dispatched a driver to fetch me and received me later in the day in an overpowering office; instead, he chose to welcome me personally, and I was flattered.

With Tony at the wheel, we drove for two hours down the M4, checked into a hotel and had lunch at the Celtic Manor complex with Alan Lewis, the coach who had been appointed to direct the Newport revival. There followed a crash course in the club, the mission and my proposed role ...

Newport RFC had apparently fallen on hard times, struggling to compete with the major club teams in Welsh rugby such as Cardiff, Swansea, Llanelli and Pontypridd, but Tony Brown had arrived to inspire a resurgence. Based in Surrey, outside London, Tony had developed Bisley Office Equipment into a successful business and one of his major factories was located in Newport. The motive for his considerable financial investment in the town's faltering rugby club was to put something back into the community.

The club was investing heavily in overseas players, and Alan Lewis' task was to weld the imported stars into a team. His initial aim was to establish a respectable standard of performance and, in the 1999/2000 season, to finish in the top five of the league and qualify for a place in the highly lucrative

European Cup for the next season. That was phase one.

Tony Brown's enthusiasm for the challenge was infectious. He made the two-and-a-half hour trip from home to watch virtually every Newport match, home or away, and his commitment to the cause was such that, on one occasion, he was to be found selling match programmes before the game. I tried to imagine one of his counterparts at a major South African provincial union taking such an active and enthusiastic approach ... but failed.

That evening, we spent time at the club which I had last visited with the 1994 Springbok touring squad, when we played Wales A in a midweek fixture. There was an undeniably special atmosphere at Rodney Parade, notably when the club's fervent supporters filled the large expanses of standing room situated along the touchline in front of the main grandstand. It took just minutes to realise this was a rugby club with a soul, with something to offer.

We had dinner with David Watkins, the club chairman, two other directors and Tony. I was starting to see positive signs in every direction. By the end of an exhausting day, I called Nicky at home in Durban and said I could almost see the sun rising for us, on a new dawn in Newport.

The following morning, we met with Tony Brown again and he placed an offer on the table. I said I would discuss his proposal with Nicky and get back to him within 48 hours. I was being cautious. I knew my wife would give the green light, and I knew Newport were presenting me with the right option at the right time.

I returned to Durban and arranged a meeting with the Natal Rugby Union, at which I informed them of my intentions and asked for an early release from the contract that tied me to them until after the World Cup. This was duly granted, Nicky was happy and I was soon calling Tony to accept the offer. Everything had happened quickly, but I had absolutely no reservations.

Henry Honiball had already agreed to join the Bristol club, just 30 minutes down the road from Newport, and Franco Smith would soon sign to complete a South African triumvirate, alongside Andy Marinos and me, at Newport. A small Springbok colony was being created in the area, making the transition to British life so much easier for our wives and children.

The closing weeks of my 15-year association with Natal rugby unfolded as an emotional and unforgettable experience. From Craven week in 1984 through to the Currie Cup triumphs of the 1990s, I had always felt comfortably at home within the realm of the NRU, and it was hard to be leaving home.

My parting ambition was to leave the field at King's Park for the last time with the Currie Cup trophy in my hands. When it emerged that Ian McIntosh and André Joubert would also be retiring from the game at the end of the season, a shared resolve started to envelop the squad and province. If this was to be the end of an era, then it was an era that should end with a bang.

We duly reached the Currie Cup final, to be played against the Golden Lions at King's Park. As thousands upon thousands packed the stadium again, I remember standing on the touchline and thinking my departure from Natal could not have been scripted more impeccably. It was a rare occasion.

As a South African male, I am neither expected nor entitled to show much emotion in public, but the astounding depth of support from the Natal public had eventually broken down even my sterling emotional defences during what had been a difficult couple of months for my family and me.

How do you respond to the schoolboy who stops you in the street and tells you not to worry about 'that Mallett'? How do you react to the lady pensioner standing at the bus stop who sees you across the street and walks over to say that, from now on, she will support Natal and Newport?

You just smile and say thank you, and consider yourself fortunate to have played for a province and lived in a town alongside such people.

Such was the level of support that surrounded us that day at King's Park, it hardly seemed to matter that the Golden Lions proved too strong for us and thoroughly deserved to take the Currie Cup to Johannesburg.

After they had left the field to continue the celebrations in their changing room, Mac, Jouba and I took the microphone and thanked the King's Park crowd for one last time. Natal had just lost a Currie Cup final, but the ovation rose to such intensity that it seemed to transcend mere results on the field.

And then it was over, and I left King's Park for the last time as a player in the knowledge that whatever I had given the province during the past 15 years, the players, coaches and supporters of Natal had given me much more.

Newport beckoned.

I turned up at Rodney Parade for my first training session with the club on the Thursday night after our arrival in Wales, and was embarrassed to discover there was no training kit for the players. Spoiled in South Africa, I had assumed kit would be made available by a sponsor. It wasn't. I had none.

In borrowed kit, I sweated through a session conducted in several centimetres of clawing mud, a far cry from the sun-kissed grass at King's Park, but the welcome could not have been friendlier and I settled swiftly.

Two days later, I made my debut for Newport in a league match against Pontypridd and was immediately impressed by the sheer physical commitment of Welsh club rugby. The invariably heavy conditions produce a much slower game than in the southern hemisphere, but the forward exchanges are certainly not for the faint-hearted. No prisoners are taken in Welsh club rugby.

We led at half-time and turned with the wind at our backs, but failed to capitalise on the conditions and lost narrowly. We would evidently require time to develop from a group of talented individuals into a genuine team; only then would we be able to produce a consistent standard of performance.

While I was quietly settling at Newport, Joost van der Westhuizen and his Springbok squad were mounting their challenge for the World Cup. Nobody was more eager for South Africa to repeat the victory of 1995, although some of the players were complaining about the spirit within the squad. I do not know if they said that because they thought it was what I wanted to hear, or whether it was an accurate reflection of events. It was no longer my business.

The team did not look impressive in the group stages, but Jannie de Beer rose to the occasion for the quarter-final against England, kicking five incredible drop goals and carrying the team to a semi-final against Australia. I watched an outstanding game of rugby on television, and was as desolate as any Springbok supporter when Larkham dropped a winning goal in extra time.

Bobby Skinstad did play at eighthman throughout the tournament, but he did not look 100% fit at any stage; towards the closing stages, he was starting to attract unfair criticism as one of the 'flops of the tournament'. His lingering knee injury would flare again, ruling him out for most of the 2000 season.

Joost van der Westhuizen appeared to have captained the team with all his customary vigour and determination, and I was pleased when he and some other players took the trouble to visit me at home, when they were in Cardiff for the Third Place match, which they won against New Zealand.

One of the guys told me that Nick Mallett had seen them leaving the hotel and asked where they were going. They had told him, whereupon the Springbok coach casually remarked: 'I would ask you to give Gary my regards, but he will probably tell me to ___ off.' In fact, I would have been pleased.

Some people have suggested to me that South Africa's performance at the 1999 World Cup proved I should not have been dropped. My captaincy had never been questioned and, the argument ran, I would certainly have offered a more significant contribution at eighthman than Mallett's choice.

To be honest, I have not considered such theories and I have no idea of what might or might not have happened if I had captained the team. There is no profit in such discussion. Joost led the side, and tried his best. Bobby played at the back of the scrum, and tried his best. Good luck to them.

As 1999 turned to 2000, I was more concerned by Newport's inability to produce consistently solid performances. We delighted our supporters by beating Llanelli at Stradey Park for the first time in 23 years, and thrilled them again when we emphatically defeated Cardiff at Rodney Parade in the Swalec Cup – I have never seen so many people in one town so downright delighted about a win – but then we went and lost a league match away to Ebbw Vale.

Midway through the season, I was asked to take over the captaincy of the team and we started to establish ourselves in the top five on the log. Our primary goals were in sight and I was happy to sign a new contract for the 2000 – 2001 season. Everyone at the club shared Tony Brown's vision, and I was starting to sense a wave of confidence and resolve sweeping through the ranks.

We were developing team spirit among our cosmopolitan band of Welsh, Fijian, Australian and South African players; as the season progressed, we were beginning to enjoy each other's company and develop the qualities of a winning side. By March, we were even laughing at the same jokes.

And we never laughed more heartily than when our reserve hooker, Gary Hicks, achieved something I had never previously witnessed on a rugby field: he succeeded in putting himself on the field as a substitute. Midway through the first half of a league game, there was a misunderstanding on the touchline and, amid the confusion, Gary stripped off his tracksuit and ran on to the field.

Our first-choice hooker saw what happened, assumed he

NEW DAWN AT NEWPORT

was being taken off, jogged to the touchline and took his place on the bench. It was five minutes before the coaching staff worked out what had taken place. By then, Gary was in the game.

As I enjoyed my rugby, so I enjoyed the Newport lifestyle that enabled me to spend more time at home with my wife and daughter than had ever been the case when I was playing for Natal and South Africa.

Our daughter, Danielle, had literally been born into the rugby life, when she arrived soon after three o'clock on a Friday afternoon, 12 September, 1997, and appeared to watch aghast as her father promptly left to play a Currie Cup match against South-Eastern Transvaal the following day.

Many professional sportsmen only see photographs of their wives and children. It goes with the territory. I am extremely fortunate to be actually with them almost every single day in Wales. These are precious times.

In many ways, Tony Brown and Newport RFC offered me a new lease on my rugby life when I needed it most; and I am resolved to reciprocate their generosity by contributing to success for Newport on the field. They offered me a new dawn; now I must generate some sunshine for them.

14

Home Thoughts

The challenge at Newport is compelling but one day, when we have realised our targets and my rugby career draws to a close, I will start living without having to check when training starts the next day. Retirement looms like a death sentence in the minds of many professional sportsmen, but not in mine.

I won't miss the limelight, because I have never sought it, and I certainly won't miss being the subject of discussion. Some people say exposure in the media is like a drug, with celebrities craving coverage of their lives every time they open a newspaper or turn on the television. If this is the case, I have certainly never inhaled.

Nicky and I have occasionally been asked whether, when my period with Newport is over, we might like to stay in Britain. At such moments, my wife and I glance at each other, weigh up all the options, consider every possibility and, within five seconds, yell in unison: 'No!'

We enjoy living in Cardiff, but our home is in Durban and we find it hard to imagine settling happily in any country other than South Africa.

I have always been extremely positive about the future of our country. Of course, there remain many problems and obstacles in national life, such as the elimination of poverty, corruption and crime, but the most instructive thought is always to wonder whether, back in the dark days of 1990, we would have settled for the relative economic stability and peace that we have today.

The answer must be yes.

So Nicky, Danielle and I will return home in due course, and I will devote some long overdue attention to Teichmann Civils, the construction company that my partners, James Teriele and Danie du Toit, have been running in my absence; and, all being well, we will thrive as normal people living normal lives.

Perhaps, on the eve of major rugby matches, a journalist will call and ask for my forecast, and my remarks will be cobbled together in paragraph 28 of the inside back page: 'Former Bok captain Gary Teichmann says that if the Natal pack can control ...'. For the time being, I suspect such interventions will be the limit of my high-profile contribution to this game.

Rugby has given me so many opportunities. I find it almost frightening to reflect on the uncertain 23-year-old attending the Cedara Agricultural College with no clear idea of what he wanted to do with his life. Since that time, in 1991, I have, in a sense, been taken under rugby's wing and transported through nine years of incredible adventure and excitement. On so many occasions and in so many ways, I have been extremely fortunate and blessed.

And I think back to the decisions that created this chance; of how my old school coaches at Hilton switched me from centre to eighthman; of how Andrew Aitken moved to Cape Town and gave me a chance in Natal; and of how three successive Springbok coaches sat down and made me their captain.

Many people have entrusted me with great responsibility over the years, and I very much hope not one of them feels I have let them down. It is strange, but when I reflect on the hundreds of matches, for my club, province and country, and even for a regional Super 12 team, it is not the results and the tries that stand out in the mind's eye; it is the people.

It would be pointless to rehearse a list of names here, but I hope each and every person who has smiled along the way understands my gratitude. In rugby, as in other forms of life, it is tempting to be brutal and rough in stampeding to the top of your field. But, in my experience, this kind of approach is followed by an equally unpleasant and ruthless fall from grace.

I have tried to be sympathetic and gentle in my approach, choosing a quieter path towards the summit. The effect of this strategy is that people tend to write you off as being too laid-back and ineffectual. If you do not rant and rave, some people assume you don't feel strongly.

This is not true.

Place a man in a room packed with other men shouting at the top of their voices and tell him to make his presence felt. What does he do? If he shouts as well, he will simply become lost in the mass of noise. No, he whispers softly; the other men are so intrigued that they fall quiet and they listen. This has tended to be my philosophy and, more often than not, it has worked.

Sooner rather than later, I would relish the opportunity of assisting in the coaching of a junior club or school team. I find the prospect of being involved in the game, of enjoying the game for the game's sake, and of being far away from the headlines and pressure, to be thoroughly appealing.

And then ... who knows? Maybe I will enjoy coaching, and move through the ranks in that field. I don't know. What I can say is that the game of rugby union still excites and inspires me as much as it ever has done. I am tired of the excesses and the controversies, but the game remains pure and apart.

Since 1995, I have heard people express concern about the state of the game, wonder whether the advent of professionalism has changed the character of rugby, fret that money has changed everything for the worse. I think there is an element of the 'nostalgia isn't what it used to be' theory here.

The Super 12 and Tri-Nations series have certainly elevated rugby union to a new level. The game has never been so fast, so powerful, so imaginatively marketed and so spectacular. As players devote more time to training, so playing standards improve and, year upon year, the game evolves.

There are thorns on the rose: specifically a book of laws that has become too finicky and involved, and could comfortably be cut by a third; and also the ongoing inability of northern hemisphere unions to transform the old amateur structures into a modern, exciting and commercially viable format.

That said, the game has moved powerfully into the new millennium, and is fast expanding beyond the boundaries of the established powers. We may still be some years, maybe even decades, from seeing the spectacle of Japan defeating the All Blacks by 50 points, but we're moving in that direction.

My paramount concern is for the players who are seduced by the rewards of professionalism, visit the BMW dealership, but are then left unemployable and helpless when their playing days are over. There is an urgent, even desperate, need for organisations to be developed that offer timely advice.

You sign a professional contract upon leaving school; you train three or four times a day; you give these crucial formative years of your life in pursuit of a dream to play international rugby: there is no time for a degree at university, no opportunity for vocational training at all. Maybe you are one of the few who make it, maybe you are one of the many who don't – either way, some time near your 30th birthday, you will be confronted by life without rugby. Such are the physical and mental demands, your career might not even take you to 30.

What will you do?

You might have some money, if you resisted the temptation to go for the convertible and put more of your salary into a pension fund; or you might have the convertible in the garage, and a mortgage, and bills … and no job.

These are the questions that need to be asked and answered when the guys are 21, not when they are 28. And, if the young heroes don't listen, then they need to be asked and asked again until they do answer.

Happily, I believe South Africa leads the field in meeting the challenge of ensuring that professional rugby claims as few victims as possible. The South African Rugby Players Association (SARPA) was formed in 1998 and, two years later, boasts a subscription-paying membership of 400 professional players, a full-time Chief Executive in a fully manned Cape Town office, with plans for expansion into the ranks of amateur players, coaches and referees.

Among its achievements, SARPA's primary gain has been the successful introduction of a standard player's contract whereby every professional player in the country is covered by full medical aid, an insurance contract, fair conditions of employment ... and makes contributions to a retirement fund.

SARPA has become an invaluable safety net and, much though players may sigh when they see the monthly deductions from their gross salary, there will come a time when they are relieved to have been forewarned.

If they can manage to play through a long and eventful career, can make lasting friends all over the world, can look back and reflect on a wonderful time and, after all that, still look forward with confidence to new challenges, projects, goals and a seat in the stands whenever the Boks play in Durban, then I believe they will be able to reflect that rugby has been good to them.

That is my happy situation.

Career Highlights

NATAL

144 Caps
Captained 57
Tries scored 23

CURRIE CUP

1995 Final Natal vs Western Province: 25-17 (Won)
1996 Final Transvaal vs Natal: 33-15 (Won)
1997 Semi-final Natal vs Free State: 22-40 (Lost)
1998 Semi-final Northern Transvaal vs Natal: 17-31 (Lost)
1999 Final Natal vs Golden Lions: 9-32 (Lost)

SOUTH AFRICA

42 Tests
Captained 36
Tries scored 6
South African Player of the Year 1998

TESTS 1996

2 July, South Africa vs Fiji, Pretoria: 43-18 (Won)
13 July, South Africa vs Australia, Australia: 16-21 (Lost)

FOR THE RECORD

20 July, South Africa vs New Zealand, New Zealand: 11-15 (Lost)
3 August, South Africa vs Australia, Bloemfontein: 25-19 (Won)
10 August, South Africa vs New Zealand, Cape Town: 18-29 (Lost)
17 August, South Africa vs New Zealand, Durban: 19-23 (Lost)
24 August, South Africa vs New Zealand, Pretoria: 26-33 (Lost)
31 August, South Africa vs New Zealand, Johannesburg: 32-22 (Won)
9 November, South Africa vs Argentina, Argentina: 46-15 (Won)
16 November, South Africa vs Argentina, Argentina: 44-21 (Won)
30 November, South Africa vs France, France: 22-12 (Won)
7 December, South Africa vs France, France: 13-12 (Won)
15 December, South Africa vs Wales, Wales: 37-20 (Won)

TESTS 1997

10 June, South Africa vs Tonga, Cape Town: 74-10 (Won)
21 June, South Africa vs Lions, Cape Town: 16-25 (Lost)
28 June, South Africa vs Lions, Durban: 15-18 (Lost)
5 July, South Africa vs Lions, Johannesburg: 35-16 (Won)
19 July, South Africa vs New Zealand, Johannesburg: 32-35 (Lost)
2 August, South Africa vs Australia, Australia: 20-32 (Lost)
9 August, South Africa vs New Zealand, New Zealand: 35-55 (Lost)
23 August, South Africa vs Australia, Pretoria: 61-22 (Won)
8 November, South Africa vs Italy, Italy: 62-31 (Won)
15 November, South Africa vs France, France: 36-32 (Won)
22 November, South Africa vs France, France: 52-10 (Won)
29 November, South Africa vs England, England: 29-11 (Won)
6 December, South Africa vs Scotland, Scotland: 68-10 (Won)

TESTS 1998

13 June, South Africa vs Ireland, Bloemfontein: 37-13 (Won)
20 June, South Africa vs Ireland, Pretoria: 33-0 (Won)
27 June, South Africa vs Wales, Pretoria: 96-13 (Won)
5 July, South Africa vs England, Cape Town: 18-0 (Won)
18 July, South Africa vs Australia, Australia: 14-13 (Won)
25 July, South Africa vs New Zealand, New Zealand: 13-3 (Won)
15 August, South Africa vs New Zealand, Durban: 24-23 (Won)
22 August, South Africa vs Australia, Johannesburg: 29-15 (Won)

CAREER HIGHLIGHTS

14 November, South Africa vs Wales, Wales: 28-20 (Won)
21 November, South Africa vs Scotland, Scotland: 35-10 (Won)
28 November, South Africa vs Ireland, Ireland: 27-13 (Won)
5 December, South Africa vs England, England: 7-13 (Lost)

TESTS 1999

12 June, South Africa vs Italy, Port Elizabeth: 74-0 (Won)
26 June, South Africa vs Wales, Wales: 19-29 (Lost)
10 July, South Africa vs New Zealand, New Zealand: 0-28 (Lost)

NEWPORT RUGBY CLUB

1999 Debut

Index

Aitken, Andrew 33, 35, 37, 46
All Blacks
   school coaching methods 22
   test matches against
      Springboks, 1981 18–19
   test series 1996 100–101
   tour of South Africa, 1992
      51–52
   tour of South Africa, 1996
      104–108
   Tri-Nations series, 1997
      135–139
   Tri-Nations series, 1998
      180–182
   Tri-Nations series, 1999 211
   see also New Zealand
Allan, John 48, 51, 60, 81–82, 148, 152, 157–158
Andrew, Rob 65
Andrews, Mark 60, 82–83, 89, 130, 146, 152, 171, 183, 190, 194–195, 210, 212
Argentina
   Springbok tour, 1993 59–64
   Springbok tour, 1996 114–115
   see also Buenos Aires XV
Atherton, Steve 24, 43, 60, 152–153
Australia
   rugby league, rights war 79
   Super 10 results, 1993 56–57
   Super 12 series 143, 148
   tour of South Africa 1992 51
   Tri-Nations Series, 1996
      95–96
   Tri-Nations Series, 1997
      137, 140
   Tri-Nations Series, 1998
      178–180, 185–186
   Tri-Nations Series, 1999 213

Badenhorst, Chris 70
Bartmann, Wahl 38, 41, 46, 48–49, 53–54, 58, 75
Beckenbauer, Franz 123
Bell, Angus 24–26
Bentley, Rob 16
Bester, André 120–121

Blakeway, Andrew 38, 46, 49, 52, 58
Blue Bulls, Currie Cup matches 34–35, 150
see also Northern Bulls and Northern Transvaal
Boome, Selborne 214
Botha, Naas 34, 36, 41, 42, 50
Breedt, Jannie 53–54
Brink, Robbie 73
British Lions, test matches 124, 134, 127–134
see also England
Brown, Tony 219–220, 224–225
Buchanan,'Bucky' 10
Buenos Aires XV, Springbok match against 62
see also Argentina
Burger, Chris, fund 13

Cabannes, Laurent 170
Campese, David 45
Catt, Mike 194
Cavaliers, tour of South Africa, 1986 77
Christie, Kitch 59, 67–69, 71–73, 89, 91–93, 129, 201
Church, Richard 23
Clontarf Club, Ireland 43–44
College Rovers club, Durban 45–46
Cotton, Fran 124
Craven Week for provincial high school teams, 1984 24–25
Cullen, Christian 101
Currie Cup
  popularity of 161–162
  results, 1984 26

results, 1990 34–35
results, 1991 39–43
results, 1992 46–54
results, 1993 58–59
results 1995–1996 143, 146–147, 149
results 1999 221–222

Dalton, James 71, 117, 171, 183, 193
Davids, George 109
Dawson, Matt 129, 195
De Beer, Jannie 136, 223
De Giorgio, Nicky
  see Teichmann, Nicky
De Villiers, Peter 164–165
Diamann Ltd 30–31
Du Plessis, Carel 114, 119, 121–129, 134–137, 140–141
Du Plessis, Morné 72–73, 84–85, 97, 102, 106, 108, 129
Du Preez, Robert 47
Du Randt, Os 97, 128, 171
Du Toit, Gaffie 210–211

Eales, John 179, 185
Eastern Province
  Currie Cup match against Natal, 1991 43
Egberink, Cliffie 43, 91
Els, Ernie 86
Engelbrecht, Jean 30
Engelbrecht, Jannie 62
England
  rugby tour of South Africa, 1994 65–66
  rugby tour of South Africa 1998 177

236

INDEX

Springbok tour of, 1997 173
Springbok tour of, 1998
  194–196
Erasmus, Rassie 170–171,
  189–190, 193, 212–213
Evennett family 14
Evennett, Geoff 27–28

Ferreira, Colonel 30
Fitzpatrick, Sean 101, 106, 139,
  148, 184–185, 216
Fourie, Pote 42
France
  Springbok tour 1996 115–119
  Springbok tour 1997 169–172
Free State
  Currie Cup match against
    Natal, 1991 43
Fyvie, Wayne 153, 179

Gage, Shaun 24, 46
Garvey, Adrian 13, 147, 151–152,
  171, 190
Golden Cats *see* Golden Lions
Golden Lions 199, 221–222
Greenway, Mike 214
Grindrod, Wally 24
Guscott, Jeremy 132, 149

Harding, Gerhard 48
Harrison, Paul 23
Harry, Phil 154
Hart, John 102, 106, 184, 216
Henry, Graham 189, 209
Hewson, Allan 19
Hick, Graeme 11
Hicks, Gary 224–225
Hill, Clive 11, 18

Hill family 14
Hillside Primary School,
  Bulawayo 11
Hilton College, Natal 15–16
  rugby matches 17–26
Honiball, Henry 47, 60, 65, 108,
  114, 131, 145, 148, 155–156,
  170, 181–182, 204, 209, 221
Horan, Tim 45, 185–186
Hulett, Sean 23

Ireland
  rugby tour of South Africa
    1998 176–177
  Springbok tour of, 1998
    193–194
Italy
  Springbok tour of, 1997
    166–167
  test match, Port Elizabeth
    1999 205

Jaguar side, match at King's
  Park, 1982 19
Jamieson, Craig 34–35, 40–42, 49
Jenkins, Neil 127, 128, 132
John, Paddy 177
Johnson, Gavin 71
Jones, Stephen 191
Joubert, André 47, 60, 68, 82–83,
  95, 115–117, 131, 149, 159,
  221–222
Joubert, Joos 158

Kayser, Deon 206–207
Keast, Andy 143–144
Kebble, Guy 60, 76, 79–80, 82, 86
Kember, Chukka 32

Kempson, Robbie 147, 151–152, 200
King, Justin 24
Krige, Corné 205
Kruger, Ruben 92, 118, 139, 184

Lacroix, Thierry 147, 170
Lamaison, Christophe 118
Laubscher, Tommy 146–147
Le Roux, Hennie 71
Le Roux, Ollie 151–152, 190
Leonard, Jason 173
Lewis, Alan 219
Livingstone, Craig 218–219
Lomu, Jonah 181
Luger, Dan 194–195
Lund, Clare
  see Teichmann, Clare
Lund family 14
Lund, Guy 5–6
Lund, Jub 6
Luyt, Louis 56, 67, 82, 84–85, 98, 139–140, 206, 216
Lynagh, Michael 65

MacDonald, Ian 74
Mackenzie, Peter 23
Mallett, Nick 102, 114, 119, 163–168, 171–174, 176, 180, 184, 188, 191, 195–197, 200–206, 208–217, 223
Mandela, Nelson 66, 74, 175
Marinos, Andy 218, 221
Maritzburg College 16, 24
Maritzburg University open side 32–33
Markgraaff, André 93–94, 98–100, 103, 106, 108–110, 112–114, 118–119–121, 127, 149, 152, 163, 215
McGeechan, Ian 124
McIntosh, Ian 10, 34, 36, 38–41, 46, 48, 52, 55, 57, 60–61, 65 68, 71, 130, 143–145, 151, 215–216, 219, 221–222
McQueen, Rod 144
Mehrtens, André 95
Mendez, Federico 152
Mexted, Murray 19
Michaelhouse
  rugby matches against Hilton College 22–23
Montgomery, Percy 131, 141, 167, 170, 175, 192, 195
Mpophomeni 5–6
Muir, Dick 41, 47, 156–157, 168–170
Mulder, Japie 71, 97
Muller, Lood 40, 48
Muller, Pieter 47, 53, 60, 157–158, 181, 186, 210
Murdoch, Rupert 79, 81–82

Natal Coastal Sharks
  Super 12 series 143, 159–160, 198–199, 202–203
  see also Natal Provincial rugby teams and Super Sharks
Natal Duikers 33
Natal provincial rugby teams
  administration 36
  Currie Cup matches, 1984 26
  Currie Cup results 1990 33–35, 37
  Currie Cup matches, 1991 41–43

INDEX

Currie Cup results 1992 46–54
Currie Cup results 1993 58–59
Currie Cup results 1995 90, 146–147
Currie Cup results 1996 108–109, 143, 149–150
Currie Cup results 1999 221–222
defeat against Free State, 1991 43
match against Springboks, 1995 74
results, 1980s 36–37
Super 10 matches, 1993–1995 56, 92
trials, 1991 38
under–21 team 32
see also Natal Coastal Sharks
Natal Rugby Union 36, 50, 56, 220
Natal Sharks
see Natal Coastal Sharks
Natal University
match against Wits University, June 1991 39
Nel, Pieter 34
New Zealand
Springbok tour, 1994 66–67
Super 10 results 56–57
Super 12 series 143, 160–161
Test matches against Springboks, 1981 18–19
tour of South Africa 51
three test series, 1996 99–108
Tri-Nations Series, 1996 95–98
Tri-Nations Series, 1997 138–139
Tri-Nations Series, 1998 180–183
Tri-Nations Series, 1999 209–212
see also All Blacks
Newport RFC, 218–220, 222, 224–225
Newscorp 79, 81–82, 94
Nkanunu, Silas 206–207
Northern Bulls 199
see also Blue Bulls and Northern Transvaal
Northern Transvaal
Currie Cup match against Natal, 1990 34–35
Currie Cup match against Natal, 1991 39–42
see also Blue Bulls and Northern Bulls

Oberholzer, Rian 120, 207–208
O'Brien, Paddy 155, 195
Olivier, Jacques 90
Olivier, Noel 64, 143–144
Oosthuizen, Theo 109
O'Shea, Conor 194
Otto, Krynauw 168, 171

Packer, Kerry 79, 81, 83, 86
Partridges XI 11
Paulse, Breyton 206–207
Penrose, Neil 55
Petersen, Arthob 129
Phipson family 14
Pienaar, François 49, 59, 61, 63, 71, 74, 88–89, 91–92, 94–99,

107, 111, 129, 149, 184, 215, 218
Pienaar, Gysie 68
Plumtree boarding school 12
Plumtree, John 38, 58, 151
Poole, Andrew 23
President's XV
   match against Northern Transvaal, 1994 65–66

Procter, Mike 16
Provincial rugby, match fees 77–85
Putt, Kevin 153–155

Quinnell brothers 189

Randall, Taine 184
Rayner, Paul 28
Reece-Edwards, Hugh 42, 47, 114, 119, 145
Retief, Dan 54
Rhodes, Digby 15
Rhodes, Jonty 15
Richards, Barry 126
Richter, Adriaan 57
Rodney Parade 220, 222
Roger, Ian 155
Roumat, Olivier 147
Rossouw, Pieter 170, 182, 194
Roux, Johan 71
Rugby World Cup *see* World Cup Rugby Championship

Saint-André, Phillipe 170
SARFU *see* South African Rugby Football Union
Schmidt, Uli 41–42, 48, 70

Scotland
   Springbok tour of, 1997 173–174
   Springbok tour of 1998 191
Short, Adrian 24
Skinstad, Bobby 183, 186, 188–194, 199, 202–204, 213–214, 223–224
Slade, John 153, 216
Smal, Gert 123, 124, 127, 141
Small, James 56, 60, 68, 82, 83, 99–100, 139–140, 158, 170, 175
Smith, Franco 160, 190, 192, 221
Smith, Ian 11, 12
Snyman, Andre 167, 170, 173
Solomons, Alan 164–165, 191, 200, 202–203, 211, 213
South African Defence Force National Service, South West Africa 27–30
South African Rugby Football Union
   affirmative action programme 206–208
   appointment of André Markgraaff 93
   appointment of Nick Mallett 163
   contracts with Springbok rugby players 82–86
   dismissal of Carel du Plessis 141
South West Africa (later Namibia)
   South African Defence Force, national service 28–30
Spencer, Carlos 136

INDEX

Springboks
  defeat by England, 1993 55
  match against Fiji, 1996 92, 94
  match against Natal, 1995 74
  match against Wales,
    September 1995 89–90
  match against Wales, 1999
    206, 209
  match against Western
    Province 1995 72
  matches against England,
    1994 65–66
  role in World Rugby
    Championship contracts
    80–81
  SARFU contracts 81–86
  squad system 204
  test matches, New Zealand,
    1981 18–19
  test match, New Zealand,
    1996 105–106
  three test home series against
    New Zealand, 106 99–106
  tour of Argentina, 1993 59–64
  tour of Argentina, France and
    Wales, 1996 108–109,
    112–120
  tour of Australia, 1993 57–58
  tour of England, 1998 187
  tour of Italy, France and
    England, 1997 167–175
  tour of New Zealand, 1994
    66–67
  tour of Wales, Scotland and
    Ireland 1994 69–71
  touring Jaguar side, King's
    Park, 1982 19
  Tri-Nations Series, 1996 94–99

Tri-Nations Series, 1997
  135–139
Tri-Nations Series, 1998
  178–186
Tri-Nations Series, 1999
  209–213
World Cup matches 71,
  73–75, 79–83, 86, 223–224
Stephenson, Kevin 159
Stewart, Christian 192
Stewart, Errol 41, 46
Straeuli, Rudolf 69–71
Stransky, Joel 24–25, 38, 47, 60,
  72, 96, 98
Strauss, Andrew 47
Strauss, Tiaan 47, 57, 60, 66,
  69–70, 72–74
Strydom, Klein 20–21, 37
Super League, professional
  global rugby competion
  development of 79–83
Super Sharks
  Super 12 series, 1998 160
  see also Natal Coastal Sharks
Super 10 series
  results 56–57, 64–65, 71–72
Super12 series
  Australia and New Zealand
    143, 176
  establishment 92, 148
  results 1996–1998 124, 159–161
  results 1999 199, 202–203
Swanepoel, Werner 169–170, 209
Swart, Balie 71

Tait, Alan 129
Teichmann Civils 6, 227
Teichmann, Clare (Mickey) 5–6

Teichmann, Danielle 225
Teichmann, David 7, 9
Teichmann, Gary
  attitude towards retirement 226–230
  childhood 7–13
  Clontarf club contract 43–44
  Defence Force experiences 27–30
  exclusion from Tri-Nations series, 1999 214–215
  final Currie Cup match, 1999 221–222
  inclusion in Springbok team, 1996 93–97
  injuries 1999 205, 212
  marriage 91–92
  match fees 76–86
  Natal provincial captaincy 146–150, 153
  Natal provincial rugby 38–43, 46–54, 76, 145
  Natal under-20 rugby 30–35
  school career 14–25
  Springbok captaincy 99–102, 104–106, 109–111, 164
  Springbok matches against British Lions 124–134, 194–197
  Springbok matches against Italy, France and England 169–174
  Springbok matches against Wales and Scotland 189–192
  Springbok tour to Argentina, France and Wales 112–121
  Super 10 series 56–57, 64–65
  Super 12 series 1996 148
  tour to England, Wales and Scotland 69–71
  tour to Argentina 60–64
  transfer to Newport Club, Wales 218–220
  Tri-Nations Series 134–140, 180–197, 211
Teichmann, George 3
Teichmann, Jack 3–5, 10, 12, 14
Teichmann, Lindsay (later Mrs Clive Alexander) 7, 14
Teichmann, Nicky (formerly De Giorgio, Nicky) 55, 60, 76, 91–92, 106, 140, 216, 218, 220
Teichmann, Robyn (later Mrs Charlie MacGillivray) 7, 14
Teichmann, Ross 7, 9, 12, 15–16, 30–31
Terblanche, Stefan 177, 192
Teriele, James 227
Thomson, Jeremy 47, 157
Transvaal Rugby Team
  Currie Cup final against Natal, 1992 53–54
  Currie Cup final against Natal, 1993 59
  see also Golden Lions
Tri-Nations Series
  1996 94–96
  1997 134–140
  1998 176, 178–186
  1999 204, 209–214
Tucuman, Springbok match, 1993 63
Turnbull, Ross 81
TWRC *see* World Rugby Championship

INDEX

Van der Schyff, Jack 104
Van der Spuy, Clive 33
Van der Valk, Rob 165, 178
Van der Watt, 20–21, 23, 37
Van der Westhuizen, Cabous 47, 68, 70, 156, 158–159
Van der Westhuizen, Joost 117–118, 120, 130, 134, 160, 169, 179, 182–183, 186, 190, 194, 204, 209, 216, 223–224
Van Heerden, Fritz 91
Van Heerden, Wickus 153–154
Van Loggerenberg, Chris 58
Van Rensburg, Theo 53
Van Rooyen, Quintus 40
Van Sloeslin, David 210–211
Van Straaten, Braam 209, 214
Van Zyl, Buurman 150
Varner, Bryce 24
Venter, André 139, 171, 189–191, 194–195
Viljoen, Harry 56–59, 81
Visagie, Rudi 43, 48

Wales
 club rugby 222–225
 Springbok tour, 1996 119–120
 match against South Africa, 1998 177–178, 189–190
 match against Springboks 1999 206, 209
Walker, Keith 43
Wallabies *see* Australia
Watkins, David 220
Watson, Tony 34, 42–43, 47–48
Western Stormers 199, 203
White, Jake 201–202
Wiese, Kobus 71, 115, 117
Williams, John 55
Wood, Keith 177, 193
Woodward, Clive 194
World Cup Rugby
 Championship
 1991 44–45
 1995 71, 73–75, 86
 1999 213, 223

243